The

If you could wish for one gift this Christmas, what would it be?

Every day Lou Suffern battles with the clock. He always has two places to be at the same time. He always has two things to do at once. When asleep he dreams. In between dreams, he runs through the events of the day while making plans for the next. When at home with his wife and family, his mind is always someplace else.

On his way into work one early winter morning, Lou meets Gabe, a homeless man sitting outside the office building. Intrigued by him and on discovering that he could also be very useful to have around, Lou gets Gabe a job in the post room.

But soon Lou begins to regret helping Gabe. His very presence unsettles Lou – and how does Gabe appear to be in two places at the same time?

As Christmas draws closer, Lou starts to understand the value of time. He sees what is truly important in life yet at the same time he learns the harshest lesson of all.

This is a story about people who, not unlike parcels, hide secrets. They cover themselves in layers until the right person unwraps them and discovers what's inside. Sometimes you have to be unravelled in order to find out who you really are.

About Cecelia

Before embarking on her writing career, Cecelia Ahern completed a degree in Journalism and Media Communications. At twenty-one years old, she wrote her first novel, *PS I Love You* which became an international bestseller and was adapted into a major motion picture starring Hilary Swank. Her successive novels, *Where Rainbows End*, *If You Could See Me Now*, *A Place Called Here*, *Thanks for the Memories* and *The Book of Tomorrow* were also number one best-sellers. Her books are published in forty-six countries and have collectively sold over nine million copies. Cecelia has also co-created the hit ABC Network comedy series *Samantha Who?* which stars Christina Applegate. Cecelia lives in Dublin, Ireland.

To sign up for the exclusive Cecelia Ahern HarperCollins newsletter and discover all about her books, as well as interviews, photographs and much more, log onto **www.cecelia-ahern.com**.

P.S Don't forget to read Cecelia's other novels:

PS, I Love You

Where Rainbows End

If You Could See Me Now

A Place Called Here

Thanks for the Memories

The Book of Tomorrow

CECELIA AHERN

THE GIFT

HARPER

Harper
An imprint of HarperCollins*Publishers*
77–85 Fulham Palace Road,
Hammersmith, London W6 8JB

www.harpercollins.co.uk

Published by HarperCollins*Publishers* 2008
1

A catalogue record for this book
is available from the British Library

ISBN: 978 0 00 788213 7

Typeset in Bembo by Palimpsest Book Production Limited,
Grangemouth, Stirlingshire

Printed and bound in Great Britain by
Clays Ltd, St Ives plc

Mixed Sources
Product group from well-managed
forests and other controlled sources
www.fsc.org Cert no. SW-COC-001806
© 1996 Forest Stewardship Council
FSC

FSC is a non-profit international organisation established
to promote the responsible management of the world's forests.
Products carrying the FSC label are independently certified
to assure consumers that they come from forests that are managed
to meet the social, economic and ecological needs
of present and future generations.

Find out more about HarperCollins and the environment at
www.harpercollins.co.uk/green

*All my love to my family for your friendship,
encouragement and love; Mim, Dad, Georgina,
Nicky, Rocco and Jay. David, Thank You.
Huge thanks to all my friends for making life a joy;
to Yo Yo and Leoni for the Rantaramas.
Thanks Ahoy McCoy for sharing your boating knowledge.
Thank you to the HarperCollins team for such support and belief
which I find endlessly encouraging and motivating;
thank you Amanda Ridout and my editors
Lynne Drew and Claire Bord.
Thank you Fiona McIntosh and Moira Reilly.
Thank you Marianne Gunn O' Connor for being You.
Thank you Pat Lynch and Vicki Satlow.
Thank you to all who read my books, I'm eternally grateful for
your support.*

Rocco and Jay;
The greatest gifts,
Both, at the same time

Chapters

1.

An Army of Secrets

If you were to stroll down the candy-cane façade of a surburban housing estate early on Christmas morning, you couldn't help but observe how the houses in all their tinselled glory are akin to the wrapped parcels that lie beneath the Christmas trees within. For each holds their secrets inside. The temptation of poking and prodding at the packaging is the equivalent of peeping through a crack in the curtains to get a glimpse of a family in Christmas-morning action; a captured moment that's kept away from all prying eyes. For the outside world, in a calming yet eerie silence that exists only on this morning every year, homes stand shoulder to shoulder like painted toy soldiers: chests pushed out, stomachs tucked in, proud and protective of all within.

Houses on Christmas morning are treasure chests of hidden truths. A wreath on a door like a finger upon a lip; blinds down like closed eyelids. Then, at some unspecific time, beyond the pulled blinds and drawn curtains, a warm glow will appear, the smallest hint of something happening inside. Like stars in the night sky which appear to the naked eye one by one, and like tiny pieces of gold revealed as they're sieved from a stream, lights go on behind the blinds and curtains in the half-light of dawn. As the sky becomes star-filled and as millionaires are made, room by room, house by house, the street begins to awaken.

On Christmas morning an air of calm settles outside. The emptiness on the streets doesn't instil fear; in fact it has the opposite effect. It's a picture of safety, and, despite the seasonal chill, there's warmth. For varying reasons, for every household this day of every year is just better spent inside. While outside is sombre, inside is a world of bright frenzied colour, a hysteria of ripping wrapping paper and flying coloured ribbons. Christmas music and festive fragrances of cinnamon and spice and all things nice fill the air. Exclamations of glee, of hugs and thanks, explode like party streamers. These Christmas days are indoor days; not a sinner lingering outside, for even they have a roof over their heads.

Only those in transit from one home to another dot the streets. Cars pull up and presents are unloaded. Sounds of greetings waft out to the cold air from open doorways, teasers as to what is happening inside. Then, while you're right there with them, soaking it up and sharing the invitation – ready to stroll over the threshold a common stranger but feeling a welcomed guest – the front door closes and traps the rest of the day away, as a reminder that it's not your moment to take.

In this particular neighbourhood of toy houses, one soul wanders the streets. This soul doesn't quite see the beauty in the secretive world of houses. This soul is intent on a war, wants to unravel the bow and rip open the paper to reveal what's inside door number twenty-four.

It is not of any importance to us what the occupants of door number twenty-four are doing, though, if you must know, a ten-month-old, confused as to the reason for the large green flashing prickly object in the corner of the room, is beginning to reach for the shiny red bauble that so comically reflects a familiar podgy hand and gummy mouth. This, while a two-year-old rolls around in wrapping paper, bathing herself in glitter like a hippo in muck. Beside them, *He* wraps a new necklace of diamonds around *Her* neck, as she gasps, hand flying to her chest, and shakes her head in disbelief, just as she's seen women in the black and white movies do.

None of this is important to *our* story, though it means a great deal to the individual that stands in the front garden of house number twenty-four looking at the living room's drawn curtains. Fourteen years old and with a dagger through his heart, he can't see what's going on, but his imagination was well nurtured by his mother's daytime weeping, and he can guess.

And so he raises his arms above his head, pulls back, and with all his strength pushes forward and releases the object in his hands. He stands back to watch, with bitter joy, as a fifteen-pound frozen turkey smashes through the window of the living room of number twenty-four. The drawn curtains act once again as a barrier between him and them, slowing the bird's flight through the air. With no life left to stop itself now, it − and its giblets − descend rapidly to the wooden floor, where it's sent, spinning and skidding, along to its final resting place beneath the Christmas tree. His gift to them.

People, like houses, hold their secrets. Sometimes the secrets inhabit them, sometimes they inhabit their secrets. They wrap their arms tight to hug them close, twist their tongues around the truth. But after time truth prevails, rises above all else. It squirms and wriggles inside, grows until the swollen tongue can't wrap itself around the lie any longer, until the time comes when it needs to spit the words out and send truth flying through the air and crashing into the world. Truth and time always work alongside one another.

This story is about people, secrets and time. About people who, not unlike parcels, hide secrets, who cover themselves with layers until they present themselves to the right ones who can unwrap them and see inside. Sometimes you have to give yourself to somebody in order to see who you are. Sometimes you have to unravel things to get to the core.

This is a story about a person who finds out who they are. About a person who is unravelled and whose core is revealed to all that count. And all that count are revealed to them. Just in time.

2.

A Morning of Half-Smiles

Sergeant Raphael O'Reilly moved slowly and methodically about the cramped staff kitchen of Howth Garda Station, his mind going over and over the revelations of the morning. Known to others as Raphie, pronounced *Ray-fee*, at fifty-nine years old he had one more year to go until his retirement. He'd never thought he'd be looking forward to that day until the events of this morning had grabbed him by the shoulders, turned him upside down like a snow-shaker, and he'd been forced to watch all his preconceptions sprinkle to the ground. With every step he took he heard the crackle of his once-solid tight beliefs under his boots. Of all the mornings and moments he had experienced in his forty-year career, what a morning this one had been.

He spooned two heaps of instant coffee into his mug. The mug, shaped like an NYPD squad car, had been brought back from New York by one of the boys at the station, as his Christmas gift. He pretended the sight of it offended him, but secretly he found it comforting. Gripping it in his hands during that morning's Kris Kringle reveal, he'd time-travelled back over fifty years to when he'd received a toy police car one Christmas from his parents. It was a gift he'd cherished until he'd abandoned it outside overnight and the rain had done enough rust damage to force his men into early retirement. He held the mug in his hands now, feeling that he should run it along the countertop making siren noises with his mouth before crashing it into the bag of sugar, which – if nobody was around to see – would consequently tip over and spill onto the car.

Instead of doing that, he checked around the kitchen to ensure he was alone, then added half a teaspoon of sugar to his mug. A little more confident, he coughed to disguise the crinkling sound of the sugar bag as the spoon once again pushed down and then quickly fired a heaped teaspoon into the mug. Having gotten away with two spoons, he became cocky and reached into the bag one more time.

'Drop your weapon, sir,' a female voice from the doorway called with authority.

Startled by the sudden presence, Raphie jumped, the sugar from his spoon spilling over the counter. It was a mug-on-sugar-bag pile-up. Time to call for back-up.

'Caught in the act, Raphie.' His colleague Jessica joined him at the counter and whipped the spoon from his hand.

She took a mug from the cupboard – a Jessica Rabbit novelty mug, compliments of Kris Kringle – and slid it across the counter to him. Porcelain Jessica's voluptuous breasts brushed against his car, and the boy in Raphie thought about how happy his men inside would be.

'I'll have one too.' She broke into his thoughts of his men playing pat-a-cake with Jessica Rabbit.

'Please,' Raphie corrected her.

'Please,' she imitated him, rolling her eyes.

Jessica was a new recruit. She'd just joined the station six months ago, and already Raphie had grown more than fond of her. He had a soft spot for the twenty-six-year-old, five-foot-four athletic blonde who always seemed willing and able, no matter what her task was. He also felt she brought a much-needed feminine energy to the all-male team at the station. Many of the other men agreed, but not quite for the same reasons as Raphie. He saw her as the daughter that he'd never had. Or that he'd had, but lost. He shook that thought out of his head and watched Jessica cleaning the spilled sugar from the counter.

Despite her energy, her eyes – almond-shaped and such a dark brown they were almost black – buried something beneath. As though a top-layer of soil had been freshly added, and pretty soon the weeds or whatever was decaying beneath would begin to show. Her eyes held a mystery that he didn't much want to explore, but he knew that whatever it was, it drove her forward during those stand-out times when most sensible people would go the opposite way.

'Half a spoon is hardly going to kill me,' he added grumpily after tasting his coffee, knowing that just one more spoon would have made it perfect.

'If pulling that Porsche over almost killed you last week, then half a spoon of sugar most certainly will. Are you actually *trying* to give yourself another heart attack?'

Raphie reddened. 'It was a heart *murmur*, Jessica, nothing more, and keep your voice down,' he hissed.

'You should be resting,' she said more quietly.

'The doctor said I was perfectly normal.'

'Then the doctor needs his head checked, you've never been perfectly normal.'

'You've only known me six months,' he grumbled, handing her the mug.

'Longest six months of my life,' she scoffed. 'Okay then, have the brown,' she said, feeling guilty, shovelling the spoon into the brown sugar bag and emptying a heaped spoon into his coffee.

'Brown bread, brown rice, brown this, brown that. I remember a time when my life was in Technicolor.'

'I bet you can remember a time when you could see your feet when you looked down too,' she said without a second's thought.

In an effort to dissolve the sugar in his mug completely, she stirred the spoon so hard that a portal of spinning liquid appeared in the centre. Raphie watched it and wondered: If he dived into that mug, where would it bring him.

'If you die drinking this, don't blame me,' she said, passing it to him.

'If I do, I'll haunt you until the day you die.'

She smiled but it never reached her eyes, fading somewhere between her lips and the bridge of her nose.

He watched the portal in his mug begin to die down, his chance of leaping into another world disappearing fast along with the steam that escaped the liquid. Yes, it had been one hell of a morning. Not much of a morning for smiles. Or maybe it was. A morning for half-smiles, perhaps. He couldn't decide.

Raphie handed Jessica a mug of steaming coffee – black with no sugar, just as she liked – and they both leaned against the countertop, facing one another, their lips blowing on their coffee, their feet touching the ground, their minds in the clouds.

He studied Jessica, hands wrapped around the mug and staring intently into her coffee as though it were a crystal ball. How he wished it was; how he wished they had the gift of foresight to stop so many of the things they witnessed. Her cheeks were pale, a light red rim around her eyes the only give-away to the morning they'd had.

'Some morning, eh, kiddo?'

Those almond-shaped eyes glistened but she stopped herself and hardened. She nodded and swallowed the coffee in response.

He could tell by her attempt to hide the grimace that it burned, but she took another sip as if in defiance. Standing up even against the coffee.

'My first Christmas Day on duty, I played chess with the sergeant for the entire shift.'

She finally spoke. 'Lucky you.'

'Yeah,' he nodded, remembering back. 'Didn't see it that way at the time, though. Was hoping for plenty of action.'

Forty years later he'd gotten what he'd hoped for and now he wanted to give it back. Return the gift. Get his time refunded.

'You win?'

He snapped out of his trance. 'Win what?'

'The chess game.'

'No,' he chuckled. 'Let the sergeant win.'

She ruffled her nose. 'You wouldn't see me letting you win.'

'I wouldn't doubt it for a second.'

Guessing the hot drink had reached the right temperature, Raphie finally took a sip of coffee. He immediately clutched at his throat, coughing and spluttering, feigning death and knowing immediately that despite his best efforts to lift the mood, it was in poor taste.

Jessica merely raised an eyebrow and continued sipping.

He laughed and then the silence continued.

'You'll be okay,' he assured her.

She nodded again and responded curtly as though she already knew. 'Yep. You call Mary?'

He nodded. 'Straight away. She's with her sister.' A seasonal lie; a white lie for a white Christmas. 'You call anyone?'

She nodded but averted her gaze, not offering more, never offering more. 'Did you, em . . . did you tell her?'

'No. No.'

'Will you?'

He gazed into the distance again. 'I don't know. Will you tell anyone?'

She shrugged, her look as unreadable as always. She nodded down the hall at the holding room. 'The Turkey Boy is still waiting in there.'

Raphie sighed. 'What a waste.' Of a life or of his own time, he didn't make clear. 'He's one that could do with knowing.'

Jessica paused just before taking a sip, and fixed those near-black almond-shaped eyes on him from above the rim of the mug. Her voice was as solid as faith in a nunnery, so firm and devoid of all doubt that he didn't have to question her certainty.

'Tell him,' she said firmly. 'If we never tell anybody else in our lives, at least let's tell him.'

3.

The Turkey Boy

Raphie entered the interrogation room as though he was entering his living room and was about to settle himself on his couch with his feet up for the day. There was nothing threatening about his demeanour whatsoever. Despite his height of six foot two, he fell short of filling the space his physical body took up. His head was, as usual, bent over in contemplation, his eyebrows mirroring the angle by dropping to cover his pea-sized eyes. The top of his back was slightly hunched, as though he carried a small shell as shelter. On his belly was an even bigger shell. In one hand was a Styrofoam cup, in the other his half-drunk NYPD mug of coffee.

The Turkey Boy glanced at the mug in Raphie's hand. 'Cool. Not.'

'So is throwing a turkey through a window.'

The boy smirked at the sentence and started chewing on the end of the string on his hooded top.

'What made you do that?'

'My dad's a prick.'

'I gathered it wasn't a Christmas gift for being father of the year. What made you think of the turkey?'

He shrugged. 'My mam told me to take it out of the freezer,' he offered, as if by way of explanation.

'So how did it get from the freezer to the floor of your dad's house?'

'I carried it most of the way, then it flew the rest.' He smirked again.

'When were you planning on having dinner?'

'At three.'

'I meant what day. It takes a minimum of twenty-four hours of defrosting time for every five pounds of turkey. Your turkey was fifteen pounds. You should have taken the turkey out of the freezer three days ago if you intended on eating it today.'

'Whatever, Ratatouille.' He looked at Raphie like he was crazy. 'If I'd stuffed it with bananas too would I be in less trouble?'

'The reason I mention it, is because if you had taken it out when you should have, it wouldn't have been hard enough to go through a window. That may sound like planning to a jury, and no, bananas and turkey isn't a clever recipe.'

'I didn't plan it!' he squealed, and his age showed.

Raphie drank his coffee and watched the young teenager.

The boy looked at the cup before him and ruffled his nose. 'I don't drink coffee.'

'Okay.' Raphie lifted the Styrofoam cup from the table and emptied the contents into his mug. 'Still warm. Thanks. So, tell me about this morning. What were you thinking, son?'

'Unless you're the other fat bastard whose window I threw a bird through, then I'm not your son. And what's this, a therapy session or interrogation? Are you charging me with something or what?'

'We're waiting to hear whether your dad is going to press charges.'

'He won't.' He rolled his eyes. 'He can't. I'm under sixteen. So if you just let me go now, you won't waste any of your time.'

'You've already wasted a considerable amount of it.'

'It's Christmas Day, I doubt there's much else for you to do around here.' He eyed Raphie's stomach. 'Other than eat doughnuts.'

'You'd be surprised.'

'Try me.'

'Some idiot kid threw a turkey through a window this morning.'

He rolled his eyes and looked at the clock on the wall, ticking away. 'Where are my parents?'

'Wiping grease off their floor.'

'They're not my parents,' he spat. 'At least, *she's* not my mother. If she comes with him to collect me, I'm not going.'

'Oh, I doubt very much that they'll come to take you home with them.' Raphie reached into his pocket and took out a chocolate sweet. He unwrapped it slowly, the wrapper rustling in the quiet room. 'Did you ever notice the strawberry ones are always the last ones left over in the tin?' He smiled before popping it in his mouth.

'I bet nothing's ever left in the tin when you're around.'

'Your father and his partner –'

'Who, for the record,' Turkey Boy interrupted Raphie and leaned close to the recording device, 'is a whore.'

'They may pay us a visit to press charges.'

'Dad wouldn't do that.' He swallowed, his eyes puffy with frustration.

'He's thinking about it.'

'No he's not,' the boy whined. 'If he is it's probably because she's making him. Bitch.'

'It's more probable that he'll do it because it's now snowing in his living room.'

13

'Is it snowing?' He looked like a child again, eyes wide with hope.

Raphie sucked on his sweet. 'Some people just bite right into chocolate; I much prefer to suck it.'

'Suck on this.' The Turkey Boy grabbed his crotch.

'You'll have to get your boyfriend to do that.'

'I'm not gay,' he huffed, then leaned forward and the child returned. 'Ah, come on, is it snowing? Let me out to see it, will you? I'll just look out the window.'

Raphie swallowed his sweet and leaned his elbows on the table. He spoke firmly. 'Glass from the window landed on the ten-month-old baby.'

'So?' the boy snarled, bouncing back in his chair, but he looked concerned. He began pulling at a piece of skin around his nail.

'He was beside the Christmas tree, where the turkey landed. Luckily he wasn't cut. The baby, that is, not the turkey. The turkey sustained quite a few injuries. We don't think he'll make it.'

The boy looked relieved and confused all at the same time.

'When's my mam coming to get me?'

'She's on her way.'

'The girl with the', he cupped his hands over his chest, 'big jugs told me that two hours ago. What happened to her face by the way? You two have a lovers' tiff?'

Raphie bristled over how the boy spoke about Jessica, but kept his calm. He wasn't worth it. Was he even worth sharing the story with at all?

'Maybe your mother is driving very slowly. The roads are very slippy.'

The Turkey Boy thought about that and looked a little worried. He continued pulling at the skin around his nail.

'The turkey was too big,' he added, after a long pause. He clenched and unclenched his fists on the table. 'She bought the same-sized turkey she used to buy when he was home. She thought he'd be coming back.'

'Your mother thought this about your dad,' Raphie confirmed, rather than asked.

He nodded. 'When I took it out of the freezer it just made me crazy. It was too big.'

Silence again.

'I didn't think the turkey would break the glass,' he said, quieter now and looking away. 'Who knew a *turkey* could break a window?'

He looked up at Raphie with such desperation that, despite the seriousness of the situation, Raphie had to fight a smile at the boy's misfortune.

'I just meant to give them a fright. I knew they'd all be in there playing happy families.'

'Well, they're definitely not any more.'

The boy didn't say anything but seemed less happy about it than when Raphie had entered.

'A fifteen-pound turkey seems very big for just three people.'

'Yeah, well, my dad's a fat bastard, what can I say.'

Raphie decided he was wasting his time. Fed up, he stood up to leave.

'Dad's family used to come for dinner every year,' the boy caved in, calling out to Raphie in an effort to keep him in the room. 'But they decided not to come this year either. The turkey was just too bloody big for the two of us,' he repeated, shaking his head. Dropping the bravado act, his tone changed. 'When will my mam be here?'

Raphie shrugged. 'I don't know. Probably when you've learned your lesson.'

'But it's Christmas Day.'

'As good a day as any to learn a lesson.'

'Lessons are for kids.'

Raphie smiled at that.

'What?' the boy spat defensively.

'I learned one today.'

'Oh, I forgot to add *retards* to that too.'

Raphie made his way to the door.

'So what lesson did you learn then?' the boy asked quickly, and Raphie could sense in his voice that he didn't want to be left alone.

Raphie stopped and turned, feeling sad, looking sad.

'It must have been a pretty shit lesson.'

'You'll find that most lessons are.'

The Turkey Boy sat slumped over the table, his unzipped hooded top hanging off one shoulder, small pink ears peeping out from his greasy hair that sat on his shoulders, his cheeks covered in pink pimples, his eyes a crystal blue. He was only a child.

Raphie sighed. Surely he'd be forced into early retirement for telling this story. He pulled out the chair and sat down.

'Just for the record,' Raphie said, '*you* asked *me* to tell you this.'

The Beginning of the Story

4.

The Shoe Watcher

Lou Suffern always had two places to be at the one time. When asleep, he dreamed. In between dreams, he ran through the events of that day while making plans for the next, so that when he was awakened by his alarm at six a.m. every morning, he found himself to be very poorly rested. When in the shower, he rehearsed presentations and, on occasion, with one hand outside of the shower curtain he responded to emails on his BlackBerry. While eating breakfast he read the newspaper, and when being told rambling stories by his five-year-old daughter, he listened to the morning news. When his thirteen-month-old son demonstrated new skills each day, Lou's face displayed interest while at the same time the inner workings of his brain were analysing why he felt the exact opposite. When kissing his wife goodbye, he was thinking of another.

Every action, movement, appointment, a doing or thought of any kind, was layered by another. Driving to work was also a conference call by speakerphone. Breakfasts ran into lunches, lunches into pre-dinner drinks, drinks into dinners, dinners into after-dinner drinks, after-dinner drinks into . . . well, that depended on how lucky he got. On those lucky nights at whatever house, apartment, hotel room or office that he felt himself appreciating his luck and the company of another, he of course would convince those who wouldn't share his appreciation – namely his wife – that he was in another place. To them, he was stuck in a meeting, at an airport, finishing up some important paperwork, or buried in the maddening Christmas traffic. Two places, quite magically, at once.

Everything overlapped, he was always moving, always had someplace else to be, always wished that he was elsewhere or that, thanks to some divine intervention, he could be in both places at the same time. He'd spend as little time as possible with each person and leave them feeling that it was enough. He wasn't a tardy man, he was precise, always on time. In business he was a master timekeeper; in life he was a broken pocket watch. He strove for perfection and possessed boundless energy in his quest for success. However, it was these bounds – so eager to attain his fast-growing list of desires and so full of ambition to reach new dizzying heights – that caused him to soar above the heads of the most important. There was no appointed time in his schedule for those whom, given the time of day, could lift him higher in more ways than any new deal could possibly accomplish.

On one particular cold Tuesday morning along the continuously developing dockland of Dublin city, Lou's black leather shoes, polished to perfection, strolled confidently across the eyeline of one particular man. This man watched the shoes in movement that morning, as he had yesterday and as he assumed he would tomorrow. There was no best foot forward, for both were equal in their abilities. Each stride was equal in length, the heel-to-toe combination so precise; his shoes pointing forward, heels striking first and then pushing off from the big toe, flexing at the ankle. Perfect each time. The sound rhythmic as they hit the pavement. There was no heavy pounding to shake the ground beneath him, as was the case with the decapitated others who raced by at this hour with their heads still on their pillows despite their bodies being out in the fresh air. No, his shoes made a tapping sound as intrusive and unwelcome as raindrops on a conservatory roof, the hem of his trousers flapping slightly like a flag in a light breeze on an eighteenth hole.

The watcher half-expected the slabs of pavement to light up as he stepped on each, and for the owner of the shoes to break out into a tap dance about how swell and dandy the day was turning out to be. For the watcher, a swell and dandy day it was most certainly going to be.

Usually the shiny black shoes beneath the impeccable black suits would float stylishly by the watcher, through the revolving doors and into the grand marble entrance of the latest modern glass building to be squeezed through the cracks of the quays and launched up into the Dublin sky. But that morning the shoes stopped directly before the watcher. And then they turned, making a gravelly noise as they pivoted on the cold concrete. The watcher had no choice but to lift his gaze from the shoes.

'Here you go,' Lou said, handing him a coffee. 'It's an Americano, hope you don't mind, they were having problems with the machine so they couldn't make a latte.'

'Take it back then,' the watcher said, turning his nose up at the cup of steaming coffee offered to him.

This was greeted by a stunned silence.

'Only joking.' He laughed at the startled look, and very quickly – in case the joke was unappreciated and the gesture was rethought and withdrawn – reached for the cup and cradled it with his numb fingers. 'Do I look like I care about steamed milk?' he grinned, before his expression changed to a look of pure ecstasy. 'Mmmm.' He pushed his nose up against the rim of the cup to smell the coffee beans. He closed his eyes and savoured it, not wanting the sense of sight to take away from this divine smell. The cardboard-like cup was so hot, or his hands so cold, that it burned right through them, sending torpedoes of heat and shivers through his body. He hadn't known how cold he was until he'd felt the heat.

'Thanks very much indeed.'

'No problem. I heard on the radio that today's going to be the coldest day of the year.' The shiny shoes stamped the concrete slabs and his leather gloves rubbed together as proof of his word.

'Well, I'd believe them all right. Never mind the brass monkeys, it's cold enough to freeze my own balls off. But this will help.' The watcher blew on the drink slightly, preparing to take his first sip.

'There's no sugar in it,' Lou apologised.

'Ah well then.' The watcher rolled his eyes and quickly pulled the cup away from his lips, as though in it there was contained a deadly disease. 'I can let you off the steamed milk, but forgetting to add sugar is a step too far.' He offered it back to Lou.

Getting the message, and the joke this time, Lou laughed. 'Okay, okay, I get the point.'

'Beggars can't be choosers, isn't that what they say? Is that to say choosers can be beggars?' The watcher raised an eyebrow, smiled, and finally took his first sip. So engrossed in the sensation of heat and caffeine travelling through his cold body, he hadn't noticed that suddenly the watcher became the watched.

'Oh. I'm Gabe.' He reached out his hand. 'Gabriel, but everyone who knows me calls me Gabe.'

Lou reached out and shook his hand. Warm leather to cold skin. 'I'm Lou, but everyone who knows me calls me a prick.'

Gabe laughed. 'Well, that's honesty for you. How's about I call you Lou until I know you better.'

They smiled at one another and then were quiet in the

sudden sliver of awkwardness. Two little boys trying to make friends in a schoolyard. The shiny shoes began to fidget slightly, tip-tap, tap-tip, Lou's side-to-side steps a combination of trying to keep warm and trying to figure out whether to leave or stay. They twisted around slowly to face the building next door. He would soon follow in the direction of his feet.

'Busy this morning, isn't it?' Gabe said easily, bringing the shoes back to face him again.

'Christmas is only a few weeks away, always a hectic time,' Lou agreed.

'The more people around, the better it is for me,' Gabe said as a twenty cent went flying into his cup. 'Thank you,' he called to the lady who'd barely paused to drop the coin. From her body language one would almost think it had fallen through a hole in her pocket rather than being a gift. He looked up at Lou with big eyes and an even bigger grin. 'See? Coffee's on me tomorrow,' he chuckled.

Lou tried to lean over as inconspicuously as possible to steal a look at the contents of the cup. The twenty-cent piece sat alone at the bottom.

'Oh, don't worry. I empty it now and then. Don't want people thinking I'm doing too well for myself,' he laughed. 'You know how it is.'

Lou agreed, but at the same time didn't.

'Can't have people knowing I own the penthouse right across the water,' Gabe added, nodding across the river.

Lou turned around and gazed across the Liffey at Dublin quay's newest skyscraper, which Gabe was referring to. With its mirrored glass it was almost as if the building was the Looking Glass of Dublin city centre. From the re-created Viking longship that was moored along the quays, to the many cranes and new corporate and commercial buildings that framed the Liffey, to the stormy, cloud-filled sky that filled the higher floors, the building captured it all and played it back to the

23

city like a giant plasma. Shaped like a sail, at night the building was illuminated in blue and was the talk of the town, or at least had been in the months following its launch. The next best thing never lasted for too long.

'I was only joking about owning the penthouse, you know,' Gabe said, seeming a little concerned that his possible pay-off had been sabotaged.

'You like that building?' Lou asked, still staring at it in a trance.

'It's my favourite one, especially at night-time. That's one of the main reasons I sit here. That and because it's busy along here, of course. A view alone won't buy me my dinner.'

'We built that,' Lou said, finally turning back around to face him.

'Really?' Gabe took him in a bit more. Mid to late thirties, dapper suit, his face cleanly shaven, smooth as a baby's behind, his groomed hair with even speckles of grey throughout, as though someone had taken a salt canister to it and, along with grey, sprinkled charm at a ratio of 1:10. Lou reminded him of an old-style movie star, emanating suaveness and sophistication and all packaged in a full-length black cashmere coat.

'I bet it bought you dinner,' Gabe laughed, feeling a slight twinge of jealousy at that moment, which bothered him as he hadn't known any amount of jealousy until he'd studied Lou. Since meeting him he'd learned two things that were of no help, for there he was, all of a sudden cold and envious when previously he had been warm and content. Bearing that in mind, despite always being happy with his own company, he foresaw that as soon as this gentleman and he were to part ways, he would experience a loneliness he had never been previously aware of. He would then be envious, cold *and* lonely. The perfect ingredients for a nice homemade bitter pie.

The building had bought Lou more than dinner. It had gotten the company a few awards, and for him personally, a house in Howth and an upgrade from his present Porsche to the new model – the latter after Christmas, to be precise, but Lou knew not to announce that to the man sitting on the freezing cold pavement, swaddled in a flea-infested blanket. Instead, Lou smiled politely and flashed his porcelain veneers, as usual doing two things at once. Thinking one thing and saying another. But it was the in-between part that Gabe could clearly read, and this introduced a new level of awkwardness that neither of them was comfortable with.

'Well, I'd better get to work. I just work –'

'Next door, I know. I recognise the shoes. More on my level,' Gabe smiled. 'Though you didn't wear those yesterday. Tan leather, if I'm correct.'

Lou's neatly tweezed eyebrows went up a notch. Like a pebble dropped in a pool, they caused a series of ripples to rise on his as yet un-botoxed forehead.

'Don't worry, I'm not a stalker.' Gabe allowed one hand to unwrap itself from the hot cup so he could hold it up in defence. 'I've just been here a while. If anything, you people keep turning up at my place.'

Lou laughed, then self-consciously looked down at his shoes, which were the subject of conversation. 'Incredible.'

'I've never noticed you here before,' Lou thought aloud, and at the same time as saying it he was mentally reliving each morning he'd walked this route to work.

'All day, every day,' Gabe said, with false perkiness in his voice.

'Sorry, I never noticed you . . .' Lou shook his head. 'I'm always running around the place, on the phone to someone or late for someone else. Always two places to be at the same time, my wife says. Sometimes I wish I could be cloned, I get so busy,' he laughed.

Gabe gave him a curious smile at that. 'Speaking of running around, this is the first time I haven't seen those boys racing by.' Gabe nodded towards Lou's feet. 'Almost don't recognise them standing still. No fire inside today?'

Lou laughed. 'Always a fire inside there, believe you me.' He made a swift movement with his arm and, like the unveiling of a masterpiece, his coat sleeve slipped down just far enough to reveal his gold Rolex. 'I'm always the first into the office so there's no great rush now.' He observed the time with great concentration, in his head already leading an afternoon meeting.

'You're not the first in this morning,' Gabe said.

'What?' Lou's meeting was disturbed and he was back on the cold street again, outside his office, the cold Atlantic wind whipping at their faces, the crowds of people all bundled up and marching in their armies to work.

Gabe scrunched his eyes shut tight. 'Brown loafers. I've seen you walk in with him a few times. He's in already.'

'Brown loafers?' Lou laughed, first confused, then impressed and quickly concerned as to who had made it to the office before him.

'You know him – a pretentious walk. The little suede tassels kick with every step, like a mini can-can, it's like he throws them up there purposely. They've got soft soles but they're heavy on the ground. Small wide feet, and he walks on the outsides of his feet. Soles are always worn away on the outside.'

Lou's brow furrowed in concentration.

'On Saturdays he wears shoes like he's just stepped off a yacht.'

'Alfred!' Lou laughed, recognising the description. 'That's because he probably *has* just stepped off his ya—' but he stopped himself. 'He's in already?'

'About a half-hour ago. Plodded in, in a kind of a rush by the looks of it, accompanied by another pair of black slip-ons.'

'Black slip-ons?'

'Black shoes. Male shoes. A little shine but no design. Simple

26

and to the point, they just did what shoes do. Can't say much else about them apart from the fact they move slower than the other shoes.'

'You're very observant.' Lou examined him, wondering who this man had been in his previous life, before landing on cold ground in a doorway, and at the same time his mind was on overdrive in its attempt to figure out who all these people were. Alfred showing up to work so early had him flummoxed. A colleague of theirs – Cliff – had suffered a nervous breakdown and this had left them excited, yes, excited, about the opening up of a new position. Providing Cliff didn't get better, which Lou secretly hoped for, major shifts were about to take place in the company, and any unusual behaviour by Alfred was questionable. In fact, any of Alfred's behaviour at any stage was questionable.

Gabe winked. 'Don't happen to need an observant person in there for anything, do you?'

Lou parted his gloved hands. 'Sorry.'

'No problem, you know where I am if you need me. I'm the fella in the Doc Martens.' He laughed, lifting the blankets to reveal his high black boots.

'I wonder why they're in so early.' Lou looked at Gabe as though he had special powers.

'Can't help you out there, I'm afraid, but they had lunch last week. Or at least, they left the building at what's considered the average joe's lunchtime, and came back together when that time was over. What they did in between is just a matter of clever guesswork,' he chuckled. 'No flies on me. Not today anyway,' he added. 'Far too cold for flies.'

'What day was that lunch?'

Gabe closed his eyes again. 'Friday, I'd say. He's your rival, is he, brown loafers?'

'No, he's my friend. Kind of. More of an acquaintance really.' On hearing this news Lou, for the first time, showed signs of being rattled. 'He's my colleague, but with Cliff having a breakdown it's a great opportunity for either of us to, well, you know . . .'

'Steal your sick friend's job,' Gabe finished for him with a smile. 'Sweet. The slow-moving shoes? The black ones?' Gabe continued. 'They left the office the other night with a pair of Louboutins.'

'Lou— Loub— what are they?'

'Identifiable by their lacquered red sole. These particular ones had one-hundred-and-twenty-millimetre heels.'

'Millimetres?' Lou questioned, then, 'Red sole, okay,' he nodded, absorbing it all.

'You could always just *ask* your friend-slash-acquaintance-slash-colleague who he was meeting,' Gabe suggested with a glint in his eye.

Lou didn't respond directly to that. 'Right, I'd better run. Things to see, people to do, and both at the same time, would you believe,' he winked. 'Thanks for your help, Gabe.' He slipped a ten-euro note into Gabe's cup.

'Cheers, man,' Gabe beamed, immediately grabbing it from the cup and tucking it into his pocket. He tapped his finger. 'Can't let them know, remember?'

'Right,' Lou agreed.

But, at the exact same time, didn't agree at all.

5.

The Thirteenth Floor

'Going up?'

There was a universal grunt and nodding of heads from inside the crammed elevator as the enquiring gentleman on the second floor looked at sleepy faces with hope. All but Lou responded, that was, for Lou was too preoccupied with studying the gentleman's shoes, which stepped over the narrow gap that led to the cold black drop below, and into the confined space. Brown brogues shuffled around one hundred and eighty degrees, in order to face the front. Lou was looking for red soles and black shoes. Alfred had arrived early and had lunch with black shoes. Black shoes left the office with red soles. If he could find out who owned the red soles, then he'd know who she worked with, and then he'd know who Alfred was secretly meeting. This process made more sense to Lou than simply asking Alfred, which said a lot about the nature of Alfred's honesty. This, he thought about at the exact same time as sharing the uncomfortable silence that only an elevator of strangers could bring.

'What floor do you want?' a muffled voice came from the corner of the elevator, where a man was well-hidden – possibly squashed – and, as the only person with access to the buttons, was forced to deal with the responsibility of commandeering the elevator stops.

'Thirteen, please,' the new arrival said.

There were a few sighs and one person tutted.

'There is no thirteenth floor,' the body-less man replied.

The elevator doors closed and it ascended quickly.

'You'd better be quick,' the body-less man urged.

'Em . . .' The man fumbled in his briefcase for his schedule.

'You either want the twelfth floor or the fourteenth floor,' the muffled voice offered. 'There's no thirteen.'

'Surely he needs to get off on the fourteenth floor,' somebody else offered. 'The fourteenth floor *is* technically the thirteenth floor.'

'Do you want me to press fourteen?' the voice asked a little more tetchily.

'Em . . .' The man continued to fumble with papers.

Lou couldn't concentrate on the unusual conversation in the usually quiet elevator, as he was preoccupied with studying the shoes around him. Lots of black shoes. Some with detail, some scuffed, some polished, some slip-ons, some untied. No obvious red soles. He noticed the feet around him beginning to twitch and shift from foot to foot. One pair moved away from him ever so slightly. His head shot up immediately as the elevator pinged.

'Going up?' the young woman asked.

There was a more helpful chorus of male yeses this time.

She stepped in front of Lou and he checked out her shoes while the men around him checked out other areas of her body in that heavy silence that only women feel in an elevator of men. The elevator moved up again. Six . . . seven . . . eight . . .

Finally, the man with the brown brogues emerged from his briefcase empty-handed, and with an air of defeat announced, 'Patterson Developments.'

Lou pondered the confusion with irritation. It had been his suggestion that there be no number thirteen on the elevator panel, but of course there was a thirteenth floor. There wasn't a gap with *nothing* before getting to the fourteenth floor; the fourteenth didn't hover on some invisible bricks. The fourteenth *was* the thirteenth, and his offices were on the thirteenth. But it was known as the fourteenth. Why it confused everybody, he had no idea: it was as clear as day to him. He exited on the fourteenth and stepped out, his feet sinking into the spongy plush carpet.

'Good morning, Mr Suffern.' His secretary greeted him without looking up from her papers.

He stopped at her desk and looked at her with a puzzled expression. 'Alison, call me Lou, like you always do, please.'

'Of course, Mr Suffern,' she said perkily, refusing to look him in the eye.

While Alison moved about, Lou tried to get a glimpse of the soles of her shoes. He was still standing at her desk when she returned and once again refused to meet his eye as she sat down and began typing. As inconspicuously as possible, he bent down to tie his shoelaces and peeked through the gap in her desk.

She frowned and crossed her long legs. 'Is everything okay, Mr Suffern?'

'Call me Lou,' he repeated, still puzzled.

'No,' she said rather moodily and looked away. She grabbed the diary from her desk. 'Shall we go through today's appointments?' She stood and made her way around the desk.

Tight silk blouse, tight skirt, his eyes scanned her body before getting to her shoes.

'How high are they?'

'Why?'

'Are they one hundred and twenty millimetres?'

'I've no idea. Who measures heels in millimetres?'

31

'I don't know. Some people. *Gabe*,' he smiled, following her as they made their way into his office, trying to get a glimpse of her soles.

'Who the hell is Gabe?' she muttered.

'Gabe is a homeless man,' he laughed.

As she turned around to question him, she caught him with his head tilted, studying her. 'You're looking at me the same way you look at the art on these walls,' she said smartly.

Modern impressionism. He'd never been a fan of it. Regularly throughout the days he'd find himself stopping to stare at the blobs of nothing that covered the walls of the corridors of these offices. Splashes and lines scraped into the canvas that somebody considered something, and which could easily be hung upside down or back to front with nobody being any the wiser. He'd contemplate the money that had been spent on them too – and then he'd compare them to the pictures lining his refrigerator door at home; home art by his daughter Lucy. And as he'd tilt his head from side to side, as he was doing with Alison now, he knew there was a playschool teacher out there somewhere with millions of euro lining her pockets, while four-year-olds with paint on their hands, their tongues dangling from their mouths in concentration, received gummy bears instead of a percentage of the takings.

'Do you have red soles?' he asked Alison, making his way to his gigantic leather chair that a family of four could live in.

'Why, did I step in something?' She stood on one foot and hopped around lightly, trying to keep her balance while checking her soles, appearing to Lou like a dog trying to chase its tail.

'It doesn't matter.' He sat down at his desk wearily.

She viewed him with suspicion before returning her attention to her schedule. 'At eight thirty you have a phone call with Aonghus O'Sullibháin about needing to become a fluent Irish speaker in order to buy that plot in Connemara. However, I have arranged for your benefit for the conversation to be *as Béarla . . .*' She smirked and threw back her head, like a horse would, pushing her mane of highlighted hair off her face. 'At eight forty-five you have a meeting with Barry Brennan about the slugs they found on the Cork site –'

'Cross your fingers they're not rare,' he groaned.

'Well, you never know, sir, they could be relatives of yours. You have some family in Cork, don't you?' She still wouldn't look at him. 'At nine thirty –'

'Hold on a minute.' Despite knowing he was alone with her in the room, Lou looked around hoping for back-up. 'Why are you calling me *sir*? What's gotten into you today?'

She looked away, mumbling what Lou thought sounded like, 'Not you, that's for sure.'

'What did you say?' But he didn't wait for an answer. 'I've a busy day, I could do without the sarcasm, thank you. And since when did the day's schedule become a morning announcement?'

'I thought that if you heard how packed your day is, *aloud*, then you might decide to give me the go-ahead to make less appointments in future.'

'Do you want less work to do, Alison, is that what this is all about?'

'No,' she blushed. 'Not at all. I just thought that you could change your work routine a little. Instead of these manic days spent darting around, you could spend *more* time with *fewer* clients. Happier clients.'

'Yes, then me and Jerry Maguire will live together happily ever after. Alison, you're new to the company so I'll let this go by, but this is how I like to do business, okay? I like to be busy, I don't need two-hour lunchbreaks and schoolwork at the kitchen table with the kids.' He narrowed his eyes. 'You mentioned happier clients; have you had any complaints?'

'Your mother. Your *wife*,' she said through gritted teeth. 'Your brother. Your sister. Your daughter.'

'My daughter is five years old.'

'Well, she called when you forgot to pick her up from Irish dancing lessons last Thursday.'

'That doesn't count,' he rolled his eyes, 'because my five-year-old daughter isn't going to lose the company hundreds of millions of euro, is she?' Once again he didn't wait for a response. 'Have you received any complaints from people who do *not* share my surname?'

Alison thought hard. 'Did your sister change her name back after the separation?'

He glared at her.

'Well then, no, sir.'

'What's with the *sir* thing?'

'I just thought,' her face flushed, 'that if you're going to treat me like a stranger, then that's what I'll do too.'

'How am I treating you like a stranger?'

She looked away.

He lowered his voice. 'Alison, we're at the office, what do you want me to do? Tell you how much I enjoyed screwing your brains out in the middle of discussing our appointments?'

'You didn't screw my brains out, we just kissed.'

'Whatever.' He waved his hand dismissively. 'What's this about?'

She had no answer to that but her cheeks were on fire. 'Perhaps Alfred mentioned something to me.'

Lou's heart did an unusual thing then, that he hadn't experienced before. A fluttering of some sort. 'What did he mention?'

She looked away, began fidgeting with the corner of the page. 'Well, he mentioned something about you missing that meeting last week −'

'Not *something*, I want specifics here, please.'

She bristled. 'Okay, em, well, after the meeting last week

34

with Mr O'Sullivan, he – as in Alfred –' she swallowed, 'suggested that I try to stay on top of you a bit more. He knew that I was new to the job and his advice to me was not to allow you to miss an important meeting again.'

Lou's blood boiled and his mind raced. He'd never felt such confusion. Lou spent his life running from one thing to another, missing half of the first in order just to make it to the end of the other. He did this all day every day, always feeling like he was catching up in order to get ahead. It was long and hard and tiring work. He had made huge sacrifices to get where he was. He loved his work, was totally and utterly professional and dedicated to every aspect of it. To be pulled up on missing one meeting that had not yet been scheduled when he had taken the morning off, angered him. It also angered him that it was family that had caused this. If it was another meeting he had sacrificed it for, he would feel better about it, but he felt a sudden anger at his mother. It was her that he had collected from hospital after a hip replacement, the morning of the meeting. He felt angry at his wife for talking him into doing it when his suggestion to arrange a car to collect his mother had sent her into a rage. He felt anger at his sister Marcia and his older brother Quentin for not doing it instead. He was a busy man, and the one time he chose family over work, he had to pay the price. He stood up and paced by the window, biting down hard on his lip and feeling such anger he wanted to pick up the phone and call his entire family and tell them, 'See? See, this is why I can't always be there. See? Now look what you've done!'

'Did you not tell him that I had to collect my mother from the hospital?' He said it quietly because he hated saying it. He hated hearing those words that he despised other colleagues using. Hated the excuses, their personal lives being brought into the office. To him, it was a lack of professionalism. You either did the job, or you didn't.

'Well, no, because it was my first week and Mr Patterson was standing with him and I didn't know what you would like me to say –'

'Mr Patterson was with him?' Lou asked, his eyes almost popping out of his head.

She nodded up and down, wide-eyed, like one of those toys with a loose neck.

'Right.' His heart began to slow down, now realising what was going on. His dear friend Alfred was up to his tricks. Tricks that Lou had assumed up until now that he was exempt from. Alfred could never get by a day doing things by the book. He looked at things from an awkward angle, came at conversations from an unusual perspective too; always trying to figure out the best way he could come out of any situation.

Lou's eyes searched his desk. 'Where's my post?'

'It's on the twelfth floor. The work-experience boy got confused by the missing thirteenth floor.'

'The thirteenth floor isn't missing! *We are on it!* What is *with* everyone today?'

'We are on the fourteenth floor, and having no thirteenth floor was a terrible design flaw.'

'It's not a design flaw,' he said defensively. 'Some of the greatest buildings in the world have no thirteenth floor.'

'Or roofs.'

'What?'

'The Colosseum has no roof.'

'What?!' he snapped again, getting confused. 'Tell the work-experience boy to take the stairs from now on and count his way up. That way he won't get confused by a missing number. Why is a work-experience person handling the mail anyway?'

'Harry says they're short-staffed.'

'Short-staffed? It only takes one person to get in the elevator and bring my bloody post up. How can they be short-staffed?'

His voice went up a few octaves. 'A monkey could do his job. There are people out there on the streets who'd die to work in a place like . . .'

'In a place like what?' Alison asked, but she was asking the back of Lou's head because he'd turned around and was looking out of his floor-to-ceiling windows at the pavement below, a peculiar expression on his face reflected in the glass for her to see.

She slowly began to walk away, for the first moment in the past few weeks feeling a light relief that their fling, albeit a fumble in the dark, was going no further, for perhaps she'd misjudged him, perhaps there was something wrong with him. She was new to the company and hadn't quite sussed him out yet. All she knew of him was that he reminded her of the White Rabbit in *Alice in Wonderland*, always seeming late, late, late for a very important date but managing to get to every appointment just in the nick of time. He was a kind man to everybody he met and was successful at his job. Plus he was handsome and charming and drove a Porsche, and those things she valued more than anything else. Sure, she felt a slight twinge of guilt about what had happened last week with Lou, when she had spoken to his wife on the phone, but then it was quickly erased by, in Alison's opinion, his wife's absolute naiveté when it came to her husband's infidelities. Besides, everybody had a weak spot, and any man could be forgiven if their Achilles heel just happened to be her.

'What shoes does Alfred wear?' Lou called out, just before she closed the door.

She stepped back inside. 'Alfred who?'

'Berkeley.'

'I don't know.' Her face flushed. 'Why do you want to know?'

'For a Christmas present.'

37

'Shoes? You want to get Alfred a pair of *shoes*? But I've already ordered the Brown Thomas hampers for everyone, like you asked.'

'Just find out for me. But don't make it obvious. Just casually enquire, I want to surprise him.'

She narrowed her eyes with suspicion. 'Sure.'

'Oh, and that new girl in accounts. What's her name . . . Sandra, Sarah?'

'Deirdre.'

'Check her shoes too. Let me know if they've got red soles.'

'They don't. They're from Top Shop. Black ankle boots, suede with water marks. I bought a pair of them last year. When they were in fashion.'

With that, she left.

Lou sighed, collapsed into his oversized chair and held his fingers to the bridge of his nose, hoping to stop the migraine that loomed. Maybe he was coming down with something. He'd already wasted fifteen minutes of his morning talking to a homeless man, which was totally out of character for him, but he'd felt compelled to stop. Something about the young man demanded he stop and offer him his coffee.

Unable to concentrate on his schedule, Lou once again turned to look out at the city below. Gigantic Christmas decorations adorned the quays and bridges; giant mistletoe and bells that swayed from one side to the other thanks to the festive magic of neon. The river Liffey was at full capacity and gushed by his window and out to Dublin Bay. The pavements were aflow with people charging to work, keeping in time with the currents, following the same direction as the tide. They pounded the pavement as they powerwalked by the gaunt copper figures dressed in rags, which had been constructed to commemorate those during the famine forced to walk these very quays to emigrate. Instead of small parcels of belongings in their hands, the Irish people of this district now carried Starbucks coffee in one hand, briefcases in the other. Women walked to the office wearing trainers with their skirts, their high heels tucked away in their bags. A whole different destiny and endless opportunities awaiting them.

The only thing that was static was Gabe, tucked away in a doorway, near the entrance, wrapped up on the ground and watching the shoes march by, the opportunities for him still not quite as equal as for those that trampled by. Though only slightly bigger than a dot on the pavement thirteen floors down, Lou could see Gabe's arm rise and fall as he sipped on his coffee, making every mouthful last, even if by now it was surely cold. Gabe intrigued him. Not least because of his talent for recalling every pair of shoes that belonged in the building as though they were a maths timetable, but, more alarmingly, because the person behind those crystal-blue eyes was remark-ably familiar. In fact, Gabe reminded Lou of himself. The two men were similar in age and, given the right grooming, Gabe could very easily have been mistaken for Lou. He seemed a personable, friendly, capable man. It could so easily be Lou sitting on the pavement outside, watching the world go by, yet how different their lives were.

At that very instant, as though feeling Lou's eyes on him, Gabe looked up. Thirteen floors up and Lou felt like Gabe was staring straight at his soul, his eyes searing into him.

This confused Lou. His involvement in the development of this building entitled him to the knowledge that, beyond any reasonable doubt, from the outside the glass was reflective. Gabe couldn't possibly have been able to see him as he stared up, his chin to the air, with a hand across his forehead to block out the light, almost in salute. He could only have been looking at a reflection of some kind, Lou reasoned, a bird perhaps had swooped and caught his eye. That's right, a reflection was all it could be. But so intent was Gabe's gaze, which reached up the full thirteen floors to Lou's office window and all the way into Lou's eyes, that it caused Lou to put aside his water-tight belief. He lifted up his hand, smiled tightly and gave a small salute. Before he could wait for a reaction from Gabe, he wheeled his chair away from the window and spun around, his pulse rate quickening, as though he'd been caught doing something he shouldn't.

The phone rang. It was Alison and she didn't sound happy.

'Before I tell you what I'm about to tell you, I just want to let you know that I qualified from UCD with a business degree.'

'Congratulations,' Lou said.

She cleared her throat. 'Here you go. Alfred wears size eight brown loafers. Apparently he's got ten pairs of the same shoes and he wears them every day, so I don't think the idea of another pair as a Christmas gift would go down too well. I don't know what make they are but the sad thing is I can find out for you.' She took a breath. 'As for the shoes with the red soles, Louise bought a new pair and wore them last week but they cut the ankle off her so she took them back, but the shop wouldn't take them back because it was obvious she'd worn them because the red sole had begun to wear off.'

'Who's Louise?'

'Mr Patterson's secretary.'

'I'll need you to find out from her who she left work with every day last week.'

'No way, that's not in my job description!'

'You can leave work early if you find out for me.'

'Okay.'

'Thank you for cracking under such pressure.'

'No problem, I can get started on my Christmas shopping.'

'Don't forget my list.'

So, despite Lou learning very little, the same odd feeling rushed into his heart, something others would identify as panic. But Gabe had been right about the shoes and so wasn't a lunatic, as Lou had secretly suspected. Earlier, Gabe had asked if Lou needed an observant eye around the building, and so, picking up the phone, Lou rethought his earlier decision.

'Can you get me Harry from the mailroom on the phone, and then get one of my spare shirts, a tie and trousers from the closet and take them downstairs to the guy sitting at the door. Take him to the men's room first, make sure he's tidied up, and then take him down to the mailroom. His name is Gabe and Harry will be expecting him. I'm going to cure his little short-staffing problem.'

'What?'

'Gabe. It's short for Gabriel. But call him Gabe.'

'No, I meant –'

'Just do it. Oh, and Alison?'

'What?'

'I really enjoyed our kiss last week and I look forward to screwing your brains out in the future.'

He heard a light laugh slip from her throat before the phone went dead.

He'd done it again. While in the process of telling the truth, he had the almost admirable quality of telling a total and utter lie. And through helping somebody else – Gabe – Lou was also helping himself; a good deed was indeed a triumph for the soul. Despite that, Lou knew that somewhere beneath his plotting and soul-saving there lay another plot, which was the beginning of a saving of a very different kind. That of his own skin. And even deeper in this onion man's complexities, he knew that this outreach was prompted by fear. Not just by the very fear that – had all reason and luck failed him – Lou could so easily be in Gabe's position at this very moment, but in a layer so deeply buried from the surface that it almost wasn't felt and certainly wasn't seen, there lay the fear of a reported crack – a blip in Lou's engineering of his own career. As much

41

as he wanted to ignore it, it niggled. The fear was there, it was there all the time, but it was merely disguised as something else for others to see.

Just like the thirteenth floor.

6.

A Deal Sealed

While Lou's meeting with Mr Brennan about the — thankfully not rare but still problematic — slugs on the development site in County Cork was close to being wrapped up, Alison appeared at his office door, looking anxious, and with the pile of clothes for Gabe still draped in her outstretched arms.

'Sorry, Barry, we'll have to wrap it up now,' Lou rushed. 'I have to run, I've two places to be right now, both of them across town, and you know what the traffic is like.' And just like that, with a porcelain smile and a firm warm handshake, Mr Brennan found himself back in the elevator descending to the ground floor, with his winter coat draped over one arm and his paperwork stuffed into his briefcase and tucked under the other. Yet, at the same time, it had been a pleasant meeting.

'Did he say no?' Lou asked Alison.

'Who?'

'Gabe? Did he not want the job?'

'There was no one there.' She looked confused. 'I stood at reception calling and calling his name — God it was so embarrassing — and nobody came. Was this part of a joke, Lou?

43

I can't believe that after you made me show the Romanian rose-seller into Alfred's office that I'd fall for this again.'

'It's not a joke.' He took her arm and dragged her over to his window.

'But there was no man there,' she said with exasperation.

He looked out the window and saw Gabe still in the same place on the ground. A light rain was starting to fall, spitting against the window at first and then quickly making a tapping sound as it turned to hailstones. Gabe pushed himself back further into the doorway, tucking his feet in closer to his chest and away from the wet ground. He lifted the hood from his sweater over his head and pulled the drawstrings tightly, which from all the way up on the thirteenth floor seemed to be attached to Lou's heartstrings.

'Is that not a man?' he asked, pointing out the window.

Alison squinted and moved her nose closer to the glass. 'Yes, but –'

He grabbed the clothes from her arms. 'I'll do it myself,' he said.

As soon as Lou stepped through the lobby's revolving doors, the icy air whipped at his face. His breath was momentarily taken away by a great gush and the rain alone felt like ice-cubes hitting his skin. Gabe was concentrating intently on the shoes that passed him, focusing his mind on something else, no doubt to try to ignore the elements that were thrashing around him. In his mind he was elsewhere, anywhere but there. On a beach where it was warm, where the sand was like velvet and the Liffey before him was the endless sea. While in this other world he felt a kind of bliss that a man in his position shouldn't.

His face, however, didn't reflect that. Gone was the look of warm contentment of that morning. His blue eyes were colder than the heated pools of earlier as they followed Lou's shoes from the revolving doors all the way to the edge of his blanket.

As Gabe watched the shoes, he was imagining them to be the feet of a local man working at the beach he was currently lounging on. The local was approaching him with a cocktail balanced dangerously in the centre of a tray, the tray held out and high from his body like the arms of a candelabra. Gabe had ordered this drink quite some time ago but he'd let the man away with the small delay. It was a hotter day than usual, the sand was crammed with glistening coconut-scented bodies and so he would forgive this local his shortcomings. The muggy air was slowing everybody down. The flipflop-clad feet that approached him sank into the sand, spraying grains of sand into the air with each step. As they neared him, the grains of sand became splashes of raindrops, and the flipflops became a familiar pair of shiny shoes. Gabe looked up, hoping to see a multicoloured cocktail filled with fruit and umbrellas on a tray. Instead, he saw Lou with a pile of clothes over his arm, and it took him a moment to adjust once again to the cold, the noise of the traffic and the hustle and bustle that had replaced his tropical paradise.

Lou's appearance of earlier that morning had also altered. His hair had lost its Cary Grant-like sheen and neatly combed quiff, and the shoulders of his suit appeared to be covered in dandruff as the little white balls of ice falling from the sky nested in his expensive suit and took their time to melt. When they did, they left dark patches on the fabric. He was uncharacteristically windswept and his usually relaxed shoulders were instead hunched high in an effort to shield his ears from the cold. His body trembled, missing his cashmere coat like a sheep who'd just been sheared and now stood knobbly-kneed and naked.

'You want a job?' Lou asked confidently, but it came out quiet and meek as half of his volume was taken away by the wind and the question asked instead to a stranger further down the pavement.

45

Gabe simply smiled. 'You're sure?'

Confused by his reaction, Lou nodded. He wasn't expecting a hug and a kiss but his offer seemed almost *expected*. This he didn't like. He was more atuned to a song and a dance, an ooh and an ahh, a thank you and a declaration of indebtedness. But he didn't get this from Gabe. What he did get was a quiet smile and, after Gabe had thrown off the blanket from his body and raised himself to his full height, a firm, thankful – and, in spite of the temperature, a surprisingly warm – handshake. Without Gabe hearing another word, it was as though they were already sealing a deal Lou couldn't recall negotiating.

Standing at exactly the same height, their blue eyes gazed directly into one another's, Gabe's from under the hood that was pulled down low over his eyes, monk-like, boring into Lou's with such intensity that Lou blinked and looked away. At the same time as that blink occurred, a doubt entered Lou's mind, now that the mere thought of a good deed was becoming a reality. The doubt came breezing through like a stubborn guest through a hotel lobby with no booking, and Lou stood there, confused as to what decision to make. Where to put this doubt. Keep it or turn it away. He had many questions to ask Gabe, many questions he probably should have asked, but there was only one that he could think of right then.

'Can I trust you?' Lou asked.

He had wanted to be convinced, for his mind to be put at ease, but he did not count on receiving the kind of response he was given.

Gabe barely blinked. 'With your life.'

The Presidential Suite for the gentleman and his word.

7.

On Reflection

G abe and Lou left the icy air and entered the warmth of the marble entrance hall. With walls, floors and pillars of granite covered by swirls of creams, caramels and Cadbury-chocolate colours, Gabe was just short of licking the surfaces. He had known he was cold, but until he felt this warmth he'd had no idea of the extent. Lou felt all eyes on him as he led the rugged-looking man through reception and into the Gents on the ground floor. Unsure of why, Lou took it upon himself to check each toilet cubicle before talking.

'Here, I brought you these.' Lou handed Gabe the pile of clothes, which were slightly damp now. 'You can keep them.'

He turned to face the mirror to comb his hair back into its perfect position, wiped away the hailstones and raindrops from his shoulders and tried his best to return to normality, physically and mentally, as Gabe slowly sifted through the belongings. Grey Gucci trousers, a white shirt, a grey and white striped tie. He fingered them all delicately as though a single touch would reduce them to shreds.

While Gabe discarded his blanket in the sink and then went into one of the cubicles to dress, Lou paced up and down the urinals responding to phone calls and emails. He was so busy with his work that when he looked up from his device, he didn't recognise the man before him and returned his attention to his BlackBerry. But then he slowly reared his head again, realising with a start that it was Gabe.

The only thing to show that this was the same man were the dirty pair of Doc Martens beneath the Gucci trousers. Everything fitted perfectly, and Gabe stood before the mirror, looking himself up and down as though in a trance. The woollen hat that had covered Gabe's head now revealed a thick head of black hair, similar to Lou's, though far more tousled. The warmth had replaced the coldness in his body and his lips were now full and red, his cheeks a nice rosy instead of the frozen pallid colour of before.

Lou didn't quite know what to say but, sensing a moment that was far deeper than he was comfortable with, he splashed around in the shallow end instead.

'That stuff you told me about the shoes, earlier?'

Gabe nodded.

'That was good. I wouldn't mind if you kept your eyes open for more of that kind of thing. Let me know now and then about what you see.'

Gabe nodded.

'Have you somewhere to stay?'

'Yes.' Gabe looked back at his reflection in the mirror. His voice was quiet.

'So you've an address to give Harry? He's your boss.'

'You won't be my boss?'

'No.' Lou took his BlackBerry out of his pocket and began scrolling for nothing in particular. 'No, you'll be in another . . . department.'

'Oh, of course.' Gabe straightened up, seeming a little

embarrassed for thinking otherwise. 'Right. Great. Thanks so much, Lou, really.'

Lou nodded it off, feeling embarrassed. 'Here.' He handed Gabe his comb while looking the other way.

'Thanks.' Gabe took it, held the comb under the tap and then began to shape his messed hair. Lou hurried him on and led him back out of the Gents and through the marble lobby to the elevators.

Gabe offered the comb back to Lou.

Lou shook his head and waved his hand dismissively, looking around to make sure nobody waiting with them by the elevators had seen the gesture. 'Keep it. You have an employer number, PRSI number, things like that?' he rattled off at Gabe.

Gabe shook his head, looking concerned. His fingers ran up and down the silk tie, as though it were a pet and he was afraid it would run off.

'Don't worry, we'll sort that out. Okay,' Lou started to move away as his phone began ringing, 'I'd better run, I've so many places to be right now.'

'Of course. Thanks again. Where do I —?'

But Gabe was cut off as Lou wandered around the lobby, his movements jittery as he spoke on the mobile in that half-walk, half-dance that people on mobile phones do. His left hand was jingling the loose change in his pocket, his right hand glued to his ear. 'Okay, gotta run, Michael.' Lou snapped the phone shut and tutted when he found an even bigger crowd still waiting at the elevators. 'These things really need to be fixed,' he said aloud.

Gabe fixed him with a look that Lou couldn't quite read. 'What?'

'Where do I go?' Gabe asked again.

'Oh, sorry, you're going down a floor. The mailroom.'

'Oh.' Gabe looked taken aback at first, and then his pleasant face returned again. 'Okay, great, thanks,' he nodded.

'Ever worked in one before? I bet they're, um . . . exciting places to be.' Lou knew that offering Gabe a job was a great gesture, and that there was nothing wrong with the job he was being offered, but somehow he felt that it wasn't enough, that the young man standing before him was not only capable but expectant of much more. There was no reasonable explanation for why on earth he felt this, as Gabe was as soft, friendly and appreciative as he had been the very first moment Lou had met him, but there was something about the way he . . . there was just something.

'Do you want to meet for lunch or anything?' Gabe asked hopefully.

'No can do,' Lou replied, his phone starting to ring again in his pocket. 'I've such a busy day ahead and I've . . .' He trailed off as the elevator doors opened and people began filing in. Gabe moved to step in with Lou.

'This one's going up,' Lou said quietly, his words a barrier to Gabe's entrance.

'Oh, okay.' Gabe took a few steps back. Before the doors closed and a few last people ran to scurry in, Gabe asked, 'Why are you doing this for me?'

Lou swallowed hard and shoved his hands deep into his pockets. 'Consider it a gift.' And the doors closed.

When Lou finally reached the fourteenth floor, he was more than surprised to enter his office area and see Gabe pushing a mail cart around the floor, depositing packages and envelopes on people's desks.

Unable to think of what to say but running through the time in which it had taken him to get to his floor, he merely stared at Gabe open-mouthed.

'Eh,' Gabe looked left and right with uncertainty, 'this is the thirteenth floor, isn't it?'

'It's the fourteenth,' Lou replied breathlessly, speaking the words more out of habit and barely noticing what he was saying. 'Of course you should be here, it's just that . . .' He held his hand to his forehead, which was hot. He hoped his moments in the rain without his coat hadn't made him ill. 'You got here so quickly that I just . . . never mind.' He shook his head. 'Those bloody lifts,' he mumbled to himself, making his way to his office.

Alison jumped up from her chair and blocked him from entering his office. 'Marcia's on the phone,' she called loudly. 'Again.'

Gabe pushed his cart down to the end of the plush corridor to another office, one of the wheels squeaking loudly. Lou watched him for a moment in wonder, and then snapped out of it.

'I don't have time, Alison, really, I've somewhere else to be right now and I have a meeting before I can even leave. Where are my keys?' He searched through the pockets of his coat, which was hanging from the coat stand in the corner.

'She's called three times this morning,' Alison hissed, blocking the receiver and holding it away from her body as though it were poison. 'I don't think she believes that I'm passing on her messages.'

'Messages?' Lou teased. 'I don't remember any messages.'

Alison squeaked with panic, moving the receiver high up in the air, further from Lou's grasp. 'Don't you dare do that to me, don't blame me! There are three messages already on your desk from this morning alone! And besides, your family hate me as it is.'

'They're right to, aren't they?' He stood close against her, backing her into her desk. Giving her a look that withered every part of her insides, he allowed two of his fingers to slowly crawl up her arm and to her hand, where he took the phone from her grasp. He heard a cough coming from behind him and he quickly moved away and pulled the phone to his ear. Pretending he didn't care, he casually spun around to check out who had interrupted them.

Gabe. With the squeaking mail cart that had miraculously failed to alert Lou this time.

'Yes, Marcia,' he said down the phone to his sister. 'Yes, of course I received your ten thousand messages. Alison very kindly passed them all on.' He smiled sweetly at Alison, who stuck her tongue out at him before leading Gabe into Lou's office. Lou stood up a little taller then and watched Gabe.

Following Alison into Lou's office, Gabe looked around the huge room like a child at the zoo. Lou noticed him take in the large en suite to the right, the floor-to-ceiling windows that displayed the city, the giant oak desk that took up more room than necessary, the couch area in the left-hand corner, the boardroom table to seat ten, the fifty-inch plasma on the wall. It was as big or bigger than any Dublin city apartment.

Gabe's head moved around the room, his eyes taking in everything. His expression was curiously unreadable and then their eyes met and Gabe smiled. It was an equally curious smile. It wasn't quite the face of admiration that Lou was hoping for, it most certainly wasn't of jealousy. More a look of amusement. Whatever it was, it immediately killed the pride and satisfaction that were lined up in the queue of emotions Lou planned to experience next. It was a smile that seemed only for Lou, but the problem was, Lou wasn't sure whether the joke was on him or if he and Gabe were sharing it. Feeling a lack of confidence he wasn't used to, he nodded back at Gabe in acknowledgement.

Meanwhile, over the phone, Marcia continued her mindless chat, and Lou felt as though his head was getting hotter and hotter.

'Lou? Lou, are you listening?' she asked in her soft voice.

'Absolutely, Marcia, but I really can't stay on right now because I've two places to be and neither of them are here,' he said, then, after a pause, added a laugh to soften the blow.

'Yes, I know you're so busy,' she said, and without any jibes intended she added, 'I wouldn't disturb you at work if we saw you on a Sunday once in a while.'

'Oh, here we go.' He rolled his eyes and waited for the usual rant.

'No, I'm not going there, please, just listen. Lou, I really need your help on this. Usually I wouldn't bother you, but Rick and I are going through the divorce papers and . . .' she sighed. 'Anyway, I want to get this right and I can't do it alone.'

'I'm sure you can't.' He wasn't sure of what it was she could or could not do as he had no idea what she was talking about, and he was so preoccupied with his growing paranoia over Gabe's movements around his office.

He stretched the phone cord to the corner of the room so that he could reach for his coat. In a messy twist of trying to get his coat on while keeping the phone tucked between his ear and shoulder, he dropped the receiver. He fixed his coat before swooping down to retrieve the receiver. Marcia was still talking.

'So can you at least answer my one question about the venue?'

'The venue,' he repeated. His phone rang in his pocket and he covered the speaker to silence the ring tone, wanting nothing more than to answer it.

She was quiet for a moment. 'Yes. The venue,' she said, her voice so quiet now he had to strain his ear to hear.

'Ah, yes, the venue for the . . .' He looked at Alison with his best look of alarm and she abandoned her study of Gabe to charge out from his office towards him with a bright yellow Post-it.

'A-ha!' Lou exclaimed, plucking it from her hand, saying the words as though clearly reading them. 'For your dad's – that would be *my* dad's – birthday party. You want a venue for Dad's birthday party.'

Lou felt a presence behind his back once again.

'Yes,' Marcia said, relieved. 'But I don't need a venue, we already have two, remember, I told you this? I just need you to help me choose one. Quentin thinks one and I think the other, and Mum just really wants to stay out of it, and –'

'Can you call my mobile, Marcia, I really have to run. I'm going to be late for a lunch meeting.'

'No, Lou! Just tell me where –'

'Look, I've got a great venue,' he interrupted her again, looking at his watch. 'Dad will love it and everyone will have a great time,' he rushed her off the phone.

'I don't want to introduce somewhere new at this point. You know what Dad's like. Just a small, intimate family gathering somewhere he feels comfort—'

'Intimate and comfortable. Got it.' Lou grabbed a pen from Alison's fingers and made a note of the party he was entrusting her to start organising. 'Great. What date are we having it?'

'On his birthday.' Marcia's voice was quieter with each response.

'Right, his birthday.' Lou looked up at Alison questioningly, who dove for her diary and began flicking at top speed. 'I thought we'd want to have it on a weekend so that everybody could really let themselves go. You know, let Uncle Leo really go for it on the dancefloor,' he smirked.

'He's just been diagnosed with prostate cancer.'

'Not really my point. So what date is the nearest weekend?' he improvised.

'Daddy's birthday falls on a Friday,' she said, tired now. 'It's December twenty-first, Lou. The same as it was last year and every year before that.'

'December twenty-first, right.' He looked at Alison accusingly, who wilted for not getting there first. 'That's next weekend, Marcia, why have you left it so late?'

'I haven't, I told you, everything's arranged. Both venues are ready to go.'

Lou stopped listening to her response once again, grabbed the diary from Alison and started flicking through it. 'Ah, no can do, would you believe. That's the date of the office party, and I really have to be here. We're having some important clients over. Dad's party can be on the Saturday, I'll have to move some things around,' he thought aloud, 'but the Saturday could work.'

'It's your father's *seventieth*, you can't change the date because of an *office* party,' she said disbelievingly. 'Besides, the music, the food, everything has already been decided on for that date. All we need is to decide which one of the two venues –'

'Well, cancel all that,' Lou said, hopping off the corner of the desk and getting ready to hang up. 'The venue I have in mind does its own catering and music, you won't have to lift a finger, okay? So that's all sorted. Great. I'll put you back on to Alison so she can take all the details.' He put the phone down on the desk and grabbed his briefcase.

Despite feeling Gabe's presence behind him, he didn't turn around. 'Everything okay, Gabe?' he asked, lifting files from Alison's desk and arranging them into his open briefcase.

'Yep, great. I just thought I'd ride down in the elevator with you, seeing as we're going the same way.'

'Oh.' Lou snapped the case closed, turned and didn't slow in his walk to the elevator, suddenly afraid that he'd made a big mistake and that he'd now have to show Gabe that his intentions behind getting him a job were not to find a playdate. He pressed the elevator button and, while waiting for the floor numbers to climb up, busied himself with his phone.

'So you have a sister?' Gabe asked softly.

'Yep,' Lou replied, still texting, feeling like he was back at school and trying to shake off the nerd he'd once been nice to. Of all the times his phone decided not to ring.

'That's great.'

'Mmm.'

'What was that?'

Gabe had responded so curtly that Lou's head snapped up. 'I didn't hear you,' Gabe said, like a schoolteacher.

Then, for some unknown reason, guilt overcame Lou and he placed his phone into his pocket. 'Sorry, Gabe,' he wiped his brow, 'it's been a funny day. I'm not myself today.'

'Who are you then?'

Lou looked at him with confusion but Gabe just smiled.

'You were saying about your sister.'

'I was? Well, she's just being the usual Marcia.' Lou sighed. 'She's driving me crazy about organising my dad's seventieth party. Unfortunately it's on the same day as the office party, which causes some problems, you know. Always a good night here.' He looked at Gabe and winked. 'You'll see what I mean. But I'm taking the whole organisation off her hands now, to give her a break,' he said.

'You don't think she's enjoying organising it?' Gabe asked.

Lou looked away. Marcia loved organising the party, she'd been planning it for the past year. In taking it out of her hands he was in fact making it easier on himself. He couldn't stand the twenty calls a day about cake-tasting and whether or not he'd allow three of their decrepit aunts to stay overnight in his house or if he'd lend a few of his serving spoons for the buffet. Ever since her marriage had ended she'd focused on this party. If she'd given her marriage as much attention as she did the bloody party, she wouldn't find herself crying to her friends at Curves every day, he thought. Taking this off her hands was a favour for her and a favour for him. Two things accomplished at once. Just what he liked.

'You *will* go to your dad's party, though, won't you?' Gabe asked. 'Your dad turning seventy,' he whistled. 'That's not one you want to miss.'

Irritation and uneasiness settled in on Lou again. Unsure if

Gabe was preaching or was just trying to be friendly, he quickly stole a glance at him to judge, but Gabe was just looking through the envelopes on his trolley, figuring out which floor to go to next.

'Oh, of course I'll *go.*' Lou plastered a fake smile on his face. 'I'll drop in for a while, at some stage. That was *always* the plan.' Lou's voice sounded forced. Why the hell was he explaining himself?

Gabe didn't respond and, after a few loaded seconds of silence, Lou punched the elevator call button a few times in a row.

'These things are so bloody slow,' he grumbled.

Finally, the doors opened and the crammed lift revealed room for only one person.

Gabe and Lou looked at one another.

'Well, one of you get in,' a crank barked from the lift.

'Go ahead,' Gabe said. 'I've got to bring this down.' He nodded at the cart. 'I'll get the next one.'

'You sure?'

'Just kiss already,' one man called, and the rest laughed.

Lou rushed in and couldn't take his eyes away from Gabe's cool stare as the doors closed and the lift slowly lowered.

After only two stoppages, they reached ground level and, finding himself crammed at the back, Lou waited for every-body to unload. He watched the workers rush to the doors of the lobby for lunch, bundled up and ready for the elements.

The crowd cleared and his heart skipped a beat as he caught sight of Gabe standing by the security desk with the trolley beside him, searching the crowds for Lou.

Lou slowly disembarked and made his way towards him.

'I forgot to leave this on your desk.' Gabe handed him a thin envelope. 'It was hidden beneath someone else's stack.'

Lou took the envelope and didn't even look at it before crushing it into his coat pocket.

'Is something wrong?' Gabe asked, but there was no concern detectable in his voice.

'No. Nothing's wrong.' Lou didn't move his eyes away from Gabe's face once. 'How did you get down here so quickly?'

'Here?' Gabe pointed at the floor.

'Yeah, here,' Lou said sarcastically. 'The ground level. You were going to wait for the next elevator. From the fourteenth floor. Just less than thirty seconds ago.'

'Oh yeah,' Gabe agreed, and he smiled. 'I wouldn't say it was quite thirty seconds ago, though.'

'And?'

'And . . .' he stalled. 'I guess I got here quicker than you.' He shrugged, then unlatched the brake at the wheel of the trolley with his foot, and prepared to move. At the same time, Lou's phone started ringing and his BlackBerry signalled a new email.

'You'd better run,' Gabe said, moving away. 'Things to see, people to do,' he echoed Lou's words. Then he flashed a porcelain smile that had the opposite effect to the warm fuzzy feeling it had given Lou that same morning. Instead, it sent torpedoes of fear and worry right to his heart and straight into his gut. Those two places. Right at the same time.

8.

Puddin' and Pie

I t was ten thirty at night by the time the city spat Lou out and waved him off to the coast road that led him home to his house in Howth, County Dublin. Bordering the sea, a row of houses lined the coast, like an ornate frame to the perfect watercolour. Windswept and eroded from a lifetime of salty air, they got into the great American spirit of housing giant Santas and reindeers on twinkling rooftops. Every window with open curtains twinkled with the lights of Christmas trees, and Lou recalled, as a boy, trying to count as many trees on show as possible to pass the time while travelling. To Lou's right he could see across the bay to Dalkey and Killiney. The lights of Dublin city twinkled beyond the oily black of the sea, like electric eels flashing beneath the blackness of a well.

Howth had been the dream destination for as long as Lou could remember. Quite literally, his first memory began there, his first feeling of desire, of wanting to belong and then of belonging. The fishing and yachting port in north County Dublin was a popular suburban resort on the north side of

Howth Head, fifteen kilometres from Dublin city. It was a village with history; cliff paths that led past Howth village and its ruined abbey, an inland fifteenth-century castle with rhododendron gardens, and many lighthouses that dotted the coastline. It was a busy, popular village filled with pubs, hotels and fine fish restaurants. It had breathtaking views of Dublin Bay and the Wicklow Mountains or Boyne Valley beyond. Howth was a peninsular island with only a sliver of land to attach it to the rest of the country. Only a sliver of land to connect Lou from his daily life to that of his family. A mere shred, so that when the stormy days attacked, Lou would watch the raging Liffey from the window of his office and imagine the grey ferocious waves crashing over that sliver, licking at the land like flames, threatening to cut his family off from the rest of the country. Sometimes in those daydreams he was away from his family, cut off from them forever. In the nicer moments he was with them, wrapping himself around them to shield them from the elements.

Behind their large landscaped garden was land, wild and rugged, of purple heather and waist-high uncultivated grasses and hay that looked out over Dublin Bay. To the front they could see Ireland's Eye, and on a clear day the view was so stunning it was almost as though a green screen had been hung from the clouds and rolled down to the ocean floor. Stretching out from the harbour was a pier, that Lou loved to take walks along, though he walked alone. He hadn't always; his love for the pier had begun when he was a child when his parents brought him, Marcia and his elder brother Quentin to Howth every Sunday, come rain or shine, for a walk along the pier. Those days were either made up of a sun so hot he could still taste the ice-cream as soon as he set foot on the pier, or were so stormy that the wind whipped with such strength they would hang on to one another to avoid being whisked off land and lost to the sea.

On those family days, Lou would disappear into his own world. For on those days he was a pirate on the high seas. He was a lifeguard. He was a soldier. He was a whale. He was anything he wanted to be. He was everything he wasn't. For the first few moments of every walk along the pier, he would begin by walking backwards, looking at their car in the car park until the bright red colour was no longer visible and the people had turned into penguins; dark dots that waddled about the place without any defined movements.

Lou still loved walking that pier; his runway to tranquillity. He loved watching the cars and the houses perched along the cliff edges fade away as he moved further and further from land. He would stand shoulder to shoulder with the lighthouse, both of them looking out. Here, after a long week at work, he could throw all of his concerns and worries out to the water and watch them land with a plop on the waves and float down to the floor below.

But the night Lou drove home after first meeting Gabe, it was too late to walk the pier. The power button on his view was off, all he could see was blackness and the occasional standby light flashing on a lighthouse. Despite the hour and the fact it was midweek, the village wasn't its usual quiet hideaway. So close to Christmas, every restaurant was throbbing with diners, Christmas parties and annual meetings and celebrations. All the boats would be in for the night, the seals gone from the pier, their bellies full with the mackerel purchased and thrown to them by visitors. The winding road that led uphill to the summit was black and quiet now, and, sensing that home was near and that nobody else was around, he put his foot down on the accelerator of his Porsche 911. He lowered his window and felt the ice-cold air blow through his hair, and he listened to the sound of the engine reverberating through the hills and trees as he made his way to Howth summit. Below him, the city twinkled with a million lights, spying him winding his way up the wooded mountain like a spider among the grass.

As icing on the cake to the day he had just had, he heard a whoop, and then, looking in his rear-view mirror, cursed loudly at the garda car that came up behind him, lights ablazing. He eased his foot off the accelerator, hoping he'd be overtaken, but to no avail, the emergency was indeed him. He indicated and pulled in, sat with his hands on the steering wheel and watched the familiar figure climbing out of the garda car. The man slowly made his way to Lou's side of the vehicle, looking around at the night as though taking a leisurely stroll, giving Lou enough time to rack his brain for the sergeant's name. Lou turned off the music he'd been blaring and took a closer look at the man in the wing mirror, hoping it would trigger the memory of his name.

The man parked himself outside Lou's door and leaned down to look into the open window.

'Mr Suffern,' he said, without a note of sarcasm, much to Lou's relief.

'Sergeant O'Reilly.' He remembered the name right on cue and threw the man a smile, showing so many teeth he resembled a tense chimpanzee.

'We find ourselves in a familiar situation,' Sergeant O'Reilly said with a grimace. 'Unfortunately for you, we both head home at the same hour.'

'Yes, indeed, sir. My apologies, the roads were quiet, I thought it would be okay. There's not a sinner around.'

'Just a few innocents. That's always the problem.'

'And I'm one of them, your honour,' Lou laughed, holding his hands up in defence. 'It's the last stretch of road before getting home, trust me, I only put the foot down seconds before you pulled me over. Dying to get home to the family. No pun intended.'

'I could hear your engine from Sutton Cross, way down the road.'

'It's a quiet night.'

'And it's a noisy engine, I know that, but you just never know, Mr Suffern. You just never know.'

'Don't suppose you'd let me off with another warning,' Lou smiled, trying to work sincerity and apology into his best winning smile. Both at the same time.

'You know the speed limit, I assume?'

'Sixty kilometres.'

'Not *one hundred and . . .*'

The sergeant suddenly stopped talking and bolted up to stand upright, causing Lou to lose eye contact with him and instead be faced with his belt buckle. Unsure of what the sergeant was up to, he stayed seated and looked out the window to the stretch of road before him, hoping he wasn't about to gain more points on his licence. With twelve as the maximum before losing his licence altogether, he was perched danger-ously close with eight points already. He peeked at the sergeant and saw him grasping at his left pocket.

'You looking for a pen?' Lou called, reaching his hand into his inside pocket.

The sergeant winced and turned his back on Lou.

'Hey, are you okay?' Lou asked with concern. He reached for the door handle and then thought better of it.

The sergeant grunted something inaudible, the tone suggesting a warning of some sort. Through the wing mirror, Lou watched him walk slowly back to his car. He had an unusual gait. He seemed to be dragging his left leg slightly as he walked. Was he drunk? Then the sergeant opened his car door, got back inside, started up the engine, did a u-turn and was gone. Lou frowned, his day – even in its twilight hours – becoming increasingly more bizarre by the moment.

Lou pulled up to the driveway feeling the same sense of pride and satisfaction he felt every night when he arrived home. To most average people, size didn't matter, but Lou didn't want to be average and he saw the things that he owned as being a measure of the man that he was. He wanted the best of everything and, to him, size and quantity were a measure of that. Despite being in a safe cul-de-sac of only a few houses on Howth summit, he'd arranged for the existing boundary walls to be built up higher and for oversized electronic gates, with cameras, at the entrance.

The lights were out in the children's bedrooms at the front of the house, and Lou instantly felt an inexplicable relief.

'I'm home,' he called to the quiet house.

There was a faint sound of a breathless and rather hysterical woman calling out movements from the television room down the hallway. Ruth's exercise DVD.

He loosened his tie and opened the top button of his shirt, kicked off his shoes, felt the warmth of the underfloor heating soothe his feet through the marble, and started to sort through the mail on the hall table. His mind slowly began to unwind, the conversations of various meetings and telephone calls all beginning to slow. Though they were still there, the voices seemed a little quieter now. Each time he took off a layer of his clothes – his overcoat flung over the chair, his suit jacket on the table, his shoes kicked across the floor, his tie onto the table but slithering to the floor, his case here, loose change and keys there – he felt the events of the day fall away.

'Hello,' he called again, louder this second time, realising that nobody – i.e. his wife – had come to greet him. Perhaps she was busy breathing to the count of four, as the hysterical woman in the television room was doing.

'Sssh,' he heard, coming from the second level of the house, followed by the creak of floorboards as his wife made her way across the landing.

This bothered him. Not the creaking, for it was an old

house and not much could be done about that, but the being silenced was a problem. After a day of non-stop talking, of clever words of jargon, persuasion and intelligent conversation, deal opening, deal development and deal closing, not one person he had met with had at any point told him to *Sssh*. This was the language of teachers and of librarians. Not of adults in their own homes. He felt like he'd left the real world and entered a crèche. After only one minute of stepping through his front door, he felt irritated. That had been happening a lot lately.

'I've just put Pud down again. He's not having a good night,' Ruth explained from the top of the stairs, in a loud whisper. This kind of speech, though Lou understood, he did not like. Like the *Sssh* language, this adult-whispering was for children in class or teenagers sneaking out of or into their homes. He didn't like limitations, particularly in his own home. So that irritated him too.

The 'Pud' she referred to was their son Ross. A little over a year old now, he still held on to his baby fat, his flesh resembling the uncooked dough of a croissant or that of a pudding. Hence the nickname Pud, which, unfortunately for the already christened Ross, seemed to be sticking around.

'What's new?' he mumbled, referring to Pud's lack of desire to sleep, while searching through the mail for something that didn't resemble a bill. He opened a few and discarded them on the hall table. Pieces of ripped paper drifted from the surface and onto the floor.

Ruth made her way downstairs, dressed in a velour track-suit-cum-pyjamas outfit, he couldn't quite tell the difference between what she wore these days. Her long brown chocolate hair was tied back in a high ponytail and she shuffled towards him in a pair of slippers – the noise grating on his ears, worse than the sound of a vacuum cleaner, which, until that point, had been his least loved.

65

'Hi,' she smiled, and the tired face disappeared and there was a glimpse, a tiny flicker, of the woman he had married. Then, as quickly as he saw it, it disappeared again, leaving him to wonder if it was he who had imagined it, or if that part of her was there at all. The face of the woman he saw every day stepped up to kiss him on the lips.

'Good day?' she asked.

'Busy.'

'But good?'

The contents of a particular envelope took his interest. After a long moment he felt the intensity of a stare.

'Hmm?' He looked up.

'I just asked if you had a good day.'

'Yeah, and I said, "busy".'

'Yes, and I said, "but good"? All your days are busy, but all your days aren't good. I hope it was good,' she said, in a strained voice.

'You don't sound like you hope it was good,' he replied, eyes down, reading the rest of the letter.

'Well, I sound like I did the first time I asked.' She kept an easiness in her voice.

'Ruth, I'm reading my post!'

'I can see that,' she mumbled, bending over to pick up the empty ripped envelopes that lay on the ground and on the hall table.

'So what happened around here today?' he asked, opening another envelope. The paper fluttered to the floor.

'The usual madness. And then I tidied the house just before you got back, for the millionth time,' she said, making a point as she bent down to pick up another crumpled ball of paper. 'Marcia called a few times today, looking for you. When I could finally find the phone. Pud hid the handset again, it took me ages to find it. Anyway, she needs help with deciding a venue for your dad's party. She liked the idea of the marquee here, and Quentin, of course, didn't. He wants it in the yacht club. I think your dad would like either of them – no, that's a lie, I think your father would prefer none of them, but seeing as it's going ahead without his say-so, he'd be happy with either. Your mum is staying out of it. So what did you tell her?'

Silence. She patiently watched him reading the last page of the document and waited for an answer. When he had folded it and dropped it on the hall table, he reached for another.

'Honey?'

'Hmmm?'

'I asked you about Marcia,' she said, through gritted teeth, and proceeded to pick up the scraps of new paper that had fallen to the ground.

'Oh yeah.' He unfolded another document. 'She was just, eh . . .' He became distracted by the contents.

'Yes?' she said loudly.

He looked up and gazed at her, as though noticing for the first time that she was there. 'She was calling about the party.' He made a face.

'I know.'

'How do you know?' He started reading again.

'Because she – never mind.' Start again. 'She's so excited about this party, isn't she? It's great seeing her really getting her teeth into something after the year she's had. She's been talking a mile a minute about food and the music . . .' She trailed off.

Silence.

'Hmm?'

'Marcia,' she said, rubbing her tired eyes. 'We're talking about Marcia, but you're busy so . . .' She began making her way to the kitchen.

'Oh, that. I'm taking the party off her hands. Alison's going to organise it.'

67

Ruth stopped. 'Alison?'

'Yes, my secretary. She's new. Have you met her?'

'Not yet.' She slowly made her way towards him. 'Honey, Marcia was really excited about organising the party.'

'And now Alison is,' he smiled. 'Not.' Then he laughed.

She smiled patiently at the in-house joke, wanting to strangle him for taking the party out of Marcia's hands and putting it into those of a woman who knew nothing of the man who was celebrating seventy years in this life, with the people he loved and who loved him.

She took a deep breath, her shoulders relaxing as she exhaled. Started again. 'Your dinner's ready.' She began to move towards the kitchen again. 'It'll just take a minute to heat up. And I bought that apple pie you like.'

'I've eaten,' he said, folding the letter and ripping it into pieces. A few pieces of paper fluttered to the ground. It was either the sound of the paper hitting the marble or his words that stopped her on her way, but either way she froze.

'I'll pick the bloody things up,' he said with irritation.

She slowly turned around and asked in a quiet voice, 'Where did you eat?'

'Shanahans. Rib-eye steak. I'm stuffed.' He absent-mindedly rubbed his stomach.

'With who?'

'Work people.'

'Who?'

'What's this, the Spanish inquisition?'

'No, just a wife asking a husband who he had dinner with.'

'A few guys from the office. You don't know them.'

'I wish you would have told me.'

'It wasn't a social thing. Nobody else's wives were there.'

'I didn't mean – I'd like to have known so I wouldn't have bothered cooking for you.'

'Christ, Ruth, I'm sorry you cooked and bought a bloody pie,' he exploded.

'Sssh,' she said closing her eyes and hoping his raised voice wouldn't wake the baby.

'No! I won't sssh!' he boomed. 'Okay?' He made his way into the parlour, leaving his shoes in the middle of the hallway and his papers and envelopes strewn across the hall table.

Ruth took another deep breath, turned away from his mess and made her way to the opposite side of the house.

When Lou rejoined his wife, she was sitting at the kitchen table eating lasagne and salad, the pie next in line to be eaten, watching women in spandex jump around on the large plasma in the attached informal living room.

'I thought you'd eaten with the kids,' he remarked, after watching her for a while.

'I did,' she said, through a full mouth.

'So why are you eating again?' He looked at his watch. 'It's almost eleven. A bit late to eat, don't you think?'

'You eat at this hour,' she frowned.

'Yes, but I'm not the one who complains that I'm fat and then eats two dinners and a pie,' he laughed.

She swallowed the food, feeling like a rock was going down her throat. He hadn't noticed his words, hadn't intended to hurt her. He never intended to hurt her; he just did. After a long silence in which Ruth had lost the anger and built up the appetite to eat again, Lou joined her at the kitchen table, in the conservatory. On the other side of the window the blackness clung to the cold pane, eager to get inside. Beyond it were the millions of lights of the city across the bay, like Christmas lights dangling from the blackness.

'It's been a weird day today,' Lou finally said.

'How?'

'I don't know,' he sighed. 'It just felt funny. I felt funny.'

'I feel like that most days,' Ruth smiled.

'I must be coming down with something. I just feel . . . out of sorts.'

She felt his forehead. 'You're not hot.'

'I'm not?' He looked at her in surprise and then felt it himself. 'I feel hot. It's this guy at work.' He shook his head. 'So odd.'

Ruth frowned and studied him, not used to seeing him so inarticulate.

'It started out well.' He swirled his wine around his glass. 'I met a man called Gabe outside the office. A homeless guy – well, I don't know if he was homeless, he says he has a place to stay, but he was begging on the streets anyway.'

At that stage the baby monitor began crackling as Pud started to cry softly. Just a gentle sleepy moaning at first. Knife and fork down and with the unfinished plate pushed away, Ruth prayed for him to stop.

'Anyway,' Lou continued, not even noticing, 'I bought him a coffee and we got talking.'

'That was nice of you,' Ruth said. Her maternal instincts were kicking in and the only voice she could now hear was that of her child, as his sleepy moans turned to full-blown cries.

'He reminded me of me,' Lou said, confused now. 'He was exactly like me and we had the funniest conversation about shoes.' He laughed, thinking back over it. 'He could remember every single pair of shoes that walked into the building, so I hired him. Well, *I* didn't, I called Harry –'

'Lou, honey,' she cut in, 'do you not hear that?'

He looked at her blankly, irritated at first that she'd butted in, and then cocked his head to listen. Finally, the cries penetrated his thoughts.

'Fine, go on,' he sighed, massaging the bridge of his nose.

'But as long as you remember that I was telling you about my day, because you're always giving out that I don't,' he mumbled.

'What is that supposed to mean?' She raised her voice. 'Your son is crying. Do I have to sit here all night while he wails for help until you've finished your story about a homeless man who likes shoes, or would you ever go and check on him of your own accord, do you think?'

'I'll do it,' he said angrily, though not making a move from his chair.

'No, I'll do it.' She stood up from the table. 'I want you to do it without being reminded. You don't do it for brownie points, Lou, you're supposed to *want* to do it.'

'You don't seem too eager to do it yourself now,' he grumbled, fiddling with his cufflinks.

Halfway from the table to the kitchen door, she stopped. 'You know you haven't taken Ross for one single day by yourself?'

'You must be serious, you're actually using his real name. Where has all that come from?'

It was all coming out of her now that she was frustrated. 'You haven't changed his nappy, you haven't fed him.'

'I've fed him,' he protested.

The wails got louder.

'You haven't prepared one bottle, made him one meal, dressed him, played with him. You haven't spent any time with him alone, without me being here to run in every five minutes to take him from you while you send an email or answer a phone call. The child has been living in the world for over a year now, Lou. It's been over a *year*.'

'Hold on.' He ran his hand through his hair and held it there, clenching a handful of hair with a tight fist, a sign of his anger. 'How have we gotten from talking about my day, which you always want to know so much about – second for second – to this attack?'

'You were so busy talking about *you* that you didn't hear your child,' she said tiredly, knowing this conversation was going the same place as every other similar argument they'd had. Nowhere.

Lou looked around the room and held out his hands dramatically, emphasising the house. 'Do you think I sit at my desk all day twiddling my thumbs? No, I work my hardest trying to juggle everything so that you and the kids can have all this, so that I *can* feed Ross, so excuse me if I don't fill his mouth every morning with mashed banana.'

'You don't juggle anything, Lou. You choose one thing over another. There's a difference.'

'I can't be in two places at once, Ruth! If you need help around here, I've already told you, just say the word and we could have a nanny here any day you want.'

He knew he'd walked himself into a bigger argument, and as Pud's wails grew louder on the baby monitor, he prepared for the inevitable onslaught. Just to avoid the same dreaded argument, he almost added, 'And I promise not to sleep with this one.'

But the argument never came. Instead, her shoulders shrank, her entire demeanour altered, as she gave up the fight and instead went to tend to her son.

Lou reached for the remote control and held it towards the TV like a gun. He pressed the trigger angrily and powered off the TV. The sweating spandexed women diminished into a small circle of light in the centre of the screen before disappearing completely.

He reached for the plate of apple pie on the table and began picking at it, wondering how on earth this had all started from the second he walked in the door. It would end as it did so many other nights: he would go to bed and she would be asleep, or at least pretend to be. A few hours later he would wake up, work out, get showered and go to work.

He sighed, then on hearing his exhale only then noticed that the baby monitor had become silent of Pud's cries, but it still crackled. As he walked towards it to turn it off, he heard other noises that made him reach for the volume dial. Turning it up, his heart broke as the sounds of Ruth's quiet sobs filled the kitchen.

9.

The Turkey Boy 2

'So you let him get away?' A young voice broke into Raphie's thoughts.

'What's that?' Raphie snapped out of his trance and turned his attention back to the young teen who was sitting across the desk from him.

'I said, you let him get away.'

'Who?'

'The rich guy in the flash Porsche. He was speeding and you let him get away.'

'No, I didn't let him get away.'

'Yeah you did, you didn't give him any points or a ticket or anything. You just let him off. That's the problem with you lot, you're always on the rich people's sides. If that was me, I'd be locked up for life. I only threw a bloody turkey and I'm stuck here all day. And it's Christmas Day, and all.'

'Shut your whining, we're waiting for your mother, you know that, and I wouldn't blame her if she does decide to leave you here all day.'

The Turkey Boy sulked for a while at that.

'So you're new to the area. You and your mother moved here recently?' Raphie asked.

The boy nodded.

'Where from?'

'The Republic of Your Arse.'

'Very clever,' Raphie said sarcastically.

'So why did you leave the Porsche guy so quickly?' he finally asked, curiosity getting the better of him. 'Did you chicken out or something?'

'Don't be daft, son, I gave him a warning,' Raphie said, straightening up defensively in his chair.

'But that's illegal, you should have given him a ticket. He could kill someone speeding around like that.'

Raphie's eyes darkened and the Turkey Boy knew to stop his goading.

'Are you going to listen to the rest of the story or what?'

'Yeah, I am. Go on.' The boy leaned forward on the table and rested his hand under his chin. 'I've got all day,' he smiled cheekily.

10.

The Morning After

At 5.59 a.m., Lou awoke. The previous evening had gone exactly as predicted: by the time he had made it to bed, Ruth's back had been firmly turned with the bedclothes tightly tucked around her, leaving her as accessible as a fig in a roll. The message was loud and clear.

Lou couldn't find it within himself to comfort her, to cross over that line that separated them in bed, and in life, to make things okay. Even as students, broke and staying in the worst accommodations he had ever experienced, with the temperamental heating and bathrooms they had had to share with dozens of others, things had never been like this. They'd shared a single bed in a box-bedroom so small that they had to walk outside for a change of mind, but they didn't mind, in fact they loved being so close to each other. Now they had a giant six-foot-six bed, so big that even when they both lay on their backs their fingers just about brushed when they stretched out. A monstrosity of space and cold spots covered the sheets that couldn't be reached to be warmed.

Lou thought back to the beginning, when he and Ruth had first met – two young nineteen-year-olds, carefree and drunk, celebrating the end of first-year university Christmas exams. With a few weeks' break ahead of them and concerns about results far from their minds, they had met on comedy night in the International Bar on Wicklow Street. After that night, Lou had thought about her every day while back home with his parents for the holidays. With every slice of turkey, every sweet wrapper he unravelled, every family fight over Monopoly, she was in his mind. Because of her he'd even lost his title in the Count the Stuffing competition he'd had with Marcia and Quentin. Lou stared at the ceiling and smiled, remembering how each year he and his siblings – paper crowns on their heads and tongues dangling from their mouths – would get down to counting every crumb of stuffing on their plate, long after his parents had left the table. Every year, Marcia and Quentin would join together to beat him, but they couldn't sustain the desire, and his dedication – some would say obsession – could never be matched. But it was matched that year, and then beaten by Quentin, because the phone had rung and it had been her, and that had been it for Lou. Childish ways were put behind. Or that was supposed to be the theory of when he became a man. Perhaps he wasn't one yet.

The nineteen-year-old of that Christmas would have longed for this moment right now. He would have grabbed the opportunity with both hands, to be transported to the future just to have her right beside him in a fine bed, in a fine house, with two beautiful children sleeping in the next rooms. He looked at Ruth beside him in bed. She had rolled onto her back, her mouth slightly parted, her hair like a haystack on top of her head. He smiled.

She'd done better than him in those Christmas exams, which was no hard task, but she had repeated that performance the following three years too. Study had always come so easily to her, while he, on the other hand, seemed to have to burn the candle at both ends in order just to scrape by. He didn't know where she ever found the time to think, let alone study, she was so busy leading the way through their adventurous nights on the town. They'd crashed parties on a weekly basis, then been thrown out, slept on fire escapes, and Ruth still made it into college for the first lecture with her assignments completed. She could do it all at once. Ruth had led the way for everybody, always bored with sitting around. She'd needed adventure, she'd needed outrageous situations and anything that wasn't ordinary. He was the life and she had been the soul of every party and every day.

Any time he'd failed an exam and had been forced to repeat, she'd been there, writing out essays for him to learn. She'd spend the summers turning study into quiz-show games, introducing prizes and buzzers, quick-fire rounds and punishments. She'd dress up in her finery, acting as quiz-show host, assistant, model, displaying all the fine things he could win if he answered all the questions correctly. She made score cards, wrote out questions, included tacky music and fake applause into every quiz they had. Food shopping was a game; with her controlling the list of treats like a game-show host. For a box of popcorn answer her this.

'Pass,' he'd say, frustrated, trying to grab the box anyway.

'No passing, Lou, you know this one,' she'd say firmly, blocking the shelves.

He wouldn't know the answer but she'd make him know it. Somehow she'd push him until he reached deep into a part of his brain that he didn't know existed and he'd find the answer he never knew that he knew. Just before making love, she'd stall and pull away from him.

'Answer me this.'

Despite his protests and wrestling to get what he wanted, she'd hold back. 'Come on, Lou, you know this one.'

If he didn't know it, he'd make himself know it.

They planned to go to Australia together after university. A year's adventure away from Ireland before life started. Determined to succeed and follow friends over there, they spent the year saving for the flights; him working behind a bar in Temple Bar while she tended tables. They saved for the dream together, but he failed his final exams and Ruth didn't. He would have packed it all in there and then, but she wouldn't let him, influencing his decision and convincing him he could do it, as she did everything. So while he began the first few months of the same year again, Ruth celebrated passing with flying colours, receiving an honours degree at a graduation ceremony that Lou couldn't bring himself to attend. He'd attended the afters, though, had a few too many drinks and made the night miserable for her. He could at least do that for her.

In the year waiting for him to finish, Ruth completed a Business Masters Degree. Just for something to do. She never once pushed it in his face, never made him feel a failure, never celebrated any wonderful achievement of her own in order not to make him feel any less. She was always the friend, the girlfriend, the life and soul of every party, the A student and achiever.

Was that when he started resenting her? All the way back then? He didn't know if it was because he never felt good enough, whether it was a way of punishing her, or whether there was no psychology behind it and he was just too weak and too selfish to say no when an attractive woman so much as looked his way – never mind when they'd grab their handbags, their coats and then his hand. Because when that happened, he forgot all sense of himself. He knew right from wrong, of course he did, but on those occasions he didn't particularly care. He was invincible, there would be no consequences and no repercussions.

Ruth had caught him with the nanny six months previously. There had only been a few incidences with her in particular, but he knew that if there were levels of fairness for having affairs, which in his opinion there were, sex with the nanny was somewhere close to the bottom. There had been nobody since then, apart from a fumble with Alison, which had been a mistake. If there were levels of acceptable excuses for having affairs, and there were for Lou, then that would have been at the top. He'd been drunk, she was attractive, and it had happened but he regretted it deeply. It didn't count.

'Lou,' Ruth snapped, breaking into his thoughts and giving him a fright.

He looked at her. 'Morning,' he smiled. 'You'll never guess what I was just thinking ab—'

'Do you not hear that?' she interrupted him. 'You're wide awake, staring at the ceiling.'

'Huh?' He turned to his left and noticed the clock had struck six. 'Oh, sorry.' He leaned across and switched off the beeping alarm.

He'd clearly done something wrong because her face went a deep red and she fired herself out of bed as though she had been released from a catapult, then charged out of the room, her hair firing out in all directions as though she'd stuck her fingers in a socket. It was only then that he heard Pud's cries again.

'Shit.' He rubbed his eyes tiredly.

'You said a bad wud,' said a little voice from behind the door.

'Morning, Lucy,' he smiled.

Her figure appeared then, a pink-sleeping-suited five-year-old, dragging her blanket along the ground behind her, her chocolate-brown hair and fringe tousled from her sleep. Her big brown eyes were the picture of concern. She stood at the end of the bed and Lou waited for her to say something.

'You're coming tonight, aren't you, Daddy?'

'What's on tonight?'

'My school play.'

'Oh yeah, that, sweetie; you don't really want me to go to that, do you?'

She nodded.

'But why?' He rubbed his eyes tiredly. 'You know how busy Daddy is, it's very hard for me to get there.'

'But I've been practising.'

'Why don't you show me now, and then I won't have to see you later.'

'But I'm not wearing my costume.'

'That's okay. I'll use my imagination. Mum always says it's good to do that, doesn't she?' He kept an eye on the door to make sure Ruth wasn't listening. 'And you can do it for me while I get dressed, okay?'

He threw the covers off and, as Lucy started prancing around, he rushed about the room, throwing on shorts and a vest for the gym.

'Daddy, you're not looking!'

'I am, sweetheart, come downstairs to the gym with me. There are lots of mirrors there for you to practise in front of, that'll be fun, won't it?'

Once on the treadmill, he turned on the plasma and started watching Sky News.

'Daddy, you're not looking.'

'I am, sweetie.' He glanced at her once. 'What are you?'

'A leaf. It's a windy day and I fall off the tree and I have to go like this.' She twirled around the gym again and Lou looked away and back at the TV.

'What's a leaf got to do with Jesus?'

'The singer?' She stopped spinning and held on to the weights bench, slightly dizzy now.

He frowned. 'No, not the singer. What's the play about?'

She took a deep breath and then spoke as though she had

memorised the story by heart. 'The three wise men have to find a star.'

'Follow a star,' he corrected her, picking up the pace now and breaking out into a jog.

'No, they *find* a star. So they are judges on the *Find a Star* show, and then Pontius Pilate sings and everybody boos and then Judas sings and everybody boos and then Jesus sings and then he wins because he has the X-factor.'

'Jesus Christ.' Lou rolled his eyes.

'Yes, "Jesus Christ the Superstar" it's called.' She danced around some more.

'So why are you a leaf?'

She shrugged and he had to laugh.

'Will you come to see me, pleeeease?'

'Yep,' he said, wiping his face on a towel.

'Promise?'

'Absolutely,' he said dismissively. 'Okay, you go back up to your mum now, I've to take a shower.'

Twenty minutes later and already in work mode, Lou went into the kitchen to say a quick goodbye. Pud was in his highchair, rubbing banana and Liga into his hair; Lucy was sucking on a spoon and watching cartoons at top volume; and Ruth was in her dressing gown making Lucy's school lunch. She looked exhausted.

'Bye.' He kissed Lucy on the head; she didn't budge she was so engrossed in her cartoon. He hovered above Pud, trying to find a place on his face that wasn't filled with food. 'Eh, bye.' He pecked him awkwardly on the top of his head. He made his way around to Ruth.

'Do you want to meet me there at six or go together from here?'

'Where?'

'The school.'

82

'Oh. About that.' He lowered his voice.

'You have to go, you promised.' She stopped buttering the bread to look at him with instant anger.

'Lucy showed me the dance downstairs and we had a talk, so she's fine about me not being there.' He picked at a slice of ham. 'Do you know why the hell she's a leaf in a nativity play?'

Ruth laughed. 'Lou, I know you're playing with me. I told you to put this in your diary last month. And then I reminded you last week, and I called that woman Tracey at the office –'

'Ah, that's what happened.' He clicked his fingers in a gosh, darn–it kind of way. 'Wires crossed. Tracey's gone. Alison replaced her. So maybe there was a problem when they switched over.' He tried to say it playfully, but Ruth's happy face was slowly dissolving to disappointment, hatred, disgust, all rolled into one and all directed at him.

'I mentioned it twice last week. I mentioned it yesterday morning, I'm like a frigging parrot with you and you still don't remember. The school play and then dinner with your mum, dad, Alexandra and Quentin. And Marcia might be coming, if she can move around her therapy session.'

'No, she really shouldn't miss that.' Lou rolled his eyes. 'Ruthy, please, I would rather stick pins in my eyes than have dinner with them.'

'They're your family, Lou.'

'All Quentin talks about are boats. Boats, boats, and more bloody boats. It is totally beyond him to think of any other conversation that doesn't involve the words boom and cleat.'

'You used to love sailing with Quentin.'

'I used to love sailing. Not necessarily with Quentin, and that was years ago, I'd hardly know my boom from my cleat at this stage.' He groaned. 'Marcia ... it's not therapy she needs, it's a good kick up the arse. Alexandra's fine.' He trailed off, lost in thought.

'The boat or his wife,' Ruth asked sarcastically, giving him a long sidelong look.

Lou didn't hear her or ignored her. 'I don't know what she sees in Quentin, I can never figure it out. She's in a totally different league to him.'

'Your league, you mean?' Ruth snapped.

'It's just that she's a *model*, Ruth.'

'So?'

'The only thing Quentin has in common with a model is the fact he collects model boats.' He laughed, then moved on, irritation quickly setting in. 'Mum and Dad are coming too?' he asked. 'No way.'

'Tough,' she said, continuing with her lunch-making. 'Lucy is expecting you at the play, your parents are excited, and I need you here. I can't do the dinner and play host all on my own.'

'Mum will help you.'

'Your mother just had a hip replacement.' Ruth tried her best not to shriek.

'Don't I know it, I collected her from hospital and got into trouble for it, like I said I would,' he grumbled. 'While Quentin was off on his boat.'

'He was racing, Lou!' She dropped the knife and turned to him, softening. 'Please.' She kissed him softly on the lips and he closed his eyes, lingering in the rare moment.

'But I've so much to do at work,' he said softly amid their kiss. 'It's important to me.'

Ruth pulled away. 'Well, I'm glad something is, Lou, because for a moment there I almost thought you weren't human.' She was silent as she buttered the bread fiercely, the knife hitting the brown bread so roughly that it made holes. She slapped down slices of ham, tossed a slice of cheese at it then pushed down on the bread and sliced it diagonally with a sharp knife. She moved about the kitchen, slamming

84

presses and violently ripping tin foil from the teeth of the packaging.

'Okay, what's up?'

'What's up? We're not in this life just to work, we're in it to *live*. We have to start doing things together, and that means you doing things for me even when you don't want to, and vice versa. Otherwise, what's the point?'

'What do you mean *vice versa*, when do I ever make you do anything you don't want to?'

'Lou,' she gritted her teeth, 'they're *your* bloody family, not mine.'

'So cancel it! I don't care.'

'You have family responsibilities.'

'But I have more work responsibilities, family can't fire me if I don't turn up to a bloody dinner, can they?'

'Yes, they can, Lou,' she said quietly, 'they just don't call it being fired.'

'Is that a threat?' He lowered his voice angrily. 'You can't throw comments like that at me, Ruth, it's not fair.'

She opened a Barbie lunch box, slammed it down on the counter, threw in the sandwich, pineapple rings and kidney beans in Tupperware, a Barbie napkin was laid on top and she banged it closed. Despite being tossed around, Barbie didn't blink once.

Ruth just looked at him and said nothing, allowing her stare to speak for her.

'Okay, fine, I'll do my best to be there,' Lou said, both to please her and to get out of the house at the very same time, yet not meaning a word of it. On her look, he rephrased it with more meaning. 'I'll be there.'

Lou arrived at his office at eight a.m. A full hour before another soul would arrive, it was important for him to be the first in, it made him feel efficient, ahead of the pack. Pacing the small empty space of the elevator and wishing it was like that every day, he revelled in not having to stop at any other floors before getting to the fourteenth. He stepped out of the elevator into the quiet corridor. He could smell the products left behind from the cleaning staff last night. The carpet shampoo, furniture polish and air-fresheners still lingered, as yet untainted by morning coffee and body smells. Outside the glistening windows it was still pitch black at the early winter hour, and the windows seemed cold and hard. The wind whipped outside and he looked forward to leaving the eerily empty corridors and getting to his office for his morning routine.

En route to his office he stopped suddenly in his tracks. He could see that, as usual for this hour, Alison's desk was empty, but his office door was ajar and the lights were on. He walked briskly towards the door and his heart began pounding with anger as, through the open door, he saw Gabe moving around his office. He yelled, then ran and fired his fist at the door, punching it open and watching it swing violently. He opened his mouth to yell again, but before he could get his words out he heard another voice coming from behind the door.

'My goodness, who's that?' came the startled voice of his boss.

'Oh, Mr Patterson. I'm sorry,' Lou said breathlessly, quickly stopping the door from slamming against his face, 'I didn't realise you were in here.' He rubbed his hand, his fist stinging and beginning to throb from punching the door.

'Lou,' the man said, catching his breath after taking a leap away from the door, 'call me Laurence, for Christ's sake, I keep telling you that. You're full of . . . energy today, aren't you?' He tried to get his bearings after the shock.

'Good morning, sir.' Lou looked from Mr Patterson to Gabe uncertainly. 'I'm sorry to have frightened you. I just thought that there was somebody in here who shouldn't be.' His eyes landed on Gabe.

'Good morning, Lou,' Gabe said politely.

'Gabe.' Lou slowly nodded at him in acknowledgement, wanting nothing more right then than an explanation as to why exactly Gabe and his boss were standing in his office at eight a.m.

He looked down at Gabe's empty mail cart and then at the unfamiliar files lying on his desk. He thought back to the previous night, replayed finishing up his paperwork and filing them away, as always, unable to leave his desk with unfinished work. Knowing that neither he nor Alison, who'd finished work at four, had left the files there, he narrowed his eyes suspiciously at Gabe.

Gabe stared back unblinkingly.

'I was just chatting to young Gabe here,' Mr Patterson explained. 'He told me that he started the job yesterday, and isn't he just wonderful being the first into the office? That shows such dedication to the job.'

'First in? Really?' Lou faked a smile. 'Wow. Looks like you beat me to it this morning because I'm usually the first in.' Lou turned to Mr Patterson and offered his big white smile. 'But you already knew that, didn't you, Gabe?'

Gabe returned the smile with an equal sincerity. 'You know what they say, the early bird catches the worm.'

'Yes it does. It catches it indeed.' Lou glared at him with a grin. A glare and a grin. Both at the same time.

Mr Patterson watched the exchange with growing discomfort. 'Well, it's just after eight, I should leave.'

'After eight, you say. That's funny,' Lou perked up. 'The mail hasn't even arrived yet. What, em, what exactly are you doing in my office, Gabe?' His voice had an edge to it that was clearly recognisable, as Mr Patterson looked uncomfortable and Gabe took on a peculiar smile.

'Well, I came in early to familiarise myself with the building. There are so many floors for me to get through in such a short period of time, I wanted to figure out who was where.'

'Isn't that wonderful?' Mr Patterson said, breaking the silence.

'Yes, it is, but you already knew where my office was,' Lou said tightly. 'You had familiarised yourself with it yesterday . . . so what, may I ask, are you doing *inside* my office?'

'Now, now, Lou, I fear I must jump in here,' Mr Patterson said awkwardly. 'I met young Gabe in the hallway and we got talking. As a favour for me, I'd asked him to bring some files to your office. He was delivering them to the desk when I realised I'd left one in my briefcase. Though he moved very quickly, I have to say that I'd just turned around when he was gone. Poof! Just like that!' Mr Patterson chuckled.

'Poof!' Gabe grinned at Lou. 'That's me all right.'

'I like fast workers, I must say, but I prefer fast *and* efficient, and my goodness you certainly are that.'

Lou almost said thank you, but Gabe jumped in.

'Thank you, Mr Patterson, and if there's anything else at all you'd like me to do for you, please let me know. I finish my shift at lunchtime and would be only too happy to help out around here for the rest of the afternoon. I'm keen to work.'

Lou's stomach tightened.

'That's wonderful, Gabe, thank you, I'll keep that in mind. Right Lou,' Mr Patterson turned to face him and Lou expected Gabe, no longer a part of this conversation, to leave. But he didn't. 'I wonder if you'd be able to meet with Bruce Archer this evening, you remember him.'

Lou nodded, his heart sinking.

'I was supposed to meet him, but I was reminded this morning of something else I have to attend.'

'This evening?' Lou asked, his mind racing.

While thinking about the offer he was picturing Lucy twirling around the gym in her sleeping suit and Ruth's face when he'd opened his eyes prematurely from that kiss and caught her looking as beautiful and serene as he'd ever remembered her.

He realised they were both staring at him, Gabe's eyes in particular searing into him.

'Yes, this evening. Only if you're free. I can ask Alfred to do it otherwise, so please don't worry.' Mr Patterson waved his hand dismissively.

'No, no,' Lou jumped in quickly. 'This evening is no problem. That's no problem.'

In his mind, Lucy, dizzy from the twirling, fell to the ground, and Ruth opened her eyes and pulled away from their kiss, his promise of less than an hour ago having broken the spell.

'Great. Great. Well, Melissa can fill you in on the details, time and venue, etc. I have a big night tonight,' he winked at Gabe. 'It's my little one's Christmas play, I'd forgotten about it until he came running to me dressed as star, would you believe. But I wouldn't miss it for the world,' Mr Patterson smiled.

'Right, yeah.' Lou felt a lump in his throat. 'That's important, all right.'

'Right, so, enjoy tonight and well done for finding this lad.' Mr Patterson patted Gabe on the back.

While Lou turned to glare at Gabe, he heard a familiar cheery call behind him.

'Morning, Laurence.'

'Ah, Alfred,' Mr Patterson said.

Alfred was a tall man, six foot with white-blond hair, kind of like an oversized Milky Bar kid who had melted and been moulded back together by the hands of a child. He always spoke with a smirk on his face and in the kind of accent that came with being privately schooled in England, despite spending the summers in Ireland, where he was from. His nose was disjointed from his rugby days and he swanned around the office, as Gabe had observed the previous day, kicking the tassels of his boat shoes in the air, one hand in his pocket, with the air of someone – a naughty schoolboy – who was up to tricks.

Alfred's eyes fell upon Gabe, then quite obviously looked him up and down in silence and waited to be introduced. Gabe imitated him, confidently giving Alfred the once-over.

'Nice shoes,' Gabe finally said, and Lou looked down at the brown loafers Gabe had described yesterday.

'Thank you.' Alfred was a little put out.

'I also like your shoes, Mr Patterson,' Gabe commented, looking across.

In a slightly awkward moment, all eyes looked down at the men's feet. A peculiar thing for most, apart from Lou, whose heart was pumping at a ridiculous rate at the sight of the black slip-ons and the brown loafers. The exact shoes Gabe had described to Lou the previous morning. So Alfred was meeting with Mr Patterson. Lou looked from Alfred to Mr Patterson, feeling a sense of betrayal. It wasn't official that Cliff's job was up for grabs, but if it was, Lou was hellbent on making sure it would be his, not Alfred's.

Mr Patterson bid farewell and took off down the corridor, swinging his briefcase jollily in his hand.

'Who are you?' Alfred asked Gabe, bringing Lou back into the room.

'I'm Gabriel.' Gabe held out his hand. 'Friends call me Gabe, but you can call me Gabriel,' he smiled.

'Charming. Alfred.' Alfred reached out his hand.

Their shake was cold and limp and their hands quickly fell by their sides. Alfred even wiped his on his trouser leg, whether it was consciously done or not.

'Do I know you?' Alfred narrowed his eyes.

'No, we've never actually met, but you may recognise me.'

'Why's that, were you in a reality show or something?' Alfred studied him again, with a smirk but a less confident one.

'You used to pass by me every day, just outside this building.'

Alfred narrowed his eyes, studying Gabe, and he looked back at Lou with a slightly nervous smile. 'Help me out here, pal.'

'I used to sit at the doorway next door. Lou gave me a job.'

Alfred's face broke into a smile, the relief more than obvious on his arrogant face. His demeanour shifted and he became the big man of the fraternity again, knowing that his position wasn't threatened by a homeless man.

He laughed as he turned to Lou, making a face and using a tone that he didn't even attempt to disguise in Gabe's company. 'You gave him a job, Lou?' he said, turning his back on Gabe. 'Well isn't it the season to be jolly, indeed. What the hell is going on with you?'

'Alfred, just leave it,' Lou replied, embarrassed.

'Okay.' Alfred held his hands up in defence and chuckled to himself. 'Stress affects us all in different ways, I suppose. Hey, can I use your bathroom?'

'What? No, not here, Alfred, just use the restrooms.'

'Come on, don't be a dick.' His tongue sounded too big for his mouth as it rolled around his words. 'I'll just be a second. See you around, Gabe, I'll try to aim my coins at your cart when you pass by,' Alfred joked, giving Gabe the once-over again. He smirked and winked at Lou before making his way to the toilet.

From the office, Lou and Gabe could hear loud sniffing.

'There seems to be a nasty cold going around this district,' Gabe smiled.

Lou rolled his eyes. 'Look, I'm sorry, Gabe – he's, you know, don't take him seriously.'

'Oh, nobody should ever take anybody seriously really, you can't control anything but what's inside this circle.' Gabe's arms made a movement around his body. 'Until we all do that, *nobody* can be taken seriously. Here, I got you this.' He leaned down to the bottom tray of the cart and lifted up a Styrofoam cup of coffee. 'I owe you from yesterday. It's a latte, the machine was back working again.'

'Oh, thanks.' Lou felt even worse, now totally conflicted as to how he felt about this man.

'So, you're going for dinner tonight?' Gabe undid the brake on the cart and started to move away, one of the wheels squeaking as he pushed it.

'No, just a coffee. Not dinner.' Lou was unsure if Gabe wanted to be invited. 'It's no big deal really. I'll be in and out in an hour at most.'

'Oh, come on, Lou,' Gabe smiled, and he sounded alarmingly like Ruth. *Oh, come on, Lou, you know this one.* But he didn't finish the sentence in quite the same way. 'You know these things always turn into dinner,' Gabe continued. 'Then drinks and then *whatever*,' he winked. 'You'll be in trouble at home, won't you, Aloysius,' he said, in a sing-song voice that chilled Lou to the bone.

Gabe exited the office and made his way towards the elevator, the squeaking of the wheel loud in the empty hallway.

'Hey!' Lou called after him, but he didn't turn around. 'Hey!' he repeated. 'How did you know that? Nobody knows that!'

Even though he was alone in the office, Lou quickly looked around to make sure no one had heard.

'Relax! I won't tell anyone,' Gabe called back to him in a voice that made Lou feel far from reassured. Lou watched as Gabe pressed the call button for the elevator and lingered by the doors, while the elevator began to rise from the ground floor.

The bathroom door opened and Alfred exited, rubbing at his nose and sniffing. 'What's all the shouting about? Hey, where did you get the coffee?'

'Gabe,' Lou replied, distracted.

'Who? Oh, the homeless guy,' Alfred said with disinterest. 'Really, Lou, what the hell were you thinking, he could wipe you out.'

'What do you mean, wipe me out?'

'Come on, were you born yesterday? You've taken a man who has nothing and put him in a place where there is everything. Ever heard of a thing called temptation? Actually, forget I asked, it's *you* I'm talking to,' he winked. 'You give in to that every time. Perhaps you and the homeless man aren't so different,' he added. 'You look alike, that's for sure. Maybe sing "Feed the Birds", or something, and we'll see,' he laughed, his chest wheezing, the result of a forty-a-day habit.

'Well, that says a lot about your upbringing, Alfred, that your only reference to a homeless person would be something from *Mary Poppins*,' Lou snapped.

Alfred's wheezing broke out into a cough. 'Sorry, pal. Did I hit a sore point?'

'We're nothing alike,' Lou spat, looking back down at the elevators to Gabe.

But Gabe was gone. The elevator pinged and the doors opened, revealing nobody inside, and with nobody to step in. In the reflection in the mirror that lined the back wall of the elevator, Lou could see the confusion written all over his face.

11.

The Juggler

At five p.m., at exactly the same time that Lou should have been leaving the building in order to get home for Lucy's school play, he instead paced the floor of his office. From the door to the desk, from the desk to the door, and back again. Over and over again. The door was wide open, prepared for Lou's eventual catapult launch down the corridor and into Mr Patterson's office, where he would announce he was unable to meet Bruce Archer for coffee. Not unlike Mr Patterson, he too had family commitments. Tonight, Laurence, his daughter was going to be a leaf. For some reason it made him weaken at the knees. Each time he reached the doorway he stopped short, and instead he'd turn around and continue his pace around his desk.

Alison eyed him curiously from her desk, looking up from her typing each time he reached the doorway. Finally, the sounds of her acrylic nails against the keys stopped.

'Lou, is there something I can do for you?'

He'd looked at her then, as though realising for the first time that he was in an office; that Alison had been there all along. He straightened himself up, fixed his tie, and cleared his throat.

'Eh . . . no, thank you, Alison,' he said, more formally than he'd meant, so intent on convincing her of his sanity that he came across as a drunken man trying to appear sober.

He began pacing towards his desk again but then stopped himself and poked his head outside the door. 'Actually, Alison, this coffee meeting . . .'

'With Bruce Archer, yes.'

'It's just coffee, isn't it?'

'So Mr Patterson said.'

'And he knows that it's me that's going to meet him?'

'Mr Patterson?'

'No, Bruce Archer.'

'Mr Patterson called him earlier to explain that he wouldn't be able to make it but that a colleague of his would be more than happy to meet him instead.'

'Right. So he might not be expecting me?'

'Would you like me to confirm that for you? Again?'

'Eh . . . no. I mean yes.' He thought about that while Alison's hand hovered over the receiver. 'No,' he said, then headed back into his office. Seconds later he poked his head out the door again. 'Yes. Confirm.' And then he quickly ducked inside again.

While he was pacing, he heard Alison call cheerily, 'Hi Gabe.'

Lou froze, and then for reasons unknown found himself rushing to the door, where he stood with his back to the wall and listened to their conversation through the open door.

'Hi Alison.'

'You look smart today.'

'Thanks. Mr Patterson has asked me to do a few jobs for him around here, so I thought it would be a good idea to look a bit more respectable.'

Lou peeked through the gap in the hinges of the door and spied Gabe, his new haircut combed neatly like Lou's. A new dark suit, similar to one that Lou owned, was draped over his shoulder and covered in plastic.

'Is the new suit for up here too?' Alison asked.

'Oh, this? This is just for me to have. You never know when a suit will come in handy,' he gave what Lou considered a very curious answer. 'Anyway, I'm here to give you these. I think they're plans. I believe Lou wanted to see them.'

'Where did you get these from?'

'I collected them from the architect.'

'But he was working from home today,' Alison said, looking inside the manila envelope with confusion.

'Yes, I collected them from his home.'

'But Lou just asked Mr Patterson for these five minutes ago. How did you get them so quickly?'

'Oh, I don't know, I just, you know . . .' Lou could see Gabe's shoulders shrugging.

'No, I don't know,' Alison laughed. 'But I wish I did. Keep working like this and I wouldn't be surprised if Mr Patterson gives you Lou's job.'

They laughed and Lou bristled, making a note to make Alison's life hell right after this conversation.

'Is Lou in right now?'

'Yes, he is. Why?'

'Is he going to meet with Bruce Archer today?'

'Yes. At least, I think so. Why?'

'Oh, no reason. Just wondering. Is Alfred free this evening?'

'Lou asked me the very same thing earlier, that's funny. Yes, Alfred's free, I checked with his secretary. That's Louise, you'd like her.' She giggled flirtatiously.

'So let me get this straight. Lou knows that Alfred is available to meet with Bruce, if Lou decides to back out.'

'Yes, I already told him. Why, what's going on?' She lowered her voice. 'What's the big deal about this evening? Lou's been acting funny about it.'

'He has? Hmm.'

That was it. Lou couldn't take it any more. He closed his office door, no doubt startling them both. He sat down at his desk and picked up the phone.

'Yes?' Alison answered.

'Get me Harry from the mailroom on the phone, and after that call Ronan Pearson and check with him if Gabe collected the plans from him personally. Do this without Gabe knowing.'

'Yes, of course, just one moment please,' she said professionally in her best telephone voice.

The phone rang and Lou adjusted his tie once again, cleared his throat and spun around in his oversized leather chair to face the window. The day was cold but crisp, there wasn't a breeze as shoppers rushed to and fro worshipping the new religion this season, their arms laden down with bags amid flashing primary colours of the numerous neon signs.

'Yello,' Harry barked down the phone.

'Harry, it's Lou.'

'What?' Harry asked loudly, the sounds of machines and voices loud behind him, and Lou had no choice but to speak up. He looked behind him to make sure he had the all-clear before speaking. 'It's Lou, Harry.'

'Lou who?'

'Suffern.'

'Oh, Lou, hi, how can I can help you? Your post end up on twelve again?'

'No, no, I got it, thanks.'

'Good. That new boy you sent my way is genius, isn't he?'

'He is?'

'Gabe? Absolutely. Everyone's calling me with nothing but good reviews. It's like he fell from the stars. I'm telling you that he couldn't have come at a better time, that's no word of a lie. We were struggling, you know that. In all of my years in this job, this Christmas season is the wildest. Everything's getting faster and faster it seems. Well it must be because it's not me that's getting slower, that's for sure. You picked a good one, Lou, I owe you. How can I help you today?'

'Well, about Gabe,' he said slowly, his heart pounding in his chest. 'You know he's taken on some other commitments in the building. Other work outside of the mailroom.'

'I heard that all right. He was as excited as anything this morning. Got a new suit, and all, on his break. I don't know where he found the time to get it, some of them in here can't even light their cigarette in the time given. He's quick, that boy. I'd say it won't be long before he's out of here and up there with you. Mr Patterson seems to have taken a shine to him. I'm happy for him, he's a good kid.'

'Yeah . . . anyway, I was just calling to let you know. I didn't want it to conflict with his work with you.' Lou tried one more time. 'You wouldn't want him to be *distracted*, with his mind on other things that he's doing on these floors. You know? It gets so manic up here and distraction can so easily happen.'

'I appreciate that, Lou, but what he does after one p.m. is his own business. To be honest with you, I'm glad he's found something else. He gets the job done so quickly it's a struggle to keep him busy till the first break.'

'Right. Okay. So, if he acts up in any way you just go ahead and do what you have to do, Harry. I don't want you to feel in any way obligated to keep him on for me. You know?'

'I know that, Lou, I do. He's a good lad, you've nothing to worry about.'

'Okay. Thanks. Take care, Harry.'

The phone went dead. Lou sighed and slowly spun around in his chair to replace the receiver. As he turned he came face-to-face with Gabe, who was standing behind his desk, watching him intently.

Lou jumped, dropping the receiver, and let out a yelp.

'Jesus Christ.' He held his hand over his pounding heart.

'No. It's just me,' Gabe said, blue eyes searing into Lou's.

'Have you ever heard of knocking? Where's Alison?' Lou leaned sideways to check her station and saw that it was empty. 'How long have you been there?'

'Long enough.' Gabe's voice was soft, and it was that which unnerved Lou most. 'Trying to get me in trouble, Lou?'

'What?' Lou's heart pounded wildly, still unrecovered from the surprise, and also alarmingly discomfited by Alison's absence and Gabe's proximity. The man's very presence disconcerted him.

'No,' he swallowed, and he hated himself for his sudden weakness. 'I just called Harry to see if he was happy with you. That's all.' He was aware of the fact he sounded like a schoolboy defending himself.

'And is he?'

'As it turns out, yes. But you must understand how I feel a responsibility to him for finding you.'

'Finding me,' Gabe smiled, and said the words as though he'd never heard them or pronounced them before.

'What's so funny about that?'

'Nothing,' Gabe continued the smile, and began looking around Lou's office, hands in his pockets, with that same patronising look that was neither jealousy nor admiration.

'It's five twenty-two p.m. and thirty-three seconds now,' Gabe said, not even looking at his watch. 'Thirty-four, thirty-five, thirty-six . . .' He turned and smiled at Lou. 'You get the idea.'

'So?' Lou put his suit jacket on and secretly tried to get a glimpse at his watch to make sure. It was spot-on five twenty-two.

'You have to leave now, don't you?'

'What does it look like I'm doing?'

Gabe wandered over to the meeting table and picked up three pieces of fruit from the bowl – two oranges and an apple – which he inspected closely, one by one. 'Decisions, decisions,' he said. He held the three pieces of fruit in his hand.

'Hungry?' Lou asked, agitated.

'No,' Gabe laughed again. 'You any good at juggling?'

That same feeling struck Lou's heart, and he remembered exactly what it was that he didn't like about Gabe. It was questions like that, statements and comments that pierced Lou somewhere other than where they should.

'You'd better get that,' Gabe added.

'Get what?'

Before Gabe could respond, the phone rang and, despite preferring having Alison screen his calls, he dove for it.

It was Ruth.

'Hi honey.' He motioned to Gabe for privacy, but Gabe began juggling the fruit in response. Lou turned his back, and then, feeling uncomfortable with Gabe behind him, he faced front to keep an eye on Gabe. He lowered his voice.

'Em, yeah, about tonight, something's come up and –'

'Lou, don't do this to me,' Ruth said. 'Lucy's heart will be broken.'

'It's just the play I won't make, sweetheart, and Lucy won't even notice I'm not there, the place will be so dark. You can tell her I was there. The rest of the night is fine. Mr Patterson asked me to meet with a client of ours. It's a big deal, and it could help me with getting Cliff's job, you know?'

'I know, I know. And then if you do get a promotion, you'll be away from us even more.'

'No, no, I won't be. I just have to really slog for these months to prove myself.'

'Who are you trying to prove yourself to? Laurence already knows your capabilities, you've been with the company five years. Anyway, I don't want to get into this conversation now. Will you make the play or not?'

'The play?' Lou bit his lip and looked at his watch. 'No, no, I won't make it.'

Gabe dropped the apple, which rolled across the carpet towards Lou's desk, and continued juggling with the oranges. Lou felt a childish sense of satisfaction that Gabe had failed.

'So you'll make it home for dinner? With your parents and Alexandra and Quentin? Your mum has just been on the phone saying how much she's looking forward to it. You know, it's a month since you've called to see them.'

'It's not been a month since I've seen them. I saw Dad just,' he went quiet while calculating the time in his head, 'well, you know, maybe it's *almost* a month.' A month? How the time had flown.

For Lou, visiting his parents was a chore, like making the bed. After not doing it for some time, the sight of the untidy blankets would play on his mind until he'd do it to get it over and done with. He'd instantly feel a satisfaction that it had been completed, and just when he thought it was over with and out of the way, he'd wake up and know he had to go and do it all over again. The thought of his father complaining to him about how it had been so long since he'd seen him made Lou want to run in the other direction. It was the same one whinging sentence that drove him insane. Though partly it made him feel guilty, it mostly made him want to stay away longer to avoid hearing those words. He needed to be in the mood to hear it, to detach the sentiments from his head so that he wouldn't bark back and rattle off the hours he'd been working and the deals he'd negotiated, just to shut his father up. He was most certainly not in the mood today. Maybe if he got home when they'd all had a few drinks it would be easier.

'I might not make dinner but I'll be there for dessert. You have my word on that.'

Gabe dropped an orange and Lou felt like punching the

ceiling with celebration. Instead he pursed his lips and continued to make excuses to Ruth for everything, refusing to apologise for something that was totally out of his control. Lou finally hung up the phone and folded his arms across his chest.

'What's so funny?' Gabe asked, throwing the one remaining orange up and down in his hand, the other hand in his pocket.

'Not such a good juggler, are you?' he smirked.

'Touché,' Gabe smiled. 'You're very observant. Indeed, I'm not a good juggler, but it's not really juggling if I'd already chosen to drop those two and keep this one in my hand, is it?'

Lou frowned at the peculiar response and busied himself at his desk, putting on his overcoat and preparing to leave.

'No, Gabe, it's certainly not juggling if you *choose . . .*' He stopped suddenly, realising what he was saying and hearing Ruth's voice in his head. His head snapped up, feeling that cold chill again, but Gabe was gone and the orange was before him on his desk.

'Alison,' Lou marched out of his office with the orange in his hand, 'did Gabe just walk out of here?'

Alison lifted a finger up to signal for him to wait, while she took notes on a notepad and listened to the voice at the other end of the phone.

'Alison,' he interrupted her again, and she panicked slightly, writing faster, nodding quickly and holding up her full hand this time.

'Alison,' he snapped, holding his hand down over the receiver to end her call. 'I don't have all day.'

She stared at him with her mouth open, receiver dangling from her hand. 'I can't believe you just −'

'Yeah, well, I did, get over it. Did Gabe walk by?' he asked. His voice was rushed, running along, skipping and jumping to keep up with his heart.

'Em . . .' she thought slowly, 'he came up to my desk about twenty minutes ago and −'

'Yeah, yeah, I know all that. He was in my office a second ago and then he was gone. Just now. Did he walk by?'

'Well, he must have, but –'

'Did you see him?'

'No, I was on the phone and –'

'Jesus.' He punched the desk with his already sore fist. 'Ah, crap.' He cradled it close to him.

'What's wrong, Lou? Calm down.' Alison stood up and reached her hand out towards him.

Lou pulled away. 'Oh, by the way,' he dropped his voice and leaned closer again, 'does any of my post ever come to me under a different name?'

'What do you mean?' she frowned.

'You know –' He looked left and right and barely moved his lips as he spoke. 'Aloysius,' he mumbled.

'Aloysius?' she said loudly.

He threw his eyes up. 'Keep it down,' he mumbled.

'No.' She lowered her voice. 'I've never seen the name Aloysius on any of the mail.' As though there were a time delay from her voice to her ears, she smiled, then snorted, and then started laughing. 'Why the hell would there be Aloy—' On his look, her words disappeared and her smile faded. 'Oh. Oh dear. That's a –' her voice went an octave higher, '*lovely* name.'

Lou walked across the newly constructed Seán O'Casey pedestrian bridge that linked the two rejuvenated north and south quays, the North Wall Quay to Sir John Rogerson's Quay. One hundred metres across the bridge brought him to his destination, The Ferryman, the only authentic pub left on this stretch of quays. It wasn't a place for cappuccinos or ciabattas, and because of that the clientele was specific. The bar contained a handful of Christmas shoppers who'd wandered off the beaten track to take a break and to wrap purple-fingered hands around their heated glasses. Apart from the few shoppers it was filled with workers, young and old, winding down after their day's work. Suits filled the seats, pints and shorts filled the surfaces. Just after six p.m. and already people had escaped the business district and into their nearest place of solace to worship at the altar of beers on tap.

Bruce Archer was one such person, propped at the bar, Guinness in hand, roaring with laughter over something somebody beside him had said. Another suit. And then there was another. Shoulder pads to shoulder pads. Pin-striped suits and diamond socks. More polished shoes and briefcases containing spreadsheets, pie charts and forward-looking market predictions. None of them were drinking coffee after all. He should have known. He hadn't known, but as he watched them back-slapping and laughing loudly, he wasn't in the least bit surprised, and so, at the very same time, he had known all along.

Bruce turned around and spotted him. 'Lou!' he shouted across the room in his heavy Boston accent, which caused heads to turn, not at Bruce but at the handsome and quite pristine man that he was shouting at. 'Lou Suffern! Good to see ya!' He stood from the stool, walked towards Lou with his hand extended, and then, gripping Lou's hand firmly, he pumped it up and down while thumping him enthusiastically on the back. 'Let me introduce you to the guys. Guys, this is Lou, Lou Suffern, works at Patterson Developments. We worked together on the Manhattan Building I was telling you about and had a real wild experience one night together, wait till we tell you about it, you'll never believe it. Lou, this is Derek from . . .' And so Lou was lost in a sea of introductions, forgetting each name the second they were introduced and pushing the image of his wife and daughter out of his head each time he shook a hand that either squeezed his too hard, was too clammy, limp, or pumped his shoulder up and down. He tried to forget that he had forsaken his family for this. He tried to forget as they poo-poohed his order of coffee and instead filled him with beer, as they ignored his attempt to leave after one pint. Then after the second. And after the third. Tired of a discussion each time a round came around, he let them change his order to a Jack Daniel's, and as his mobile phone rang he also let their adolescent jeers convince him not to answer. And then, after all that, they needed to convince him no more. He was there with them for the long haul, with his phone on silent and vibrating every ten minutes with a call from Ruth. He knew at this point that Ruth would understand; if she didn't then she was an extremely unreasonable person.

There was a girl catching his eye across the bar; there was another whisky and Coke on the counter. All sense and reason had gone outside with the smokers, and it was shivering outside, half thinking of hailing a taxi, the other half looking around for someone to take it home and love it. And then, too cold and frustrated, sense turned on reason and resorted to fisticuffs outside the bar, while Lou turned his back and took sole care of his ambition.

12.

The Fast Lane

Lou realised he was far too drunk to chat up the attractive woman in the bar who had been giving him eyelashes all night when, in the process of joining her table, he stumbled over his own feet and without noticing managed to knock over her friend's drink into her lap. Not the pretty one's lap, just her friend's. And while he mumbled something he regarded as highly smooth and clever, it seemed to her to come across as rather sleazy and offensive. For there was a fine line between sleazy and offensive and a sexy chat-up line when you'd had as much to drink as Lou Suffern. He appeared to have lost the swagger of charm and sophistication that he'd possessed in heaps when he had first walked in. The droplets of whisky and Coke that stained his crisp white shirt and tie appeared to be more of a fashion don't for these sophisticated businesswomen, and his blue eyes, which usually caused women to feel like they were falling from a height directly into his aqua pools, were now bloodshot and glassy and so didn't have the desired effect. When intending to undress her with his eyes, he'd instead appeared shifty, and so, too drunk to get anywhere with her

– or her friend, whom he'd also tried to come on to after bumping into her coming back from the toilet, where she was trying to clean the red wine he'd spilled on her suit – the more sensible option seemed to be to walk back to his car. And drive home.

When he reached the cold and dark basement car park underneath his office building – a walk that took twenty minutes longer than it should have – he realised he had forgotten where he'd parked his car. He circled the centre of the car park, pressing the button on his key and hoping the sound of the alarm or the flashing lights would give it away. Unfortunately he was enjoying the spinning so much, he kept forgetting to study the cars. Finally, a light caught his eye, and when he spotted his car in his allocated car space, he closed one eye and focused on making his way to his Porsche.

'Hello baby,' he purred, rubbing up alongside of it – though not deliberately out of love but because he'd lost his footing. He kissed the bonnet and climbed inside. Then, finding himself in the passenger seat, where there was no steering wheel, he got back out and made his way around to the driver's side. He climbed to the right-hand side and, once settled, he focused on the columns of cement that held the roof up and watched them swaying. He hoped they wouldn't sway on top of his car as he was driving home. That would be both irresponsible of them and an expensive misfortune for him.

After a few moments of trying to get the key into the ignition and scraping the metal around it with the tip of the key, he finally turned it around the right way and it slotted inside. At the sound of the engine he cheered, then pushed his foot on the accelerator to the floor. Finally remembering to look up at where he was going, he screamed with fright. At the bonnet of the car stood a motionless Gabe.

'Jesus Christ!' Lou shouted, taking his foot off the accelerator and banging on the windscreen with his bruised right hand. 'Are you crazy? You're going to get yourself killed!'

Gabe's face blurred then, but Lou would have bet his life that he was smiling. He heard a knock, he jumped, and when he looked up he saw Gabe peering in the driver's window at him. The engine was still running and so Lou lowered the window a slit.

'Hi.'

'Hi Gabe,' he replied sleepily.

'You want to turn the engine off, Lou?'

'No. No, I'm driving home.'

'You won't get very far if you don't take it out of neutral. I don't think it's such a good idea to drive home. Why don't you get out and we'll get you a taxi home?'

'No, can't leave the Porsche here. Some crazy will steal it. Some looney tune. Some homeless vagabond.' He started laughing at that, quite hysterically. 'Oh, I know. Why don't you drive me home?'

'No, no, I don't think that's a good idea, Lou. Come on out and we'll get you a taxi,' Gabe said, opening the door of the car.

'Nope. No taxi,' Lou slurred, moving the clutch from neutral to drive. He pushed his foot down on the accelerator and the car jumped forward with the door wide open, then it stopped, then lurched forward again and stopped. Gabe rolled his eyes and hung on to the passenger door as it jumped forward like a cricket with an anxiety disorder.

'Okay, fine,' Gabe said finally after Lou had driven – although driven not being the operative word – all the way to the exit slope. '*Fine*, I said.' He raised his voice as Lou lurched forward again. 'I'll drive you home.'

Lou climbed over the gear stick into the passenger seat and Gabe sat in the driver's seat with trepidation. He didn't need to adjust the seat or mirrors as he and Lou, it seemed, were exactly the same height.

'You know how to drive?' Lou asked.

'Yes.'

'Have you driven one of these before?' Lou asked, and then began laughing hysterically. 'Maybe there's one parked beneath your penthouse,' he laughed.

'Buckle up, Lou.' Gabe ignored his comments and concentrated on getting Lou home alive. That task was very important at this point, very important indeed.

14.

The Turkey Boy 3

'So, you caught him speeding again in the car?' The Turkey Boy lifted his head from where his chin was resting on his hands on the table. 'I hope you arrested him this time. He could have almost killed somebody again. And what are you doing hanging around the same place in your car all the time? Sounds to me like you're stalking him.'

'I didn't catch him speeding,' Raphie explained, ignoring the last question. 'They went through a red light is all.'

'Is all? I hope you arrested the flashy bastard.'

'Well, how could I arrest Lou, now, really, come on,' Raphie explained, sounding like a teacher. 'You're not listening. Stop jumping the gun here.'

'But you're so bloody slow at telling the story. Just get to the point.'

'I am, and I won't tell you the story at all if that's going to be your attitude.' Raphie glared at the Turkey Boy, who didn't snap back this time, and so he continued the story. 'It wasn't Lou that ran the red light because it wasn't Lou that was driving, I told you that.'

'Gabe wouldn't have run the red light. He wouldn't do that,' Turkey Boy piped up.

'Well, how was I to know that? I hadn't met the chap before, had I?'

'They must have swapped over on the way home.'

'*Gabe* was behind the wheel. Mind you, they were so similar they could easily have swapped, but no, I know it was Lou in the passenger seat, totally blazooed with both eyes in one socket.'

'How come you just happened to catch him in the same place again?'

'I was just keeping an eye on someone's house, is all.'

'A murderer?' The Turkey Boy's eyes lit up.

'No, not a bloody murderer, somebody I know, is all.'

'Were you following your wife?' the boy perked up again.

Raphie shifted uncomfortably in his seat. 'What do you mean?'

'To see if she's having an affair.'

Raphie rolled his eyes. 'Son, you watch far too much television.'

'Oh.' The Turkey Boy was disappointed. 'So what did you do when you caught them?'

15.

Home Sweet Home

'Hello Sergeant,' Gabe said, big blue eyes wide and honest. Taken aback by the man's knowledge of his position, Raphie changed his mind on his tone of approach. 'You broke a red light there, you know.'

'I know, Sergeant, I apologise profusely, it was a total accident on my behalf, I promise you that. It was amber and I thought I'd make it . . .'

'You broke it well after it was amber.'

'Well.' Gabe looked to his left at Lou, who was pretending to sleep, snoring loudly and laughing between snores. In his hand was a long umbrella.

Raphie examined the umbrella in Lou's hand and then followed Gabe's gaze to the accelerator.

'Jesus,' he whispered, under his breath.

'No, I'm Gabe,' Gabe responded. 'I'm a colleague of Mr Suffern's, I was just trying to get him home safely, he's had a bit to drink.'

On cue, Lou snored loudly and made a whistling noise. Then he laughed.

'You don't say.'

'I feel like I'm a dad on duty tonight,' Gabe said. 'Making sure my child is safe. That's important, isn't it?'

'What do you mean?' Raphie narrowed his eyes.

'Oh, I think you know what I mean,' Gabe smiled innocently.

Raphie fixed his gaze on Gabe and toughened his tone, unsure if he had a smart arse on his hands. 'Show me your driver's licence please.' He held out his hand.

'Oh, I, em, I don't have it on me.'

'Do you *have* a driver's licence?'

'Not on me.'

'So you said.' Raphie took out a notepad and pen. 'What's your name then?'

'My name is Gabe, sir.'

'Gabe what?' Raphie straightened himself a little.

'Are you okay?' Gabe asked.

'Why do you ask?'

'You look a little uncomfortable. Is there something wrong?'

'I'm fine.' Raphie started to back away from the car.

'You should get that looked at,' Gabe said, voice heavy with concern.

'You mind your own business,' Raphie barked, looking around to make sure nobody heard.

Gabe looked in the rear-view mirror at the garda car. There was no one else in it. No back-up. No witness.

'Make sure you drop into the Howth Garda Station this week, Gabe, bring your licence with you then and report to me. We'll deal with you then. Get that boy home safely.' He nodded at Lou and then made his way back to his car.

'S'e drunk again?' Lou asked, opening his bleary eyes and turning around to watch Raphie walk to the car.

'No, he's not drunk,' Gabe said, watching Raphie's slow walk back to the car in the rear-view mirror.

'Then what is he?' Lou snarled.

'He's something else.'

'No, you're somethin' else. Now drive me home.' He clicked his fingers and laughed. 'Actually, let me drive,' he said grumpily, and started squirming in his seat to get out. 'I don't like people thinking this is your car.'

'It's dangerous to drink and drive, Lou. You could crash.'

'So,' he huffed childishly. 'That's my problem, isn't it?'

'A friend of mine died not so long ago,' Gabe said, eyes still on the garda car that was slowly driving back down the road. 'And believe me, when you die, it's everybody else's *but* your problem. He left behind a right mess. I'd buckle up if I were you, Lou.'

'Who died?' Lou closed his eyes, ignoring the advice, and leaned his head back on the rest, giving up on his idea to drive.

'I don't think you know him,' Gabe said, indicating as soon as the garda car was out of sight and moving out onto the road again.

'How'd he die?'

'Car crash,' Gabe said, pushing his foot down on the accelerator. It jerked forward quickly, the engine loud and powerful all of a sudden in the quiet night.

Lou's eyes opened slightly and he looked at Gabe warily. 'Yeah?'

'Yep. Sad really. He was a young guy. Young family. Lovely wife. Was successful.' He pressed his foot down harder on the speed.

Lou's eyes were fully open now.

'But that's not the sad thing. The saddest thing was that he didn't sort out his will on time. Not that he's to blame, he was a young man and didn't plan on leaving so soon, but it just shows you never know.'

The speedometer neared one hundred kilometres in the fifty-kilometre zone and Lou grabbed the door handle and held on tightly. He moved from his slouched position, pushing his buttocks firmly to the back of the seat. He was sitting up poker-straight now, watching the speedometer, and the blurred lights of the city across the bay whizzing by.

He began to reach for his seat belt, but all of a sudden, as quickly as Gabe had sped up, he took his foot off the accelerator, checked his wing mirror, indicated, and turned the wheel steadily to the left. He looked at Lou's face, which had turned an interesting shade of green, and he smiled.

'Home sweet home, Lou.'

It was only over the next few days, as the hangover haze had begun to lift, that Lou realised he didn't recall once giving Gabe any directions to his home that night.

'Mum, Dad, Marcia, Quentin, Alexandra!' Lou announced at full boom, as soon as the door had been pulled open by his startled-looking mother. 'I'm ho-ome,' he sang, embracing his mother and planting a smacker on her cheek. 'I'm so sorry I missed dinner, it was such a busy evening at the office. Busy, busy, busy.'

Even Lou couldn't keep a straight face for that excuse, and so he stood in the dining room, his shoulders moving up and down, his chest wheezing in a near silent laugh, watched by startled and unimpressed faces. Ruth froze, watching her husband with mixed feelings of anger, hurt and embarrassment. Somewhere inside her there was jealousy too. She'd had a day of dealing with Lucy's uncontrollable excitement that had been channelled in all the positive and negative ways a child could possibly behave, and then later dealt with her nerves and tears as she wouldn't go on stage until her father had arrived. After returning from the school play, she'd put the kids to bed and run around the house all evening in order to get the dinner ready and bedrooms ready for guests. Her face was now bright red from the hot kitchen and her fingers burned from carrying hot dishes. She was flushed and tired, too, physically and mentally drained from trying to stimulate her children in all the ways a parent should; from being on her knees on the floor with Pud, to wiping the tears and offering advice to a disappointed Lucy, who'd failed to find her father in the audience despite Ruth's attempts to convince her otherwise.

Ruth looked at Lou swaying at the doorway, his eyes bloodshot, his cheeks rosy, and she wished that that could be her, throwing caution to the wind and acting the eejit in front of their guests. But he'd never stand for it – and she'd never do it – and that was the difference between them. But there he was, swaying and happy, and there she was, static and deeply dissatisfied, wondering why on earth she had chosen to be the glue holding it all together.

'Dad!' Lou announced. 'I haven't seen you for ages! It's been so long, hasn't it?' He smiled, walking towards his father with an extended hand. He sat down in the chair beside him, pulling it closer and scraping the floor so that their elbows were almost touching. 'Tell me what you've been up to. Oh, and I wouldn't mind some of that red wine, thanks so much. My favourite, honey, well done.' He winked at Ruth, then proceeded to spill most of it on the white linen as with an unsteady arm he poured it into an unused glass.

'Steady there now, son,' his father said quietly, reaching out to help him steady his hand.

'Dad, I'm fine.' Lou pulled away from him, splashing wine over his father's shirt sleeves.

'Ah, Aloysius,' his mother said, and Lou rolled his eyes.

'It's fine, love, I'm fine,' his father said, trying to make light of it.

'That's your good shirt,' she continued, reaching for her napkin, dunking it in her water glass and dabbing at her husband's white sleeves.

'Mum,' Lou looked around the table, laughing, 'I haven't killed the man, I just splashed wine.'

His mother threw him a look of scorn and looked away again, continuing to help her husband.

'Maybe this will help.' Lou reached for the salt and began shaking it over his father's arms.

'Lou!' Quentin raised his voice. 'Stop it!'

Lou stopped, then looked at Alexandra with a childish sheepish grin.

'Ah, Quentin,' Lou nodded at his brother, 'I didn't notice you there. How's the boat? Got any new sails? Any new equipment? Won any competitions lately?'

Quentin cleared his throat, and tried to calm himself. 'We're actually in the final in two wee—'

'Alexandra!' Lou exploded, mid Quentin's sentence. 'How can I not have kissed the lovely Alexandra?' He stood up and, bumping against the backs of everybody's chairs, he made his way over to her. 'How is the beautiful Alexandra tonight? Looking ravishing, as always.' He reached down and hugged her tight, kissing her neck.

'Hi Lou,' she smiled. 'Good night?'

'Oh, you know, busy, busy, lots of paperwork to get through.' He threw his head back and laughed again, loud like a machine gun. 'Ah dear. Oh, what's the problem in here? You all look like somebody's died. You could do with rockets shoved up your arses, come on.' He shouted a little too aggressively and clapped his hands in front of their faces. 'Bor-ing.' He turned to look at his sister Marcia. 'Marcia,' he said, followed by a sigh. 'Marcia,' he repeated. 'Hi,' he simply said, before making his way back to his chair, smiling childishly to himself.

Gabe hovered awkwardly by the dining-room door in the long heavy silence that followed.

'Who have you brought with you, Lou?' his brother Quentin interrupted, holding out his hand and moving towards Gabe.

117

'Sorry, we weren't introduced. I'm his brother, Quentin, and this is my wife, Alexandra.'

Lou wolf-whistled, then laughed.

'Hello, I'm Gabe.' Gabe shook Quentin's hand and entered the dining room. He made his way around the table, shaking hands with all the family.

'Lou,' Ruth said quietly, 'perhaps you should have some water or coffee, I'm about to make some coffee.'

Lou sighed loudly. 'Am I an embarrassment, Ruth, am I?' he snapped. 'You told me to come home. I'm home!'

There was a silence around the table as people awkwardly tried to avoid each other's gazes. Lou's father looked at him angrily, the colour rising in his face, his lips trembling slightly as though the words were rushing out of them yet weren't making any sound.

Gabe continued to make his way around the table.

'Hello, Ruth, I'm very pleased to finally meet you.'

She would barely look him in the eye as she limply took his hand.

'Hi,' she said quietly. 'Please excuse me while I just take all this away.' She stood up from the table and began carrying the leftover cheese plates and coffee cups into the kitchen.

'I'll help you,' Gabe offered.

'No, no, please, sit down.' She rushed into the kitchen with a load in her arms.

Gabe disobeyed and followed her anyway. She was leaning against the counter where she had placed the crockery, her back to him. Her head was down, her shoulders hunched, all life and soul of the woman gone at that very moment. He made a noise placing the plates beside the sink so that she knew he was there.

She jumped now, alert to his presence, composed herself, life and soul returning from their time-out, and she turned around to face him.

'Gabe,' she smiled tightly, 'I told you not to bother.'

118

'I wanted to help,' he said softly. 'I'm sorry about Lou. I wasn't out with him tonight.'

'No?' She folded her arms and looked embarrassed for not knowing.

'No. I work with him at the office. I was there late when he got back from the . . . well, from his coffee meeting.'

'When he got back to the office? Why would he . . .' She looked at him with confusion and then, ever so slowly, a shadow fell across her face as realisation dawned. 'Oh, I see. He was trying to drive home.'

It wasn't a question, more a thought aloud, and so Gabe didn't respond, but she softened towards him.

'Right. Well, thank you for bringing him home safely, Gabe. I'm sorry I was rude to you but I'm just, you know . . .' The emotion entered her voice and she stopped talking and instead busied herself scraping food from the plates into the bin.

'I know. You don't have to explain.'

From the dining room they heard Lou let out a 'Whoa' and then there was the sound of a glass smashing, and his laughter again.

She stopped scraping the plates and closed her eyes, sighing.

'Lou's a good man, you know,' Gabe said softly.

'Thank you, Gabe. Believe it or not, that is exactly what I need to hear right now, but I was rather hoping it wouldn't come from one of his work buddies. I'd like for his mother to be able to say it,' she looked up at him, eyes glassy, 'or his father, or it would be nice to hear it from his daughter. But no, at work, Lou is the man.' She scraped the plates angrily.

'I'm not a work buddy, believe me. Lou can't stand me.'

She looked at him curiously.

'He got me a job yesterday. I used to sit outside his building every morning, and yesterday, totally out of the blue, he stopped and gave me a coffee and offered me a job.'

'He mentioned something like that last night.' Ruth searched her brain. 'Lou really did that?'

'You sound surprised.'

'No, I'm not. Well, I am. I mean . . . what job did he give you?'

'A job in the mailroom.'

'How does that help him out?' she frowned.

Gabe laughed. 'You think he did it for his own good?'

'Oh, that's a terrible thing for me to say.' She bit her lip to hide her smile. 'I didn't mean it that way. I know Lou is a good man, but lately he's just been very . . . busy. Or more *distracted*; there's nothing wrong with being busy, as long as you're not distracted.' She waved her hand dismissively. 'But he's not all here. It's like he's in two places at once. His body with us, his mind constantly elsewhere. The decisions he makes lately are all to do with work, how to help his work, how to get him from one meeting to the other meeting in the quickest time possible, yada, yada, yada . . . so him offering you the job, I just thought that . . . God, listen to me.' She composed herself. 'You obviously brought out the good side in him, Gabe.'

'He's a good man,' Gabe repeated.

Ruth didn't answer, but it was almost as though Gabe read her mind when he said, 'But you want him to become a better one, don't you?'

She looked at him in surprise.

'Don't worry.' He placed his hand over hers and it was immediately comforting. 'He will be.'

When Ruth told her sister the next day about the exchange, and her sister ruffled her nose thinking it all very weird and suspicious as she did most things in life, Ruth only then wondered why on earth she hadn't questioned Gabe, why she hadn't felt it all so very odd at that moment. But it was the moments that counted, being *in* the moment, and in that moment she hadn't felt compelled to ask. She believed him, or at least she had wanted to believe him. A kind man had told her that her husband would be a better man. What good was an afterthought?

16.
The Wake-Up Call

Lou awoke the morning after to a woodpecker sitting on his head and hammering away consistently with great gregariousness at the top of his skull. The pain worked its way from his frontal lobe, through both his temples, and down to the base of his head. Somewhere outside, a car horn beeped, ridiculous for this hour, and an engine was running. He closed his eyes again and tried to disappear into the world of sleep, but responsibilities, the woodpecker, and what sounded like the front door slamming, wouldn't allow him safe haven in his sweet dreams.

His mouth was so dry, he found himself smacking his gums together and thrashing his tongue around in order to gather the smallest amount of moisture to give him the honour of avoiding the loathful task of dry-retching. And then the saliva came, and he found himself in that awful place – between his bed and the toilet bowl – where his body temperature went up, his mind dizzied and the moisture came to his mouth in waves. He kicked off his bedclothes, ran for the toilet and fell to his knees in a heavy, heaving, worshipping of the toilet bowl. It was only when he no longer had any energy, or anything left inside his stomach, for that matter, that he sat on the heated tiles in physical and mental exhaustion, and noticed that the skylight was bright. Unlike the darkness of his usual morning rises at this time of the year, the sky was a bright blue. And then panic overcame him, far worse than the dash he'd just encountered, but more like the panic that a child would experience on learning they're late for school.

Lou dragged himself up from the floor, and returned to the bedroom with the desire to grab the alarm clock and strangle the nine a.m. that flashed boldly in red. They'd all slept it out. They'd missed their wake-up call. Only they hadn't, because Ruth wasn't in bed, and it was only then he noticed the smell of a fry drifting upstairs, almost mockingly doing the can-can under his nose. He heard the clattering and clinking of cups and saucers. A baby's babbles. Morning sounds. Long, lazy sounds that he shouldn't be hearing. He should be hearing the hum of the fax machine and photocopier, the noise of the elevator as it moved up and down the shaft and every now and then pinged as though the people inside had been cooked. He should be hearing Alison's acrylic nails on the keyboard. He should be hearing the squeaking of the mail cart as Gabe made his way down the hallways . . .

Gabe.

He pulled on a robe and rushed downstairs, almost falling over the shoes and briefcase he'd left at the bottom step, before bursting through the door into the kitchen. There they were, the three usual suspects: Ruth, his mother and his father. Gabe wasn't anywhere to be seen, thankfully. Egg was dribbling down his father's grey stubbled chin, his mother was reading the newspaper, and both she and Ruth were still in their dressing gowns. Pud was the only one to make a sound as he sang and babbled, his eyebrows moving up and down with such expression it was as though his sentences actually meant something.

Lou took this scene in, but at the very same time failed to appreciate a single pixel of it.

'What the hell, Ruth?' he said loudly, causing all heads to look up and turn to him.

'Excuse me?' She looked at him with widened eyes.

'It's nine a.m. Nine o-fucking-clock.'

'Now, Aloysius,' his father said angrily. His mother looked at him in shock.

'Why the hell didn't you wake me?' He came closer to her.

'Lou, why are you talking like this?' Ruth frowned, then turned to her son. 'Come on, Pud, a few more spoons, honey.'

'Because you're trying to get me fired is what you're doing. Isn't it? Why the hell didn't you wake me?'

'Well, I was going to wake you but Gabe said not to. He said to let you rest until about ten o'clock, that a rest would do you good, and I agreed,' she said matter-of-factly, appearing unaffected by his attack in his parents' presence.

'Gabe?' He looked at her as though she were the most ludicrous thing on the planet. 'GABE?' he shouted now.

'Lou,' his mother gasped. 'Don't you dare shout like that.'

'Gabe the mailboy? The fucking MAILBOY?' He ignored his mother. 'You listened to *him?* He's an imbecile!'

'Lou!' his mother said once again. 'Fred, do something.' She nudged her husband.

'Well, that imbecile,' Ruth fought to stay calm, 'drove you home last night instead of leaving you to drive to your death.'

As though just remembering that Gabe had driven him home, Lou rushed outside to the driveway. He made his way around the perimeter of the car, hopping from foot to foot on the pebbles, his concern for his vehicle so great that he couldn't feel the occasional sharp corner breaking through his flesh. He examined his Porsche from all angles, running his fingers along the surface to make sure there weren't any scratches or dents. Finding nothing wrong, he calmed a little, though he still couldn't understand what had made Ruth value Gabe's opinion so highly. What was going on in the world that had everybody eating out of Gabe's palm?

He made his way back inside, where his mother and father threw him such a look, he couldn't for once think of anything to say to them. He turned away from them and returned to the kitchen, where Ruth was still sitting at the table feeding Pud.

'Ruthy,' he cleared his throat and made an attempt at a Lou-style apology, the kind of apology that never involved the word sorry, 'it's just that Gabe is after my job, you see. You didn't understand that, I know, but he is. So when he left bright and early this morning to get to work –'

'He left five minutes ago.' She cut him off straight away, not turning around, not looking at him. 'He stayed in one of the spare rooms because I'm not too sure if he's got anywhere else to go. He got up and made us all breakfast and then I called him a taxi, which I paid for so that he could get to work. He just left five minutes ago and so he, too, is late for work. So you can take your accusations and your behaviour and follow him in there, where you can act the bully-boy.'

'Ruthy, I –'

'You're right, Lou, and I'm wrong. It's clear from this morning's behaviour that you're totally in control of things and not in the least bit stressed,' she said sarcastically. 'I was such a fool to think you needed an extra hour's sleep. Now, Pud,' Ruth lifted the baby from his chair and kissed his food-stained face, 'let's go give you a bath,' she smiled.

Pud clapped his hands and turned to jelly under her raspberry kisses. Ruth walked towards Lou with Pud in her arms, and for a moment Lou softened at the look on his son's face, his smile so big it could light up the world if ever the moon lost its beam. He prepared to take Pud in his arms but it didn't happen. Ruth walked right on by, cuddling Pud tight while he laughed uproariously as though her kisses were the funniest thing that had happened in his short life. Lou acknowledged the rejection. For about five seconds. And then he realised that was five seconds out of the time needed for him to get to work. And so he dashed.

In record time, and thankfully due to Sergeant O'Reilly not being present when Lou put his foot down and fired his way to work, Lou arrived at the office at ten fifteen a.m.; the latest he had ever arrived at the office. He still had a few minutes before the meeting ended, and so, spitting on his hand and smoothing down his hair, which hadn't been washed, and running his hands across his face, which hadn't been shaved, he shook off the waves of dizziness that his hangover had brought, took a deep breath and then entered the boardroom.

There was an intake of breath at the sight of him. It wasn't that he looked so bad, it was just that, for Lou, he wasn't perfect. He was always perfect. He took a seat opposite Alfred, who beamed with astonishment and absolute delight at his friend's apparent breakdown.

'I'm so sorry I'm late,' Lou addressed the table of twelve more calmly than he felt, 'I was up all night with one of those tummy bugs, but I'm okay now, I think.'

Faces nodded in sympathy and understanding.

'Bruce Archer has that very same bug,' Alfred smirked, and he winked at Mr Patterson.

The switch was flicked and Lou's blood began to boil, expecting any minute for a loud whistling to drift from his nose as he reached boiling point. He sat through the meeting, fighting flushes and nausea, while the vein in his forehead pulsated at full force.

'And so, tonight is an important night, lads.' Mr Patterson turned to Lou, and Lou zoned in on the conversation.

'Yes, I have the audio-visual conference call with Arthur Lynch,' Lou spoke up. 'That's at seven thirty, and I'm sure it

126

will all go without a hitch. I've come up with a great number of responses to his concerns, which we went through during the week. I don't think we need to go through them again –'

'Hold on, hold on.' Mr Patterson lifted a finger to stall him and it was only then that Lou noticed that Alfred's cheeks had lifted into a great big smile.

Lou stared at Alfred to catch his eye, hoping for a hint, a give-away, but Alfred avoided him.

'No, Lou, you and Alfred have a dinner with Thomas Crooke and his partner, this is the meeting we've been trying to get all year,' Mr Patterson laughed nervously.

Crumble, crumble, crumble. It was all coming tumbling down. Lou shuffled through his schedule, ran shaky fingers through his hair and wiped the beads of sweat on his forehead. He ran his finger along the freshly printed schedule, his tired eyes finding it hard to focus, his clammy forefinger smudging the words as he moved it along the page. There it was, the visual conference call with Arthur Lynch. No mention of a dinner. No damn mention of a damn dinner.

'Mr Patterson, I'm well aware of the long-hoped-for meeting with Thomas Crooke,' Lou cleared his throat and looked at Alfred with confusion, 'but nobody confirmed any dinner with me, and I made it known to Alfred last week that I have a meeting with Arthur Lynch at seven thirty p.m. tonight,' he repeated with some urgency. 'Alfred? Do you know about this dinner meeting?'

'Well, yeah, Lou,' Alfred said in a ridiculing tone, with a shrug that went with it. 'Of course I do. I cleared my schedule as soon as they confirmed it. It's the biggest chance we've got to make the Manhattan development work. We've all been talking about this for months.'

The others around the table squirmed uncomfortably in their seats, though there were some, Lou was certain, who would be enjoying this moment profusely, documenting every sigh, look and word to rehash it to others as soon as they were out of the room.

'Everybody, you can all get back to work,' Mr Patterson said with concern. 'We need to deal with this rather urgently, I fear.'

The room emptied and all that were left at the table were Lou, Alfred and Mr Patterson; and Lou instantly knew by Alfred's stance and the look on his face, by his stubby fingers pressed together in prayer below his chin, that Alfred had already taken the higher moral ground on this one. Alfred was in his favourite mode, his most comfortable position of attack.

'Alfred, how long have you known about this dinner and why didn't you tell me?' Lou immediately went on the offensive.

'I told you, Lou.' Alfred addressed him as though he were slow and unable to comprehend.

With Lou a sweaty, unshaven mess and Alfred so cool, he knew he wasn't coming out of this looking the best. He removed his shaky fingers from the schedule and clasped his hands together.

'It's a mess, a bloody mess.' Mr Patterson rubbed his chin roughly with his hands. 'I needed both of you at that dinner, but I can't have you missing the call with Arthur. The dinner can't be changed, it took us too long to get it in the first place. How about the call with Arthur?'

Lou swallowed. 'I'll work on it.'

'If not, there's nothing we can do, except for Alfred to begin things, and Lou, as soon as you've finished your meeting, you make your way as quickly as you can to Alfred.'

'Lou has serious negotiations to discuss, so he'll be lucky if he makes it to the restaurant for after-dinner mints. I'll be well able to manage it, Laurence.' Alfred spoke from the side of his mouth with the same smirk that made Lou want to pick up the water jug from the middle of the table and bash it against Alfred's head. 'I'm capable of doing it alone.'

'Yes, well, let's hope Lou negotiates fast and that he's successful, otherwise this entire day will have been a waste of time,' Mr Patterson snapped, gathering his papers and standing up. Meeting dismissed.

Lou felt like he was in the middle of a nightmare; everything was falling apart, all his good work was being sabotaged.

'Well, that was a disappointing meeting. I thought he was going to tell us about who was taking over when he leaves,' Alfred said lazily. 'Not a word out of him, would you believe. I really think he owes it to us to let us know, but I have been in the company longer than you, so . . .'

'Alfred?' Lou stared at him with amazement.

'What?' Alfred took a packet of chewing gum out of his pocket and threw one into his mouth. He offered one to Lou, who shook his head wildly.

'I feel like I'm in the twilight zone. What the hell is going on here?'

'You're hungover is what's going on. You look more like the homeless man than the homeless man himself,' Alfred laughed. 'And you should really take one of these,' he offered the mint gum again, 'your breath stinks of vomit.'

Lou waved them away again.

'Why didn't you tell me about the dinner, Alfred?' he said angrily.

'I told you,' Alfred said, smacking the gum in his mouth. 'I definitely told you. Or I told Alison. Or was it Alison? Maybe it was the other one, the one with the really big boobs. You know, the one you were banging?'

Lou stormed off on him then and headed straight to Alison's desk, where he threw the details of that evening's dinner on her keyboard, stopping the acrylic nails from tapping.

She narrowed her eyes and read the brief.

'What's this?'

'A dinner tonight. A very important one. At eight p.m. That I *have* to be at.' He paced the area before her while she read it.

'But you can't, you have the conference call.'

'I know, Alison,' he snapped. 'But I need to be at this.' He stabbed a finger on the page. 'Make it happen.' He rushed into his office and slammed the door. He froze before he got to his desk. On the surface his mail was laid out.

He backtracked and opened his office door again.

Alison, who had snapped to it quickly, hung up the phone and looked up at him. 'Yes?' she said eagerly.

'The mail.'

'Yes?'

'When did it get here?'

'First thing this morning. Gabe delivered it the same time as always.'

'He can't have,' Lou objected. 'Did you see him?'

'Yes,' she said, concern on her face. 'He brought me a coffee too. Just before nine, I think.'

'But he can't have. He was at my house,' Lou said, more to himself.

'Em, Lou, just one thing before you go . . . Is this a bad time to go over some details for your dad's party?'

She'd barely finished her sentence before he'd gone back into his office and slammed the door behind him.

There are many types of wake-up calls in the world. For Lou Suffern, a wake-up call was a duty for his devoted BlackBerry to perform on a daily basis. At six a.m. every morning, when he was in bed both sleeping and dreaming at the same time, thinking of yesterday and planning tomorrow, his BlackBerry would dutifully and loudly ring in an alarming and screeching tone purposely uneasy on the ear. It would reach out from the bedside table and prod him right in the subconscious, taking him away from his slumber and dragging him into the world of the awakened. When this happened, Lou would wake up; eyes closed, then open. Body in bed, then out of bed; naked, then clothed. This, for Lou, was what waking up was about. It was the transition period from sleep to work.

For other people wake-up calls took a different form. For Alison at the office it was the pregnancy scare at sixteen that had forced her to make some choices; for Mr Patterson it was the birth of his first child that had made him see the world in a different light and affected every single decision he made. For Alfred it was his father's loss of their millions when Alfred was twelve years of age that forced him to attend state school for a year, and although they had returned to their wealthy state without anybody of importance knowing about the family hiccup, this experience changed how he saw life and people forever. For Ruth, her wake-up call was when, on their summer holidays, she walked in on her husband in their bed with their twenty-six-year-old Polish nanny. For little Lucy at only five years old, it was when she looked out at the audience of her school play and saw an empty seat beside her mother. There are many types of wake-up calls, but only one that holds any real importance.

Today, though, Lou was experiencing a very different kind of wake-up call. Lou Suffern, you see, wasn't aware that a person could be awakened when their eyes were already open. He didn't realise that a person could be awakened when they were already out of their bed, dressed in a smart suit, doing deals and overseeing meetings. He didn't realise a person could be awakened when they considered themselves to be calm, composed and collected, able to deal with life and all it had to throw at them. The alarm bells were ringing, louder and louder in his ear, and nobody but his subconscious could hear them. He was trying to knock it off, to hit the snooze button so that he could nestle down in the lifestyle he felt cosy with, but it wasn't working. He didn't know that he couldn't tell life when he was ready to learn, but that life would teach him when it was good and ready. He didn't know that he couldn't press buttons and suddenly know it all; that it was the buttons in him that would be pressed.

Lou Suffern thought he knew it all.

But he was only about to scratch the surface.

17.

Bump in the Night

At seven p.m. that evening, when the rest of his colleagues had been spat out of the office building and then sucked in by the spreading Christmas mania outside, Lou Suffern remained inside at his desk, feeling less like the dapper businessman and more like Aloysius, the schoolboy on detention, whom he'd fought so hard over the years to leave behind. Aloysius stared at the files on the desk before him with all the same excitement as being faced with a plate of veg, their very green existence presiding over his freedom. On discovering there was absolutely no possibility for Lou to cancel or rearrange the conference call, a seemingly genuinely disappointed Alfred had given Lou his best puppy eyes and gone into damage-limitation mode, sucking up any hint of involvement in the cock-up with all the strength of a Dyson, and worked on the best methods to approach the deal. As convincing as always, Alfred left Lou unable to remember what his issue had been with him in the first place, wondering why he'd blamed him for this mess at all. Alfred had this effect on people time and time again, taking the same course as a boomerang that had been dragged through shit yet still managed to find its way back to the same pair of open hands.

Outside was black and cold. Lines of traffic filled every bridge and quay as people made their way home, counting down the days of this mad rush to Christmas. Harry was right, it was all moving too quickly, the build-up feeling more of an occasion than the moment itself. Lou's head pulsated more than it had that morning, and his left eye throbbed as the migraine worsened. He lowered the lamp on his desk, feeling sensitive to the light. He could barely think, let alone string a sentence together, and so he wrapped himself up in his cashmere coat and scarf and left his office to get to the nearest shop or pharmacy for some headache pills. He knew he was hungover but he was also sure he was coming down with something; the last few days he'd felt extraordinarily unlike himself. Disorganised, unsure of himself; traits that were surely due to illness.

The office corridors were dark; lights were out in all the private offices apart from a few emergency lights that were lowly lit for security guards doing their rounds. He pressed the elevator call button and waited for the start-up sound of the ropes pulling the elevator up the shaft. All was silent. He pressed the button again and looked up at the displayed levels. The ground floor was lit up but there was no movement. He pressed the button again. Nothing happened. He pressed it a few more times until the anger could no longer be suppressed and so he began punching. Out of service. Typical.

He moved away from the elevator in search of the fire escape and his head continued to pound. With thirty minutes until his meeting, he had just enough time to run up and down thirteen floors with the pills. Leaving the familiarity of the main office corridor, he pushed through a few doors he'd never really noticed before, and found himself in corridors that had narrowed and where the plush carpets disappeared. The thick walnut doors and wall panelling of his section were replaced by white paint and chipboard and the office sizes were reduced to box rooms. Instead of the fine art collection he studied each day in the corridors of his office, photocopiers and fax machines lined the halls.

Turning the corner, he stalled and chuckled to himself, Gabe's secrets of speed revealed. Before him was a service elevator, and it all made sense. The doors were wide open, a ghastly white light of a long fluorescent strip illuminating the small grey cube. He stepped inside, his eyes aching from the light, and before he could even reach for the buttons on the panel, the doors closed and the elevator descended speedily. Its speed was twice as fast as the regular elevators, and again Lou was satisfied to have caught on to how Gabe had managed to make it from one place to another so quickly.

While the elevator continued to move downward he pressed the ground-floor button but it failed to light up. He thumped it a few times and, with growing concern, watched as the light moved from each floor number. Twelve, eleven, ten . . . The elevator picked up speed as it descended. Nine, eight, seven . . . It showed no signs of slowing. The elevator was rattling now as it sped along the ropes, and with growing fear and anxiety Lou began to press all of the buttons he could find, alarm included, but it was to no avail. The elevator continued to fall through the shaft on a course of its own choosing.

Only floors away from the ground level, Lou moved away from the doors quickly and hunched down, huddling in the corner of the elevator. He tucked his head between his knees, crossed his fingers and braced himself for the crash position.

Seconds later, the elevator slowed and suddenly stopped. Inside the elevator shaft, the cube bounced on the end of the ropes and shuddered from its sudden halt. When Lou opened his eyes, which had been scrunched shut, he saw that he'd stopped on the basement floor. As though the elevator had functioned normally the entire time, it omitted a cheery ping and the doors slid open. He shuddered at the sight, it was hardly the welcoming committee that greeted him each time he stepped off on the fourteenth floor. The basement was cold and dark, and the ground concrete and dusty. Not wanting to get off on this floor, he pressed the ground-floor button again to quickly get back to marble surfaces and carpets, to creamy toffee swirls and chromes, but again the button failed to light up, the elevator failed to respond and its doors stayed open. He had no choice but to step out and try to find the fire escape so that he could climb up a level to the ground floor. As soon as he stepped out of the elevator and placed both feet on the basement floor, the doors slid closed and the elevator ascended.

The basement was lowly lit. At the end of the corridor a fluorescent strip of light on the blink flashed on and off, which didn't help his headache and made him lose his footing a few times. There was the loud hum of machines around, the ceilings hadn't been filled in and so all the electrics and wiring were revealed. The floor was cold and hard beneath his leather shoes and dustmites bounced up to cover his polished tips. As he moved along the narrow hallway, searching for the escape exit, he heard the sound of music drifting out from under the door at the end of a hallway that veered off to the right. 'Driving Home for Christmas' by Chris Rea. Along the hallway on the opposite side, he saw the green escape sign of a man running out a door, illuminated above a metal door. He looked from the exit, back to the room at the end of the hall where music and light seeped from under the door. He looked at his watch. He still had time to make his way to the pharmacy and – providing the elevators worked – back to his office in time for the conference call. Curiosity got the better of him, and so he made his way down the hall and drummed his knuckles against the door.

The music was so loud he could barely hear his own knock, and so slowly he opened the door and tucked his head around the corner.

The sight stole words from his mouth and ran off with them under its arm, cackling.

Inside was a small stock room, the walls lined with metal shelves, from floor to ceiling filled with everything from light bulbs to toilet rolls. There were two aisles, both of them no more than ten feet in length, and it was the second aisle that caught Lou's attention. Through the shelving units, light came from the ground. Walking closer to the aisle, he could see the familiar sleeping bag laid out from the wall, reaching down the aisle and stopping short of the shelving unit. On the sleeping bag was Gabe, reading a book, so engrossed that he didn't look up as Lou approached. On the lower shelves, a row of candles were lit, the scented kind that were dotted around the bathrooms of the offices, and a small shadeless lamp sent out a small amount of orange light in the corner of the room. Gabe was wrapped up in the same dirty blanket that Lou recognised from Gabe's days out on the pathway. A kettle was on a shelf and a plastic sandwich packet was half-empty beside him. His new suit hung from a shelf, still covered in plastic and never worn. The image of the immaculate suit hanging from the metal shelf of a small stock room reminded Lou of his grandmother's parlour, something precious and saved for the big occasion that never came, or that came and was never recognised.

Gabe looked up then and his book went flying from his hands, just missing a candle, as he sat up straight and alert.

'Lou,' he said, with fright.

'Gabe,' Lou said, and he didn't feel the satisfaction he thought he should. The sight before him was sad. No wonder the man had been first at the office every morning and last there. This small store room piled high with shelves of miscellaneous junk had become Gabe's home.

'What's the suit for?' Lou asked, eyeing it up. It looked out of place in the dusty room. Everything was tired and used, left behind and forgotten, yet hanging from a wooden hanger was a clean, expensive suit. It didn't fit in.

'Oh, you never know when you'll need a good suit,' Gabe replied, watching Lou warily. 'Are you going to tell?' he asked, though he didn't sound concerned, just interested.

Lou looked back at him and felt pity. 'Does Harry know you're here?'

Gabe shook his head.

Lou thought about it. 'I won't say a word.'

'Thanks.'

'You've been staying here all week?'

Gabe nodded.

'It's cold in here.'

'Yeah. Heat goes off down here when everyone leaves.'

'I can get you a few blankets or, em, an electric heater or something, if you want,' Lou said, feeling foolish as soon as the words were out.

'Yeah, thanks, that would be good. Sit down.' Gabe pointed to a crate that was on the bottom shelf. 'Please.'

Lou rolled up his sleeves as he reached for the crate, not wanting the dust and dirt to spoil his suit, and he slowly sat down.

'Do you want a coffee? It's black, I'm afraid, the latte machine isn't working.'

'No thanks. I just stepped out to get a few headache pills,' Lou replied, missing the joke while looking around in distraction. 'I appreciate you driving me home last night.'

'You're welcome.'

'You handled the Porsche well.' Lou studied him. 'You driven one before?'

'Yeah, sure, I have one out the back.' Gabe rolled his eyes.

'Yeah, sorry . . . how did you know where I lived?'

'I guessed,' Gabe said sarcastically, pouring himself a coffee. On Lou's look he added, 'Your house was the only one on the street with a bad taste in gates. Bad tasting gates at that. They had a bird on top. A bird?' He looked at Lou as though the very thought of a metal bird caused a bad smell in the room, which it could very well have done had the scented candles not covered it.

'It's an eagle,' Lou said defensively. 'You know, last night I was . . .' Lou began to apologise, or at least to explain his behaviour last night, then rethought it, not in the mood to have to explain himself to anybody, particularly to Gabe, who was sleeping on the floor of a basement stock room and still had the audacity to raise himself above Lou. 'Why did you tell Ruth to let me sleep until ten?'

Gabe fixed those blue eyes on him, and despite the fact Lou had a six-figure salary and a multi-million-euro house in one of the most affluent areas in Dublin and all Gabe had was this, he once again felt like the underdog, like he was being judged.

'Figured you needed the rest,' Gabe responded.

'Who are you to decide that?'

Gabe simply smiled.

'What's so funny?'

'You don't like me, do you, Lou?'

Well, it was direct. It was to the point, no beating around the bush, and Lou appreciated that.

'I wouldn't say I don't *like* you,' he said.

'You're worried about my presence in this building,' Gabe continued.

'Worried? No. You can sleep where you like. This doesn't bother me.'

'That's not what I mean. Do I threaten you, Lou?'

Lou threw his head back and laughed. It was exaggerated and he knew it, but he didn't care. It had the desired effect. It filled the room and echoed in the small concrete cell and open ceiling of revealed wires, and his very presence sounded larger than Gabe's space. 'Intimidated by you? Well, let's see . . .' He held his hands out to display the room Gabe was living in. 'Do I really need to say any more?' he said pompously.

'Oh, I get it,' Gabe smiled broadly, as though guessing the winning answer to a quiz. 'I have fewer *things* than you. I forgot that meant something to you.' He laughed lightly and clicked his fingers, leaving Lou feeling stupid.

'Things aren't important to me,' Lou defended himself weakly. 'I'm involved in lots of charities. I give things away all the time.'

'Yes,' Gabe nodded solemnly, 'even your word.'

'What are you talking about?'

'You don't keep that either.' He moved on quickly and started rooting in a shoe box on the second shelf. 'Your head still at you?'

Lou nodded and rubbed his eyes tiredly.

'Here.' Gabe stopped rooting and retrieved a small container of pills. 'You always wonder how I get from place to place? Take one of these.' He threw them across to Lou.

Lou studied them. There was no label on the container.

'What are they?'

'They're a little bit of magic,' he laughed. 'When taken, everything becomes clear.'

'I don't do drugs.' Lou handed them back, placing them on the end of the sleeping bag.

'They're not drugs.' Gabe rolled his eyes.

'Then what's in them?'

'I'm not a pharmacist, just take them, all I know is that they work.'

'No thanks.' Lou stood and prepared to leave.

'They'd help you a lot, you know, Lou.'

'Who says I need help?' Lou turned around. 'You know what, Gabe, you asked me if I don't like you. That's not true, I don't really mind you. I'm a busy man, I'm not much bothered by you, but *this*, this is what I don't like about you, patronising statements like that. I'm fine, thank you very much. My life is fine. All I have is a headache, and that's all. Okay?'

Gabe simply nodded, and Lou turned around and made his way towards the door again.

Gabe started again. 'People like you are —'

'Like what, Gabe?' Lou turned around and snapped, his voice rising with each sentence. 'People like me are what? Hard working? Like to provide for their families? Don't sit on their arses on the ground all day waiting for hand-outs? People like me who help people like you, who go out of their way to give you a job and make your life better . . .'

Had Lou waited to hear the end of Gabe's sentence, he would have learned that Gabe wasn't implying anything of the sort. Gabe was referring to people like Lou who were competitive. Ambitious people, with their eye on the prize instead of the task at hand. People who wanted to be the best for all the wrong reasons and who'd take almost any path to get to that place. Being the best was as equal as being in the middle, which was as equal as being the worst. All were merely a state of being. It was how a person *felt* in that state and *why* they were in that state that was the important thing.

Gabe wanted to explain to Lou that people like him were constantly looking over their shoulders, always looking at what the next person was doing, comparing themselves, looking to achieve greater things, always wanting to be better. And the entire point of Gabe telling Lou Suffern about people like Lou Suffern, was to warn him that people who constantly looked over their shoulders bumped into things.

Paths are so much clearer when people stop looking at what everyone else is doing and instead concentrate on themselves. Lou couldn't afford to bump into things around about this point in the story. If he had, it would have surely ruined the ending, of which we've yet to get to. Yes, Lou had much to do.

But Lou didn't stick around to hear any of that. He left the store room/Gabe's bedroom, shaking his head with disbelief at Gabe's cheek as he walked back down the corridor with the dodgy fluorescent lighting that flashed from brightness to darkness. He found his way to the escape exit and ran up the stairs to the ground floor.

The ground floor was immediately brown and warm and Lou was back in his comfort zone. The security guard looked up at him from his desk as Lou emerged from the emergency exit and frowned.

'There's something wrong with the elevators,' Lou called out to him, not enough time now for him to get to a pharmacy and back in time for the conference call. He'd have to go straight up looking like this, feeling like this, head hot and mushy, with the ridiculous words of Gabe ringing in his ears.

'That's the first I've heard of it.' The security guard made his way over to Lou. He leaned over and pressed the call button, which lit up immediately and the lift door opened.

He looked at Lou oddly.

'Oh. Never mind. Thanks.' Lou got back in the lift and made his way up to the fourteenth floor. He leaned his head against the mirror and closed his eyes and dreamed of being at home in bed with Ruth, cosied up beside him, wrapping her arm and leg around him as she always did – or used to do – as she slept.

When the elevator pinged on the fourteenth floor and the doors opened, Lou opened his eyes and jumped and screamed with fright.

Gabe stood directly before him in the hall – looking solemn – his nose almost touching the doors as they slid open. He rattled the container of pills in Lou's face.

'SHIT! GABE!'

'You forgot these.'

'I didn't forget them.'

'They'll get rid of that headache for you.'

Lou snatched the container of pills from Gabe's hand and stuffed them deep into his trouser pocket.

'Enjoy.' Gabe smiled with satisfaction.

'I told you, I don't do drugs.' Lou kept his voice low, even though he knew he was alone on the floor.

'And I told you they're not drugs. Think of them as a herbal remedy.'

'A remedy for what, exactly?'

'For your problems, of which there are many. I believe I listed them out to you already.'

'Says you, who's sleeping on the floor of a bloody basement stock room,' Lou hissed. 'How's about you take a pill and go about fixing your own life? Or is that what got you in this mess in the first place? You know, I'm getting tired of you judging me, Gabe, when I'm up here and you're the one down there.'

Gabe's expression was curious at that statement, which made Lou feel guilty. 'Sorry,' he sighed.

Gabe simply nodded.

Lou examined the pills as his head pounded, heavier now. 'Why should I trust you?'

'Think of it as a gift.' Gabe repeated the words Lou had spoken only days before.

Along with it, Gabe's gift brought chills down Lou Suffern's spine.

18.

Granted

Alone in his office, Lou took the pills from his pocket and placed them on his desk. He laid his head down and finally closed his eyes.

'Christ, you're a mess,' he heard a voice say close to his ear and he jumped up.

'Alfred,' he rubbed his eyes, 'what time is it?'

'Seven twenty-five. Don't worry, you haven't missed your meeting. Thanks to me,' he smirked, running his chubby, nicotine-stained, nail-bitten fingers along Lou's desk, his one touch enough to tarnish everything and leave his dirty mark, which annoyed Lou. The term 'grubby little mitts' applied here.

'Hey, what are these?' Alfred picked up the pills and popped open the lid.

'Give them to me.' Lou reached out for them but Alfred pulled away. He emptied a few into his open clammy palm.

'Alfred, give them to me,' Lou said sternly, trying to keep the desperation out of his voice as Alfred moved about the room waving the container in the air, teasing him with the same air and issues of a school bully.

'Naughty, naughty, Lou, what are you up to?' Alfred asked in an accusing sing-song tone that chilled Lou to the core.

Knowing that Alfred was most likely to try to use these against him, Lou thought fast.

'Looks like you're concocting a story,' Alfred smiled. 'I know it when you're bluffing, I've seen you in every meeting, remember? Don't you trust me with the truth?'

Lou smiled and kept his tone easy, almost joking, but both were deadly serious. 'Honestly? Lately, no. I wouldn't be surprised if you hatched a plan to use that little container against me.'

Alfred laughed. 'Now, really. Is that any way to treat an old friend?'

Lou's smile faded. 'I don't know, Alfred, you tell me.'

They had a moment's staring match. Alfred broke it.

'Something on your mind, Lou?'

'What do you think?'

'Look,' Alfred's shoulders dropped, the bravado act over with and the new humble Alfred act begun, 'if this is about the meeting tonight, be rest assured that I did not meddle with your appointments in any way. Talk to Louise. With Tracey leaving and Alison taking over, a lot of stuff got lost in the mix,' he shrugged, 'though between you and me, Alison seems a little flakey.'

'Don't blame it on Alison.' Lou folded his arms.

'Indeed,' Alfred smiled and nodded slowly to himself, 'I forgot that you two have a thing.'

'We have no *thing*. For Christ's sake, Alfred.'

'Right, sorry.' Alfred zipped his lips closed. 'Ruth will never know, I promise.'

The very fact that he'd mentioned that unnerved Lou. 'What's gotten into you?' Lou asked him, serious now. 'What's up with you? Is it stress? Is it the crap you're putting up your nose? What the hell is up? Are you worried about the changes –'

'The changes,' Alfred snorted. 'You make me sound like a menopausal woman.'

Lou stared at him.

'I'm fine, Lou,' he said slowly. 'I'm the same as I've always been. It's you that's acting a little funny around here. Everyone's talking about it, even Mr Patterson. Maybe it's these.' He shook the pills in Lou's face, just as Gabe had done.

'They're headache pills.'

'I don't see a label.'

'The kids scratched it off, now can you please stop mauling them and give them back?' Lou held an open hand out towards Alfred.

'Oh, headache pills. I see.' Alfred studied the container again. 'Is that what they are? Because I thought I heard the homeless guy saying that they were herbal?'

Lou swallowed. 'Were you spying on me, Alfred? Is that what you're up to?'

'No,' Alfred laughed easily, 'I wouldn't do that. I'll have some of these checked out for you, to make sure they're nothing stronger than headache pills.' He took a pill, pocketed it, and handed back the container. 'It's nice to be able to find out a few things for myself when my friends are lying to me.'

'I know the feeling,' Lou agreed, glad to have the container back in his possession. 'Like my finding out about the meeting you and Mr Patterson had a few mornings ago and the lunch you had last Friday.'

Unusually for Alfred, he looked genuinely shocked.

'Oh,' Lou said softly, 'you didn't know that I knew, did you? Sorry about that. Well, you'd better get to dinner or you'll miss your appetiser. All work and no caviar makes Alfred a dull boy.' He led a silent Alfred to his door, opened it and winked at him before closing it quietly in his face.

★   ★   ★

Seven thirty p.m. came and went without Arthur Lynch appearing on the fifty-inch plasma before Lou at the board-room table. Aware that at any moment he could be seen by whoever would be present at the meeting, he attempted to relax in his chair, and tried not to sleep. At seven forty p.m., Mr Lynch's secretary informed him that Mr Lynch would be a few more minutes.

While waiting, the increasingly sleepy Lou pictured Alfred in the restaurant, brash as could be, the centre of attention, loud and doing his best to entertain; stealing the glory, making or breaking a deal that Lou wouldn't be associated with unless Alfred failed. In missing that — the most important meeting of the year — Lou was losing the biggest chance to prove himself to Mr Patterson. Cliff's job and the empty office that came with it was dangled at him day in and day out like a carrot on a string. Cliff's old office was down the hall next to Mr Patterson's, blinds open and vacant. A larger office, with better light. It called to him. It had been six months since the mem-orable morning Cliff had had his breakdown — after a long process of unusual behaviour. Lou had finally found Cliff crouched under his desk, his body trembling, with the keyboard held tightly and close to his chest. Occasionally his fingers tapped away in some sort of panicked Morse code. They were coming to get him, he kept repeating, wide-eyed and terrified.

Who exactly *they* were, Lou had been unable to ascertain. He'd tried to gently coax Cliff out from under the desk, to make him put his shoes and socks back on, but Cliff had lashed out as Lou neared and hit him across the face with the attached mouse, swinging the wire around like a cowboy rope. The force of the small plastic mouse hadn't hurt nearly as much as the sight of this young successful man falling apart. The office had lain empty for all those months and, as rumours of Cliff's further demise drifted through offices, the sympathy for him lessened as the competition for his job increased. Lou had recently heard that Cliff had started seeing people again, and he had all the best intentions to visit. He knew he should, and he would at some point, but he just couldn't seem to find the time . . .

Lou's frustration grew as he stared at the black plasma still yet to come alive. His head pounded and he could barely think as his migraine spread from the base of his head to his eyes. Feeling desperate, he retrieved the pills from his pocket and stared at them.

He thought of Gabe's knowledge of Mr Patterson and Alfred's meeting and of how Gabe had correctly judged the shoe situation, of how Gabe had provided him with coffee the previous morning, driven him home and somehow won Ruth over. Convincing himself that on every occasion Gabe had never let him down, and that he could trust him now, Lou shook the open container and one small white glossy pill rolled out onto the palm of his sweaty hand. He played with it for a while, rolling it around in his fingers, licked it; and when nothing drastic happened, he popped it into his mouth and quickly downed it with a glass of water.

Lou held on to the boardroom table with both hands, gripping it so hard that his sweaty prints were visible on the glass surface laid to protect the solid walnut. He waited. Nothing happened. He lifted his hands from the table and studied them as though the effects would be seen on his sweaty palms. Still nothing out of the ordinary happened, no unusual trip, nothing life-threatening apart from his head, which continued to pound.

At seven forty-five p.m. there was still no sign of Arthur Lynch on the plasma. Lou tapped his pen against the glass impatiently, no longer caring about how he'd appear to the people on the other side of the camera. Already paranoid beyond reasoning, Lou began to convince himself that there was no meeting at all, that Alfred had somehow orchestrated this staged meeting so that he could have dinner by himself and negotiate the deal. But Lou wouldn't allow Alfred to sabotage any more of his hard work. He stood quickly, grabbed his overcoat and charged for the door. He pulled it open and had one foot over the threshold when he heard a voice coming from the plasma behind him.

'I'm very sorry for keeping you waiting, Mr Suffern.'

The voice stalled Lou in his march. He closed his eyes and sighed, kissing his dream of the top office with the three-hundred-and-sixty-degree view of Dublin goodbye. He quickly thought about what to do: run and make it in time for dinner or turn around and face the music. Before he had time to make the decision, the sound of another voice in the office almost stopped his heart.

'No problem, Mr Lynch, and please call me Lou. I understand how things can run over time so there are no apologies needed. Let's get down to business, shall we? We have a lot to discuss.'

'Certainly, Lou. And call me Arthur, please. We do have rather a lot to get through, but before I introduce you to these two gentlemen beside me, would you like to finish your business up there? I see you have company?'

'No, Arthur, it's just me here in the office,' Lou heard himself say. 'Everyone else has deserted me.'

'That man there by the door, I can see him on our screen.'

Spotted, Lou slowly turned around and came face to face with himself. He was still seated at the boardroom table, in the same place as he had been waiting before he had planned his escape, grabbed his coat and made for the door. The face that greeted him was also a picture of shock. The ground swirled beneath Lou and he held on to the door frame to stop himself from falling.

'Lou? Are you there?' Arthur asked, and both heads in the office turned to face the plasma.

'Erm, yes, I'm here,' Lou at the board table stammered.

'I'm sorry, Arthur, that gentleman is a . . . a colleague of mine. He's just leaving, I believe he has an important *dinner* meeting to get to.' Lou turned around and threw Lou at the door a warning look. 'Don't you?'

Lou simply nodded and left the room, his knees and legs shaking with his every step. At the elevators, he held on to the wall as he tried to catch his breath and let the dizziness subside. The elevator doors opened and he fell inside, thumping the ground-floor button and hunkering down in the corner of the space, moving farther and farther away from himself on the fourteenth floor.

At eight p.m., as Lou was in the boardroom of Patterson Development offices negotiating with Arthur Lynch, at the same time as Alfred and the team of men were being led to their table, Lou entered the restaurant. He offered his cashmere coat to the host, adjusted his tie, smoothed down his hair and made his way over, one hand in his pocket with the other swinging by his side. His body was loose again, nothing rigid, nothing contained. In order to function he needed to feel the swing of his body, the casual motion of a man who personally doesn't care about the decision either way, but who will do his best to convince you otherwise, because his only concern is the client.

'Pardon me, gentlemen, for being a little delayed,' he said smoothly to the men whose noses were buried deep in their menus.

They all looked up and Lou was exceptionally happy to see the expression on Alfred's face: a Mexican wave of revealing emotions, from surprise, to disappointment, to resentment, to anger. Each look told Lou that this cock-up had indeed been caused deliberately by Alfred. Lou made his way around the table greeting his dinner guests, and by the time he reached Alfred, his friend's smug face had sent his former look of shock whimpering away into the corner.

150

'Patterson is going to kill you.' He spoke quietly from the side of his mouth. 'But at least one deal will be done tonight. Welcome, my friend.' He shook Lou's hand, his deliriousness in sensing Lou's sacking tomorrow lighting up his face.

'It's all been taken care of,' Lou simply replied, turning to take his place a few seats away.

'What do you mean?' Alfred asked, in a tone that revealed he had forgotten where he was. Lou felt Alfred's tight grip around his arm preventing him from moving away.

Lou looked around at the table and smiled, and then turned his back. He discreetly removed each of Alfred's fingers from his arm. 'I said, it's all been taken care of,' Lou repeated.

'You cancelled the conference call? I don't get it.' Alfred smiled nervously. 'Let me in on it.'

'No, no, it's not cancelled. Don't worry, Alfred, let's pay our guests some attention now, shall we?' Lou flashed his pearly whites and finally extricated himself from Alfred's grip so he could move to his chair. 'Now, gentlemen, what looks good on this menu? I can recommend the foie gras, I've had it here before, it's a treat.' He smiled at the team and immersed himself in the pleasure of deal-making.

At nine twenty p.m., after the visual conference call with Arthur Lynch, an exhausted yet exhilarated and triumphant Lou stood outside the window of The Saddle Room restaurant. He was wrapped up in his coat as the December wind picked up, his scarf tight around his neck, yet he didn't feel the cold as he watched himself through the window, suave and sophisticated and holding everyone's attention as he told a story. Everybody's face was interested, all but Alfred, and after five minutes of his animated hand gestures and facial expressions, all the men started laughing. Lou could tell from his body movements that he was telling the story of how he and his colleagues had wandered into a gay bar in London instead of the lapdancing bar they had thought it was. Looking at himself telling the story, he decided then and there never to tell it again. He looked like a prat.

He felt a presence beside him, and he didn't need to look around to know who it was.

'You're following me?' he asked, still watching through the window.

'Nah, just figured you'd come here,' Gabe responded, shivering and stuffing his hands into his pockets. 'How are you doing in there? Entertaining the crowd as usual, I see.'

'What's going on, Gabe?'

'Busy man like you? You got what you wished for. Now you can do everything. Mind you, it'll wear off by the morning so watch out for that.'

'Which one of us is the real me?'

'Neither of you, if you ask me.'

Lou looked at him then and frowned. 'Enough of the deep insights, please. They don't work on me.'

Gabe sighed. 'Both of you are real. You both function as you always do. You'll merge back into one and be as right as rain again.'

'And who are you?'

Gabe rolled his eyes. 'You've been watching too many movies. I'm Gabe. The same guy you dragged off the streets.'

'What's in these?' Lou took the pills out of his pocket. 'Are they dangerous?'

'A little bit of insight. And that never killed anyone.'

'But these things, you could really make some money from these. Who knows about them?'

'All the right people – the people who made them – and don't you go trying to make a fortune from them or you'll have a few people to answer to.'

Lou backed off for the moment. 'Gabe, you can't just double me up and then expect me to accept it without question. This could have dire medical consequences for me, not to mention life-changing psychological reactions. And the rest of the world really needs to know about this, this is insane! We really need to sit down and talk about it.'

'Sure we will.' Gabe studied him. 'And then, when you tell the world, you'll either be locked up in a padded cell or become a freakshow act, and every day you can read about yourself in exactly the same amount of column inches as Dolly the cloned sheep. If I were you I'd just keep quiet about it all and make the best of a very fortunate situation. You're very pale. Are you okay?'

Lou laughed hysterically. 'No! I'm not okay. This is not normal, why are you behaving like this is normal?!'

Gabe just shrugged. 'I'm used to it, I guess.'

'Used to it?' Lou gritted his teeth. 'Well, where do I go now?'

'Well, you've taken care of business at the office, and it looks like your other half is taking care of business here.' Gabe smiled. 'That would leave one special place for you to go.'

Lou thought about that and then slowly a smile crawled onto his face and light entered his eyes as he finally understood Gabe for the first time that evening. 'Okay, let's go.'

'What?' Gabe seemed taken aback. 'Let's go where?'

'The pub. First drink is on me. Christ, the look on your face! Why, where else were you expecting me to go?'

'*Home*, Lou.'

'Home?' Lou scrunched up his face. 'Why would I do that?' He turned back to watch himself at the dinner table, launching into yet another story. 'Oh, that's the one about the time I was stranded in Boston airport. There was this woman on the same flight as me . . .' He smiled, turning around to Gabe to tell the story, but Gabe was gone.

'Suit yourself,' Lou mumbled. He watched himself for a little bit longer, in shock and unsure whether he was really experiencing this night. He definitely deserved a pint, and if the other half of him was heading home after the dinner, that meant he could stay out all night and nobody would notice – nobody, that was, but the person he was with. Happy days.

19.

Lou Meets Lou

A triumphant Lou rolled up to his home, gratified by the sound of the gravel beneath his wheels and the sight of his electronic gates closing behind him. The dinner meeting had been a success: he had commanded the conversation, had done some of the best convincing, negotiating and entertaining that he'd ever done. They'd laughed at his jokes, all his best ones, they'd hung on his every word. All gentlemen had left the table in agreement and content. He'd shared a final drink with an equally jubilant Alfred before driving home.

The lights in the downstairs rooms were all out, but upstairs, despite this late hour, all were on, bright enough to help land a plane.

He stepped inside, into the blackness. Usually, Ruth left the entrance-hall lamp on, and he felt around the walls for the lights. There was an ominous smell.

'Hello?' he called. His voice echoed three flights up to the skylight in the roof.

The house was a mess, not the usual tidiness that greeted

him when he came home. Toys were scattered around the floor. He tutted.

'Hello?' He made his way upstairs. 'Ruth?'

He waited for her shushing to break the silence, but it didn't.

Instead, once he reached the landing, Ruth ran from Lucy's bedroom, dashing by him, hand over her mouth, eyes wide and bulging. She hurried into their bathroom and closed the door. This was followed by the sound of her vomiting.

Down the hall, Lucy started to cry and call for her mother.

Lou stood in the middle of the landing, looking from one room to the other, frozen on the spot, unsure what to do.

'Go to her, Lou,' Ruth just about managed to say, before another encounter with the toilet bowl.

He was hesitant and Lucy's cries got louder.

'Lou!' Ruth yelled, more urgently this time.

He jumped, startled by her tone, and made his way to Lucy's room. He slowly pushed open the door, peeking inside, feeling like an intruder as he entered a world he had rarely ventured into before. Dora the Explorer welcomed him inside. The smell of vomit was pungent in his daughter's room. Her bed was empty, but her sheets and pink duvet unkempt from where she'd slept. He followed her sounds into the bathroom and found her on the tiles, bunny slippers on her feet and throwing up into the toilet. She was crying, weeping quietly as she did so. Spitting and crying, crying and spitting, her sounds echoing in the base of the toilet.

Lou stood there, looking around, briefcase still in hand, unsure of what to do. He took a handkerchief out of his pocket and covered his nose and mouth, to block the smell and to prevent the infection from spreading to him.

Ruth returned, much to his relief, and noted him just idly standing by watching his five-year-old daughter being ill, and then barged by him to tend to her.

'It's okay, sweetheart.' Ruth fell to her knees and wrapped

156

her arms around her daughter. 'Lou, I need you to get me two damp facecloths.'

'Damp?'

'Run them under some cold water and rinse them out so they're not dripping wet,' she explained calmly.

'Of course, yes.' He shook his head at himself. He wandered slowly out of the bedroom, then froze once again on the landing. Looked left, looked right. He returned to the bedroom. 'Facecloths are in the . . .'

'Hotpress,' Ruth said.

'Of course.' He made his way to the hotpress and, still with his briefcase in hand and his coat on, with one hand he fingered the various colours of facecloths. Brown, beige or white. He couldn't decide. Choosing brown, he returned to Lucy and Ruth, ran them under the tap and handed them to her, hoping what he'd done was correct.

'Not just yet,' Ruth explained, rubbing Lucy's back as her daughter took a break.

'Okay, erm, where will I put them?'

'Beside her bed. And can you change her sheets? She had an accident.'

Lucy started to weep again, tiredly nuzzling into her mother's chest. Ruth's face was pale, her hair tied back harshly, her eyes tired, red and swollen. It seemed it had already been a hectic night.

'The sheets are in the hotpress too. And the Deoralite is in the medicine cabinet in the utility room.'

'The what?'

'Deoralite. Lucy likes blackcurrant. Oh God,' she said, jumping up, hand over her mouth again, and running down the hall to their own en suite.

Lou was left in the bathroom alone with Lucy, whose eyes were closed as she leaned up against the bath. Then she looked at him sleepily. He backed out of the bathroom and started to remove the soiled sheets from her bed. As he was doing so, he heard Pud's cries from the next room. He sighed, finally put down his briefcase, took off his coat and suit jacket, and threw them out of the way, into Dora's tent. He opened the top button of his shirt, loosened his tie and rolled up his sleeves.

Lou stared deep into his Jack Daniel's and ice and ignored the barman, who was leaning over the counter and speaking aggressively into his ear.

'Do you hear me?' the barman growled.

'Yeah, yeah, whatever.' Lou's tongue stumbled over his words, like a five-year-old walking with untied shoelaces, already unable to remember what he'd done wrong. He waved a limp hand dismissively through the air as though wafting away a fly.

'No, not *whatever*, buddy. Leave her alone, okay? She doesn't want you to talk to her, she doesn't want to hear your story, she is not interested in you. Okay?'

'Okay, okay,' Lou grumbled then, remembering the rude blonde who'd kept ignoring him. He'd happily not talk to her, he wasn't getting much conversation out of her anyway and the journalist he'd spoken to earlier didn't seem much interested in the amazing story that was his life. He kept his eyes down into his whisky. A phenomenon had occurred tonight, and nobody was interested in hearing his story. Had the world gone mad? Had they all become so used to new inventions and scientific discoveries that the very thought of a man being cloned no longer had shock value? No, the young occupants of this trendy bar would rather sip away at their cocktails, the young women swanning about in the middle of December with their tanned legs, short skirts and highlighted hair, designer handbags hooked over extended brown arms like candelabras, each one looking as exotic and as at home as a coconut in the north pole. This they cared more about than the greater events of the country. A man had been cloned. There were two Lou Sufferns in the city tonight. Bilocation was a reality. He laughed to himself and shook his head at the hilarity of it all. He alone knew the great depths of the universe's abilities, and nobody was interested in learning.

He felt the barman's stare searing into him and so he stopped his solo chortling and instead concentrated again on his ice. He watched it shifting in the glass as it squirmed around trying to get comfortable, falling deeper and deeper into the liquid. It made his eyes droop just watching it. The barman finally left him to his own devices and tended to the others crowded around the bar. Around the lonesome Lou, the noise continued, the sound of people being with other people: after-work flirting, after-work fighting, tables of girls huddled together with eyes locked in as they caught up, circles of young men standing with eyes locked outwards and shifty movements. Tables were dominated by drinks covered with beer mats, the empty seats around them a sign that the people belonging to the glasses were outside striking up matches and new relationships in the smokers' quarters.

Lou looked around to catch somebody's eye. He was fussy at first about his chosen confidant, preferring somebody good looking to share his story with for the second time, but then he decided to settle on anybody. Surely somebody would care about the miracle that had occurred.

The only eye he succeeded in meeting was that of the barman again.

'Gimme me nuther one,' Lou slurred when the barman neared him. 'A neat Jack on th'rocks.'

'I just gave you another one,' the barman responded, a little amused this time, 'and you haven't even touched that.'

'So?' Lou closed one eye to focus on him.

'So, what good is there in having two at the same time?'

At that, Lou started laughing, a chesty wheezy laugh with the presence of the bitter December breeze that had darted into his chest for warmth as soon as it had seen his coat open and his chest revealed, moving quick like a frazzled cat through a doorflap at the sound of a firework.

'I think I missed the joke,' the barman smiled. Now that the bar counter was quiet, he may have had no drink to give to pass the time, but he'd time to give the drunk.

'Ah, nobody here cares.' Lou got angry again, waving his hand dismissively at the crowd around him. 'All they care about is Sex on the Beach, thirty-year mortgages and St Tropez. I've been listenin' and that's all they're sayin'.'

The barman laughed. 'Just keep your voice down. What don't they care about?'

Lou turned serious now and fixed the barman with his best serious stare. 'Cloning.'

The barman's face changed, interest lighting up his eyes, finally something different for him to hear about rather than the usual woes. 'Cloning? Right, you have an interest in that, do you?'

'An interest? I have *more* than an *interest.*' Lou laughed patronisingly and then winked at the barman. He took another sip of his whisky and prepared to tell the story. 'This may be hard for you to believe, but I', he took a deep breath, 'have been cloned,' he began. 'This guy gave me pills and I took them,' he said, then hiccuped. 'You probably don't believe me but it happened. Saw it with my own two eyes.' He pointed at his eye, misjudged his proximity and poked himself. Moments later, after the sting was gone and he had rubbed away the tears, he continued chatting. 'There's two of me,' he continued, holding up four fingers, then three, then one, then finally two.

'Is that so?' the barman asked, picking up a pint glass and beginning to pour a Guinness. 'Where's the other one of you? I bet he's as sober as a judge.'

Lou laughed, wheezy again. 'He's at home with my wife,' he chuckled. 'And with my kids. And I'm here, with her.' He directed his thumb to the left of him.

'Who?'

Lou looked to the side and almost toppled off his bar stool in the process. 'Oh, she's – where is she?' He turned around to the barman again. 'Maybe she's in the toilet – she's gorgeous, we were having a good chat. She's a journalist, she's going to write about this. Anyway, it doesn't matter. I'm here having *all the fun*, and he's,' he laughed again, 'he's at home with my wife and kids. And tomorrow, when I wake up, I'm going to take a pill – not drugs, they're herbal, for my headache.' He pointed to his head seriously. 'And I'm going to stay in bed and he can go to work. Ha! All the things that I am going to do, like,' he thought hard but failed to come up with anything, 'like, oh, so, so many things. All the places I'm going to go. It's a fucking mir'cle. D'ya know when I last had a day off?'

'When was that?'

Lou thought hard. 'Last Christmas. No phone calls, no computer. Last Christmas.'

The barman was dubious. 'You didn't take a holiday this year?'

'Took a week. With the kids.' He ruffled up his nose. 'Fucking sand everywhere. On my laptop, in my phone. And this.' He reached into his pocket and took out his BlackBerry and slammed it on the bar counter.

'Careful.'

'This thing. Follows me everywhere; sand in it and it still works. The drug of the nation. This thing.' He poked it, mistakenly pressing some buttons, which lit up the screen. Ruth and the kids smiled back at him. Pud with his big silly toothless grin, Lucy's big brown eyes peeping out from under her fringe, Ruth holding them both. Holding them all together. He studied it momentarily with a smile on his face. The light went out, the picture faded to black and the device sat staring at him. 'In the B'hamas,' he continued, 'and *beep-beep*, they got me. *Beep-beep, beep-beep*, they get me,' he laughed again. 'And the red light. I see it in my sleep, in the shower, every time I close my eyes, the red light and the *beep-beep*. I hate the fucking *beep-beep*.'

'So take a day off,' the barman said.

'Can't. Too much to do.'

'Well, now that you're cloned, you can take all the days off that you want,' the barman joked, looking around so that nobody else could hear him.

'Yeah,' Lou smiled dreamily, 'there's so much I want to do.'

'Like what? What do you want to do now, more than anything in the world?'

Lou closed his eyes and, taking advantage of his closed eyelids, the dizziness swept in to knock him off his stool. 'Whoa –' He opened his eyes quickly. 'I want to go home, but I can't. He won't let me. I called him earlier and said I was tired and wanted to go home. He wouldn't let me,' he snorted. 'Mr High Almighty said no.'

'Who said?'

'The other me.'

'The other you told you to stay out?' The barman tried not to laugh.

'He's at home, so there can't be two of us. But I'm tired now.' His eyelids drooped. They opened wide again as he thought of something. He leaned in close to the barman, dropped his voice. 'I watched him from the window, you know.'

'The other you?'

'Now you're getting it. I went home and watched him from outside. He was in there, moving about with his sheets and his towels, running upstairs, running downstairs, running from room to room like he thought he was something special.' He snorted. 'One minute I'm watching him tell his stupid jokes at dinner and then the next he's making beds at home. Thinks he can do both.' He rolled his eyes. 'So I came back in here.'

'So maybe he can,' the barman smiled.

'Maybe he can what?'

'Maybe he can do both,' the barman winked. 'Go home,' he said, taking Lou's empty glass before moving down the end of the bar to serve another customer.

As the young customer rattled off his order, Lou thought long and hard about that. If he couldn't go home, he had nowhere else to go.

'It's okay, sweetie, it's okay, Daddy's here,' Lou said, holding Lucy's hair back from her face and rubbing her back as she leaned over the toilet and vomited for the twentieth time that night. He sat on the cold bathroom tiles, in a T-shirt and boxer shorts, and leaned against the bath as her tiny body convulsed one more time and expelled more vomit.

'Daddy . . .' Her voice was tiny through her tears.

'It's okay, sweetie, I'm here,' he repeated sleepily. 'It's almost over.' It had to be, how much more could her tiny body get rid of?

Every twenty minutes he'd gone from sleeping in Lucy's bed to assisting her in the bathroom, where she'd thrown up, her body going from freezing to boiling and back again in a matter of minutes. Usually it was Ruth's duty to stay up all night with the children, sick or otherwise, but unfortunately for Lou, and for Ruth, she was having the same experience as Lucy in their own bathroom down the hall. Gastroenteritis, always an end-of-year gift brought around the Christmas season for those whose systems were ready to wave goodbye to the year before the calendar was.

Lou carried Lucy to her bed again, her small hands clinging around his neck. Already she was asleep, exhausted by what the night had brought her. As he laid her down on the bed, he wrapped her now cold body in blankets and tucked her favourite bear close to her face, as Ruth had shown him before running for the toilet again. His mobile vibrated again on the pink princess bedside locker. At four a.m., it was the fifth time he'd received a phone call from himself. Glancing at the caller display, his own face flashed up on the screen.

'What now?' he whispered into the phone, trying to keep his voice and anger at a low.

'Lou! It's me, Lou!' came the drunken voice at the other end, followed by a raucous laugh.

'Stop calling me,' he said, a little louder now.

In the background there was music thumping, voices loud and a gabble of non-specific words. He could hear glasses clinking, various levels of shouts and laughter exploding every few moments from different corners of the room. Alcohol fumes almost drifted down the phone and penetrated the peaceful innocent world of his daughter. Subconsciously, he blocked the receiver with his hand, to protect her from the intrusion of the adult world seeping into her sleeping world.

'Where are you?'

'Leeson Street. Somewhere,' he shouted back. 'I met this girl, Lou,' came the voice. 'Fucking amazing! You'll be proud of me. No, you'll be proud of you!' Raucous laughter again.

'What?!' Lou barked loudly. 'No! Don't do anything!' he shouted, and Lucy's eyes fluttered open momentarily like two little butterflies, big brown eyes glancing at him with fright, but then on seeing him – her daddy – the alerted look disappeared, a small smile crept onto her lips and her eyes closed again with exhaustion. That look of trust, the faith she had put in him in that one simple look, did something to him right then. He knew he was her protector, the one that could take away the fright and put a smile on her face, and it gave him a better feeling than he'd ever felt in his life. Better than the deal at dinner; better than seeing the look on Alfred's face when he'd arrived. It made him hate the man at the end of the phone, loathe him so much that he felt like knocking him out. His daughter was at home, throwing her guts up, so much so that her entire body was so exhausted she could barely keep her eyes open or stand, and there he was, out getting drunk, chasing skirts, expecting Ruth to do all this without him. He hated the man at the end of the phone.

'But she's hot, if you could just see her,' he slurred.

'Don't you even think about it,' he said threateningly, his voice low and mean. 'I swear to God, if you do anything, I will . . .'

'You'll what? Kill me?' More raucous laughter. 'Sounds like you'd be cutting off your nose to spite your face, my friend. Well, where the hell am I supposed to go, huh? Tell me that? I can't go home, I can't go to work?'

The door to the bedroom opened then and an equally exhausted Ruth appeared.

'I'll call you back.' He hung up quickly.

'Who was on the phone at this hour?' she asked quietly. She was dressed in her robe, her arms hugging her body protectively. Her eyes were bleary and puffed, her hair pulled back in a ponytail; she looked so fragile, a raised voice might blow her over and break her. For the second time that night his heart melted again and he moved towards her, arms open.

'It was just a guy I know,' he whispered, stroking her hair. 'He's out drunk, I wish he'd stop calling. He's a loser,' he added quietly. He snapped the phone shut and tossed it aside into a pile of teddybears. 'How are you?' He pulled away and examined her face closely. Her head was boiling hot, but she shivered in his arms.

'I'm fine.' She gave him a wobbly smile.

'No, you're not fine, go back to bed and I'll get you a facecloth.' He kissed her affectionately on the forehead. Her eyes closed and her body relaxed in his arms.

He almost broke their embrace to punch the air and holler with celebration, because for the first time in a long time he felt her give up the fight with him. For the past six months, when he held her she had been rigid and taut, as though she felt by doing that she was showing him she wasn't accepting his ways, she was protesting and refusing to validate his behaviour. He revelled in the moment of feeling her relax against him; a silent but huge victory for their marriage.

Among the pile of teddies his phone vibrated again, bouncing around in Paddington Bear's arms. His face flashed up again on screen and he had to look away, not able to stand the sight of himself. He could understand how Ruth felt now.

'There's your friend again,' Ruth said, pulling away slightly, allowing him to reach for his phone.

'No, leave him.' He ignored it, bringing her closer to him again. 'Ruth,' he said gently, lifting her chin so she could look at him. 'I'm sorry.'

Ruth looked up at him in shock, and then examined him curiously for the catch. There had to be a catch. Lou Suffern had said he was sorry. Sorry was not a word in his vocabulary.

From the corner of Lou's eye, the phone vibrated, hopping around and falling out of Paddington Bear's paws and onto Winnie the Pooh's head, being passed around teddy to teddy like a hot potato. Each time the phone stopped, it quickly started again, his face lighting up on screen, smiling at him, laughing at him, telling him he was weak for uttering those words. He fought that side of him, that drunken, foolish, childish, irrational side of him, and refused to answer the phone, refused to let go of his wife. He swallowed hard.

'I love you, you know.'

It was as though it was the first time she'd ever heard it. It was as though they were back to the very first Christmas they'd spent together, sitting by the Christmas tree in her parents' house in Galway, the cat curled in a ball on its favourite cushion by the fire, the crazy dog a few years too many in this world outside in the back garden, barking at everything that moved and didn't move. Lou had told her then, by the fake white

Christmas tree that had been fought over by Ruth's parents only hours before – Mr O'Donnell wanting a real pine tree, Mrs O'Donnell not wanting to have to continuously vacuum the pine needles. The gaudy tree was slowly lit up by tiny green, red and blue bulbs, and then the lights would slowly fade again. This happened over and over, and, despite its ugliness, it was relaxing, like a chest heaving slowly up and down. It was the first moment they'd had together all day, the only moments they'd have before he'd have to sleep on the couch and Ruth would disappear to her room. He wasn't planning on saying it, in fact he was planning on never saying it, but it had popped out, as naturally as a newborn. He'd struggled with it for a while, twisting the words around in his mouth, pushing, then withdrawing, not brave enough to say them. But then the words were out and his world had immediately changed. Twenty years later in their daughter's bedroom, it felt like the same moment all over again, with that same look of pleasure, and surprise, on Ruth's face.

'Oh Lou,' she said softly, closing her eyes and savouring the moment. Then suddenly her eyes flicked open, a flash of alarm in them that scared Lou to death about what she would say. What did she know? His past behaviour came gushing at him as he panicked, like a school of ghostly piranhas, coming back to haunt him and nipping him in the backside. He thought of the other part of him, out and drunk, possibly destroying this new relationship with his wife, destroying the repairs it had taken them both so much to achieve. He had a vision of the two Lous: one building a brick wall, the other moving behind him with a hammer and knocking down everything as soon as it was built. In reality that's what Lou had been doing all along. Building his family up with one hand, while in the other his behaviour was shattering everything he'd strived so hard to create.

Ruth quickly let go of him, rushed away from him and

into the bathroom, where he heard the toilet seat go up and the contents of her insides empty into the bowl. Hating anyone being with her during moments like this, Ruth, a multi-tasker as always, mid-vomit, managed to lift her leg to kick the bathroom door closed.

Lou sighed and collapsed to the floor in the pile of teddies. He picked up the phone that had begun to vibrate for the fifth time.

'What now?' he said in a dull voice, expecting to hear his own drunken voice on the other end. But he didn't.

20.

The Turkey Boy 4

'Bullshit,' the Turkey Boy said as Raphie paused for breath. Raphie didn't say anything, instead he chose to wait for something more constructive to come out of the Turkey Boy's mouth.

'Total bullshit,' he said again.

'Okay, that's enough,' Raphie said, standing up from the table and gathering the mug, Styrofoam cup and sweet-wrappers of the chocolates that he'd managed to munch through while he told his story. 'I'll leave you alone in peace now to wait for your mother.'

'No, wait!' Turkey Boy spoke up.

Raphie continued walking to the door.

'You can't just end the story there,' he said incredulously. 'You can't leave me hanging.'

'Ah, well, that's what you get for being unappreciative,' Raphie shrugged, 'and for throwing turkeys through windows.' He left the interrogation room.

Jessica was in the station's tiny kitchen, having another coffee. Her eyes were red raw and the bags under them had blackened.

'Coffee break already?' He pretended not to notice her withering appearance.

'You've been in there for ages.' She blew and sipped, not moving the mug from her lips as she spoke, eyes on the notice-board in front of her.

'Your face okay?'

She gave a single nod, the closest she'd ever get to commenting on the cuts and scrapes across her face. She changed the subject. 'How far did you get in the story?'

'Lou Suffern's first doubling up.'

'What did he say?'

'I do believe "Bullshit" was the expression he used, which was then closely followed by "Total bullshit".'

Jessica smiled lightly, blowing on her coffee and sipping again. 'You got further than I thought. You should show him the tapes of that night.'

'We got video surveillance of the pub he was in already?' Raphie asked, flicking the switch on the kettle again. 'Who the hell was working there on Christmas Day? Santa?'

'No, we haven't got that yet. But the recorded audio-visual conference call shows a guy who looks exactly like Lou walking out of his office. Certain people at Patterson Developments don't seem to know how to take a day off. ' She rolled her eyes. 'Christmas Day, honestly.'

'It could be the Gabe guy in the conference call. They look alike.'

'Could be.'

'Where is he anyway? He was supposed to be here an hour ago.'

Jessica shrugged.

'Well, he'd better get his ass in here soon, *and* bring his driver's licence like I told him to,' Raphie fumed, 'or I'll . . .'

'Or you'll what?'

'Or I'll bring him in myself.'

She lowered the mug slowly from her lips and those intense, secretive eyes stared deep into his. 'Bring him in for what, Raphie?'

Raphie ignored her and instead poured himself another coffee, adding two sugars, which Jessica – sensing his mood – did not protest to. He filled a Styrofoam cup with water and shuffled off down the corridor again.

'Where are you going?' she called after him.

'To finish the story,' he grumbled.

The Remainder of the Story

21.

Man of the Moment

'Wakey wakey,' a sing-song voice penetrated Lou's drunken dreams, where everything was being rerun a hundred times over: mopping Lucy's brow, plugging Pud's soother back into his mouth, holding back Lucy's hair over the toilet, hugging his wife close, Ruth's body relaxing against his, then back to Lucy's heated brow again, Pud spitting out his soother, Ruth's smile when he'd told her he loved her.

He smelled fresh coffee under his nose. He finally opened his eyes and jumped back with fright at the sight that greeted him, bumping his already throbbing head against the concrete wall.

Lou took a moment to adjust to his surroundings. Sometimes the visions that greeted his newly opened eyes of a morning were more comforting than others. As opposed to the mug of coffee that at that moment was thrust mere inches from his nose, he was more accustomed to the sound of a toilet flush acting as his wake-up call. Often, the wait for the mystery toilet-flusher to exit the bathroom and show her face in the bedroom was a long and unnerving one, and on some occasions, though rare, Lou had taken it upon himself to disappear from the bed, and the building – at exactly the same time – before the mystery woman had the opportunity to show her face.

On this particular morning after Lou Suffern had been doubled up for the very first time, he was faced with a new scenario: a man of similar age was before him thrusting a mug of coffee at him with a satisfied look on his face. This was certainly a new one for the books. Thankfully, the young man was Gabe, and Lou found, with much relief, that they were both fully dressed and that there was no toilet-flushing involved. With a throbbing head and the foul stench of rotting dead rats working his mouth, like a presidential candidate working a room on a campaign trail, he took in his surroundings.

He was on the ground. That he could tell by his proximity to the concrete and the longer distance to the open panelled ceiling with wires dripping down. The floor was hard despite the sleeping bag beneath him. He had a crick in his neck from the position his head had been rather unfortunately lodged in against the concrete wall. Above him, metal shelves towered to the ceiling: hard, grey, cold and depressing, they stood like the cranes that littered Dublin's skyline, metal invaders umpiring a developing city. To the left, a shadeless lamp was the guilty party behind the unforgiving bright white light that wasn't so much thrown around the room as it was aimed at Lou's head, like a pistol in a steady hand. What was glaringly obvious was that he was in Gabe's storage room, in the basement. Gabe stood over him, his hand thrust towards him, and in it a mug of steaming coffee. The sight was familiar, a mirror-image of only a week ago, when Lou had stopped on the street to offer Gabe a coffee. Only this time the image was as distorted and disturbing as a funfair mirror, because when Lou assessed the situation, it was him that was down here, and Gabe that was up there.

'Thanks.' He took the mug from Gabe, wrapping his cold

hands around the porcelain. He shivered. 'It's freezing in here.' His first words were a croak, and as he sat up he felt the weight of the world crashing down on his head as a hangover for the second morning running reminded him that although age had brought him much to celebrate – for example, the nose that as a boy had always been too big for his face, was finally, in his thirties, in proportion – this hangover was not one of them.

'Yeah, someone promised to bring me an electric heater but I'm still waiting.' Gabe grinned. 'Don't worry, I hear blue lips are in this season.'

'Oh, sorry, I'll get Alison on to that,' Lou mumbled, and sipped on the black coffee. He had taken his initial wakening moment to figure out where he was, and once the confusion of his whereabouts had been cleared up and his position established, he relaxed and started drinking. But the one sip of caffeine that followed alerted him to another problem.

'What the hell am I doing here?' He sat up properly, attentive now, and studied himself for clues. He was dressed in yesterday's suit, a crumpled, rumpled mess with some questionable, though mostly self-explanatory, stains on his shirt, tie and jacket. In fact there was dirt just about everywhere he looked. 'What the hell is that smell?'

'I think it's you,' Gabe smiled. 'I found you around the back of the building last night throwing up into a skip.'

'Oh God,' Lou whispered, covering his face with his hands. Then he looked up, confused. 'But last night I was home. Ruth and Lucy; they were sick. And as soon as they fell asleep, Pud woke up.' He rubbed his face tiredly. 'Did I just dream that?'

'Nope,' Gabe replied chirpily, pouring hot water into his instant coffee. 'You did that too. You were very busy last night, don't you remember?'

It took a moment for last night's events to register with Lou, but the onslaught of memories of the previous night – the pill, doubling up – came to his mind and suddenly pennies were dropping all over the place like a malfunctioning coin dispenser.

'That girl I met.' He aborted the sentence, both wanting to know the answer and not wanting to know at exactly the same time. A part of him was sure of his innocence, while the other part of him wanted to take himself outside and beat himself up for possibly jeopardising his marriage again. His body broke out into a cold sweat, which added a new scent to the mix.

Gabe let him stew for a while, as he blew on his coffee and took tiny sips like a mouse nibbling on a hot piece of cheese.

'You met a girl?' he asked, wide-eyed and innocent.

'I, erm, I met a – never mind – was I alone when you found me last night?' Same question, different words. Both at the same time.

'Indeed you were, very alone. Though not lonely, you were quite content to keep yourself company, mumbling about a girl,' Gabe teased him. 'Seemed as though you'd lost her and couldn't remember where you'd put her. You didn't find her at the bottom of the skip, anyway, though perhaps if we clear away the layer of vomit you deposited in the recycle bin, your cardboard cut-out woman may be revealed.'

'What did I say? I mean, don't tell me exactly, just tell me if I said anything about – you know – shit, if I've done something, Ruth will kill me.' Tears sprang into his eyes. 'I'm the biggest fucking asshole.' He kicked away the crate that was at the end of the sleeping bag, with frustration.

Gabe's smile faded, respecting this side of Lou. 'You didn't do anything with her.'

'How do you know?'

'I know.'

Lou studied him then, warily, curiously, distrustingly and then trusting all at the same time. Gabe seemed to be his everything right then: his one parent, the kidnapper he was growing to like, the only person who understood his situation, yet the one who had put him in that situation. A dangerous relationship.

'Gabe, we really have to talk about these pills. I don't want them any more.' He took them out of his pocket. 'I mean, last night was a revelation, it really was, in so many ways.' He rubbed his eyes tiredly, remembering the sound of his drunken voice at the end of the phone. 'I mean, are there two of me now?'

'No, you're back to one again,' Gabe explained. 'Fig roll?'

'But Ruth,' Lou ignored him. 'She'll wake up and I'll be gone. She'll be worried. Did I just vanish?'

'She'll wake up and you'll be gone to work, just like always.'

He absorbed that information and calmed a little. 'But it's not right, it doesn't make sense. We really need to discuss where you got them from.'

'You're right, we do,' Gabe said seriously, taking the container from Lou and stuffing it into his pocket. 'But not yet. It's not time yet.'

'What do you mean, it's not time? What are you waiting for?'

'I mean it's almost eight thirty and you've got a meeting to get to before Alfred sweeps in and steals the limelight.'

At that, Lou's coffee was placed carelessly on a shelf, between an extension lead and a pile of mouse traps, and he jumped to his feet, instantly forgetting about his serious concerns about the peculiar pills, and also forgetting to wonder how on earth Gabe knew about his eight-thirty meeting.

'You're right, I'd better go, but we'll talk later.'

'You can't go looking like that,' Gabe laughed, looking Lou's filthy rumpled suit up and down. 'And you smell of vomit. And cat urine. Believe me, I know, I've a fine nose for it by now.'

'I'll be okay.' Lou looked at his watch while taking off his suit jacket at the same time. 'I'll grab a quick shower in my office and change into my spare suit.'

'You can't. I'm wearing it, remember?'

Lou looked over at Gabe then, and remembered how he'd provided him with his spare clothes the first day he had employed him. He'd bet Alison hadn't replaced the clothes yet, she was too new to know to do that.

'Shit! Shit, shit, shit!' He paced the small room, biting his manicured fingernails, pulling and spitting, pulling and spitting.

'Don't worry, my cleaner will see to them,' Gabe said with amusement, watching as the chewed nails fell to the cemented floor.

Lou ignored him, pacing some more. 'Shops don't open till nine, where the hell can I get a suit?'

'Never fear, I think I have something here in my walk-in wardrobe,' Gabe said, disappearing down the first aisle and reappearing with the new suit draped in plastic. 'Like I said, you never know when a new suit will come in handy. It's your size and all, fancy that. It's almost like it was made for you.' He winked at Lou. 'May your outer dignity mirror an inner dignity of your soul,' Gabe said, handing the suit over to him.

'Eh yeah, sure. Thanks,' Lou said uncertainly, quickly lifting it from Gabe's outstretched hands.

In the empty staff elevator, Lou looked at his reflection in the mirror. He was unrecognisable from the man who'd woken up on the floor half an hour earlier. The suit that Gabe had given him, despite being an unknown designer – something he wasn't used to – was surprisingly the best-fitting suit he had ever owned. With the blue of the shirt and tie against the navy jacket and trousers, Lou's eyes were popping out, innocent and cherub-like.

Things were very good for Lou Suffern that day. He was back to his groomed, handsome best, his shoes polished to perfection by Gabe and back to how they used to dance along the pavements. The swing was back in his step, his left hand casually placed in his pocket, his right arm swinging loosely by his side in rhythm with his step and available to answer the phone and/or shake a hand at every possible moment. He was the man of the moment. After a phone call with his wife and Lucy, he was father of the year according to Lucy, and the odds of him being in with the chance to be husband of the year in the next decade or two were improving. He was happy, so happy, in fact, that he whistled and didn't stop even when Alison delivered the news that his sister was on the line. He happily reached for the phone and propped his behind on the corner of Alison's desk.

'Marcia, good morning,' he said cheerily.

'Well, you're in a good mood today. I know you're busy, Lou, I won't keep you long. I just wanted to let you know that we all got Dad's birthday invitations, they were . . . very nice . . . very sophisticated . . . not what I would have chosen but . . . anyway, I've had a few people on the phone to say they haven't received theirs yet.'

'Oh, they must have got lost in the post,' Lou said, 'we'll send them out some more.'

'But it's tomorrow, Lou.'

'What?' He frowned and squinted his eyes to concentrate on the calendar on the wall.

'Yes, his birthday's tomorrow,' she said, sounding slightly panicked. 'They won't get the invites if you send them out now. I just wanted to make sure that it would be okay for everyone just to turn up without an invite, it's only a family party.'

'Don't worry, just email us through the list again and we'll have a guest list on the door. It's all under control.'

'I might just bring a few things to –'

'It's all under control,' he said more firmly.

He watched his colleagues walk down the hall and into the

boardroom, Alfred lagging behind in his slacks and blazer with big gold buttons as though he was about to captain a cruise-liner.

'What's happening at the party, Lou?' Marcia asked nervously.

'What's happening?' Lou laughed. 'Oh well, come on, Marcia, we want it to be a surprise for everyone.'

'Do you know what's happening?'

'Do I know what's happening? Are you worried about my organisational skills?'

'I'm worried that you've repeated every single one of my questions just to give yourself more thinking time,' she said easily.

'Of course I know what's going on, you think I'd just leave it up to Alison to do alone?' He laughed. 'She's never even met Dad,' he said, echoing what he'd heard a few family members mumble.

'Well, it's important for someone in the family to be involved, Lou – this Alison seems like a nice girl but she doesn't really know Dad, does she? I've been calling her to help out but she hasn't been very forthcoming. I want Dad to have the time of his life.'

'He will, Marcia, he will.' Lou's stomach turned uneasily. 'We'll all have fun, I promise. Now, you know I won't be there at the very beginning because I've got this office party. I have to be here for a little while but I'll come straight over.'

'I know, that's perfectly understandable. Oh God, Lou, I just want Dad to be happy. He's always busy making sure the rest of us are. I want him to finally relax and enjoy himself.'

'Yeah,' Lou swallowed, with the first hint of trepidation. 'Me too. Okay, I'd better hurry, I've got to go to a meeting. I'll see you all tomorrow, okay?'

He handed the phone back to Alison, his smile gone. 'It's all under control, isn't it?'

'What?'

'The party,' he said firmly. 'My dad's party.'

'Lou, I've been trying to ask you questions about it all we—'

'Is it all under control? Because if it's not, you'd tell me, wouldn't you?'

'Absolutely.' Alison smiled nervously. 'The place you picked is very, erm, cool, shall we say, and they have their own standardised events management team. I told you about this already,' she said quickly, 'a few times during the week. I also left some options of food and music on your desk for you to decide on, and when you didn't do that, I had to decide it myse—'

'Okay, Alison, a note for the future: when I ask if it's all under control, I only want a yes or a no,' he said, firmly but politely. 'I don't have time for questions and memos, really, all I need to know is if you can do it or not. If you can't, then that's fine, we just look at doing something else. Okay?'

She nodded quickly.

'Great.' He clapped his hands and hopped off the desk. 'I'd better get to this meeting.'

'Here,' she handed him his files. 'And congratulations on those two deals yesterday, everyone is talking about it.'

'They are?'

'Yes,' she said, wide-eyed. 'Some people are saying you'll get Cliff's job.'

That was like music to Lou's ears, but he played it down. 'Now, Alison, let's not jump the gun. We're all wishing a speedy recovery for Cliff.'

'Of course we are, but . . . anyway,' she smiled, 'see you at the party tomorrow?'

'Of course I will,' he smiled back, and it was only as he was marching away and heading towards the meeting room that he really understood what she had meant.

★　　★　　★

When Lou entered the boardroom, all twelve around the table stood to applaud him, their big, white-toothed smiles beaming from ear to ear, not quite meeting their tired morning eyes, and with tiny chips evident on their stressed and in-dire-need-of-a-massage shoulders. This was what everybody he knew was faced with. Not enough hours of sleep; the inability to get away from work or work-related devices like laptops, PDAs and mobiles; distractions that each of their family members wanted to flush down the toilet. Of course they were happy for him, in a frazzled, too-much-access–to-electro-magnetic-energy kind of way. They were all functioning to stay alive, to pay the mortgages, to do the presentations, to meet the quotas, to please the boss, to get in early enough to beat the traffic, hang around long enough in the evenings until it had gone. Everyone in that room was putting in all the hours under the sun trying to unload their work before Christmas, and, as they all did that, the pile of personal problems in their inboxes grew higher. That would all be dealt with over the Christmas break. Finally, time for festive family issues that had been side-lined all year. 'Twas the season for family folly.

The applause was led by a beaming Mr Patterson, and all joined in but Alfred, who was exceptionally slow to stand. While the others were on their feet, he was slowly pushing his chair back. When the others were clapping, he was adjusting his tie and fastening his gold buttons. He succeeded in clapping once before the applause died down, one single clap that sounded more like a balloon had burst.

Lou worked his way around the table, shaking hands, slapping backs, kissing cheeks. By the time he reached Alfred, his friend had already seated himself but offered Lou a limp clammy hand.

'Ah, the man of the moment,' Mr Patterson said happily, taking Lou's hand warmly and placing his left hand firmly on Lou's upper arm. He stood back and looked at Lou proudly, as a grandfather would his grandson on Communion Day, beaming with pride and admiration.

'You and I will have a conversation after this,' he said quietly as the others were still continuing their talk. 'You know there'll be changes after Christmas, that's no secret around here,' he said solemnly, maintaining respect for Cliff.

'Yes,' Lou nodded sagely, secretly loving being personally let in on the secret, despite the fact that everybody knew about it.

'Well, we'll talk, okay?' Mr Patterson said firmly, and as the other conversations died down, he took his seat and the chat was ended.

Feeling like he was floating, Lou sat down and found it hard to keep up with the rest of the morning's discussion. From the corner of his eye, Lou could see that Alfred had caught the end of Mr Patterson's comment.

'You look tired, Lou, were you out celebrating last night?' a colleague asked.

'I was up all night with my little girl. Vomiting bug. My wife had it too, so it was a busy night.' He smiled, thinking of Lucy tucked in bed, her thick fringe hiding half her face.

Alfred laughed and his wheeze was loud in the room.

'My son had that last week,' Mr Patterson said, ignoring Alfred's outburst. 'It's going around.'

'It's going around, all right,' Alfred repeated, looking at Lou.

The aggression was emanating from Alfred in waves, almost like the heat visibly rising from a desert highway. It seeped from his soul, distorting the air around him, and Lou wondered if everybody could see it. Lou felt for him; he could see how lost and fearful he was.

'It's not just me you should be congratulating,' Lou announced to the table, 'Alfred was in on the New York deal too. And a fine job he did of it.'

'Absolutely.' Alfred brightened up, coming back to the room and fidgeting with his tie, which made Lou nervous. 'It was nice of Lou to finally join me at the end, in time to see me wrap it all up.'

Everyone around the table laughed, but it hit Lou elsewhere; in a place that rather hurt. In that moment he was Aloysius again, eight years old on the local football team, taken off the field minutes before the final whistle of the football final because his own team-mate, jealous of Lou scoring more points than him, had landed a kick between his legs and sent him on his knees, gasping, red-faced, close to dizziness and vomit. Like Alfred's comment, it wasn't so much the kick to the groin that hurt as much as the person who'd delivered the blow and the reasoning behind it. He'd lain on the field, hands covering his groin, his face hot and sweaty, frustration seeping from his pores, while being crowded around by the rest of the team, who looked at him and wondered if he was faking it.

'Yes, we have already commended Alfred,' Mr Patterson said, not looking his way, 'but two deals at once, Lou, how on earth did you manage it? We all know you're a multi-tasker at the best of times, but what an extraordinary use of time management, and, of course, your negotiating skills.'

'Yes, extraordinary,' Alfred agreed, his tone playful, but underneath it there was venom. 'Almost unbelievable. Perhaps unnatural. What was it Lou, speed?'

There were a few nervous laughs, a cough and then a silence. Mr Patterson broke the tension by getting the meeting started but the damage had already been done. Alfred had left something hanging in the air. A question replaced what had previously been admiration, a seed had been planted in each mind and, whether it was believed or not, each time Lou achieved anything or his name was mentioned in future, Alfred's comment would be momentarily, perhaps subconsciously, entertained and that seed would grow, peep up from the dirty soil and then rear its ugly head.

After all his hard work, missing out on family occasions, running out of his home to reach the office, quick pecks on Ruth's cheek for the sake of long handshakes with strangers at the office, he had finally had his moment. Two minutes of handshakes and applause. Followed by a seed of doubt.

'You look happy,' Gabe commented, placing a package on a desk nearby.

'Gabe, my friend, I owe you big-time,' Lou beamed as he left the meeting, just short of reaching out to hug him. He lowered his voice. 'Can I have those . . . the container back, please? I was very tired and emotional this morning and I don't know what got into me, *of course* I believe in the herbal remedy thingies.'

Gabe didn't respond. He continued laying out envelopes and packages on the surrounding desks while Lou looked on after him with hope on his face, like a dog awaiting his walkies.

'It's just that I think I'm going to need a lot more from where they came from,' Lou winked. 'You know?'

Gabe looked confused.

'Cliff's not coming back.' Lou kept his voice down and tried to hide the excitement. 'He's totally fried.'

'Ah, the poor man who had the breakdown,' Gabe said, still placing items on desks.

'Yes,' Lou almost squealed with excitement. 'Don't tell anyone I told you.'

'That Cliff's not coming back?'

'Yes, that and . . . you know,' he looked around, 'other things. Maybe a new job, more than likely a promotion. Nice big pay rise.' He grinned. 'He's going to talk to me about it soon.' Lou cleared his throat. 'So whatever it is that he has in store for me, I'm going to need those little herbal beauties because I can't possibly sustain my previous work-rate without ending up either divorced or six feet under.'

'Ah, yes. Them. Well, you can't have them.'

Gabe continued pushing the trolley down the hall. Lou quickly followed, yapping at his heels like a Jack Russell after a postman.

'Ah, come on, I'll pay you whatever you want for them. How much do you want?'

'I don't want anything.'

'Okay, you probably want to keep them for yourself, I get it. At least tell me where I can get them?'

'You can't get them anywhere. I threw them away. You were right about them, they're not right. Psychologically. And who knows the physical side-effects? They'd probably just end up hurting people in the long run. I mean, I don't think they were made to be used continuously, Lou. Maybe they were a scientific experiment that found their way out of a lab.'

'You did *what* to them?' Lou panicked, ignoring all that Gabe had said. 'Where did you put them?'

'In the skips.'

'Well, get them for me. Climb in and get them back,' Lou said angrily. 'If you just put them there this morning, they will still be there now. Come on, hurry, Gabe.' He prodded Gabe in the back.

'They're gone, Lou. I opened the container and emptied them into the skip, and considering what you deposited inside it last night, I'd steer clear.'

Lou grabbed him by the arm and led him to the staff elevator. 'Show me.'

Once outside, Gabe pointed the skip out to Lou, large and filthy yellow. Lou charged over. Looking inside, he could see the container sitting on top, so close he could touch it, and then, beside it, the pile of pills lay among a greenish-brown ooze of some sort. The smell was dire and so he held his nose and tried not to retch. The pills were soaked in whatever the substance was and his heart sank. He took off his suit jacket and threw it at Gabe to catch. He rolled up his shirt-sleeves and prepared to shove his hands in the foul-smelling ooze. He paused before going in.

'If I can't get these pills, where can I get more?'

'Nowhere,' Gabe responded, standing by the back door and watching him, arms folded and sounding bored. 'They don't make them any more.'

'What?' Lou spun around. 'Who made them? I'll pay them to make more.'

This panic went on for a while, Lou interrogating Gabe as to how he could get his hands on more pills, until he realised the only way he could get his hands on them was by dealing with what was right in front of him. Once again distracted, he decided what needed to be dealt with was the skip, not his life.

'Shit. Maybe I can wash them.' He stepped closer and leaned in. The smell made him retch. 'What the hell is that?' He gagged again and had to step away from the skip. 'Damn it.' Lou kicked the skip and then regretted it when the pain hit.

'Oh look,' Gabe said in a bored tone. 'It looks like I dropped one on the ground.'

'What? Where?' He instantly forgot the pain in his toe and raced back to the skip like a child racing for the last seat in musical chairs. He examined the ground around the bins. Between the cracks of the cobbles he saw something white peering up at him. Leaning closer, he noticed it was a pill.

'A-ha! Found one!'

'Yeah, I had to throw them from a distance, the smell was so bad,' Gabe explained. 'A few fell on the ground.'

'A few? How many?'

Lou got down on his hands and knees and started searching.

'Lou, you really should just go back inside. You've had a good day. Why don't you just leave it at that? Learn from it and move on?'

'I have learned from it,' he said, nose close to the cobbles. 'I've learned that I'm the hero around here with these things. Ah-ha – there's another one.' Satisfied that those two were all he could salvage from the skip, he put them in his handkerchief, back into his pocket, and he stood up and wiped his knees.

'Two will do for now,' he said, wiping his forehead with his handkerchief. 'I can see two more under the skip but I'll leave them for the time being.'

When Lou climbed up from his knees, which were by then black and dirty and his hair dishevelled, he turned around and found he had more company. Alfred was standing beside Gabe, his arms folded, a smug look on his face.

'Drop something, Lou? Well, look at that. The man of the moment, indeed.'

22.

'Tis the Season...

'You'll be there, won't you, Lou?' Ruth asked, trying her best to hide the panic from her voice. She moved around their bedroom in her bare feet, the sound of her skin against the wooden floors like little feet splashing in water. Her long brown hair was up in rollers, her body was draped in a towel with beads of shower water glistening on her shoulders as they caught the light.

Lou watched his wife of ten years from their bed, his head moving back and forth as though a tennis-match spectator. They were going into the city centre in separate cars at separate times; he had his office party to get to before joining the rest of his family at a later stage for his father's party. He wasn't long home from work, had showered and dressed in the space of twenty minutes, but instead of his usual pacing downstairs and waiting for his wife impatiently, he had chosen to lie on the bed and watch her. He had just learned tonight that watching was so much more entertaining than pacing with a rising anger. Lucy had joined him on their bed only moments ago and was cuddling her blanket. Fresh out of the bath, she was dressed in her sleeping suit and smelled so freshly of strawberries that he almost wanted to eat her.

'Of course I'll be there.' He smiled at Ruth.

'It's just that you should have left the house a half-hour ago and that puts you behind as it is.' She rushed by him and disappeared into the walk-in wardrobe. The rest of her sentence disappeared along with her, as the muffled sounds drifted out into the bedroom, leaving the words behind in the wardrobe hanging on rails and folded neatly on the shelves. He lay back on the bed, rested his arms behind his head and laughed.

'She's talking fast,' Lucy whispered.

'She does that.' Lou smiled, reached out and tucked a loose strand of hair behind his daughter's ear.

Ruth reappeared dressed in her underwear.

'You look beautiful,' he smiled.

'Daddy!' Lucy giggled outrageously. 'She's in her panties!'

'Yes, well, she looks beautiful in her panties.' He kept his eyes on Ruth while Lucy rolled around the bed laughing at this idea.

Ruth turned around and studied him quickly. Lou could see her swallow, her face curious, not used to the sudden attention, perhaps worrying that he was acting this way out of guilt, another part of her afraid to become hopeful, afraid that it was yet another build-up to a later let-down. She disappeared to the bathroom for a few moments, and when she re-entered the room she hopped around in her underwear.

Lucy and Lou started laughing while watching her.

'What are you doing?' Lou laughed.

'I'm drying my moisturiser.' She ran on the spot, smiling. Lucy hopped up and momentarily joined her, giggling and dancing, before deciding her mother was dry, and joining her father back on the bed again.

'Why are you still here?' Ruth asked gently. 'You don't want to be late for Mr Patterson.'

192

'This is far more fun.'

'Lou,' she laughed, 'while I appreciate the fact that you are not constantly moving for the first time in ten years, you really have to go. I know you say you'll be there tonight, but –'

'I will be there tonight,' he replied, insulted.

'Okay, but please don't be too late,' she continued, racing around the room. 'Most people going to your dad's party are over the age of seventy, they might have fallen asleep or have gone home by the time you consider your night to be just beginning.' She darted back into the wardrobe.

'I'll be there,' he replied, more to himself.

He heard her rooting around in the drawers, pushing closed presses. She bumped into something, swore, dropped something else, and when she reappeared in the bedroom she was dressed in a black cocktail dress.

Usually he would automatically tell her she was beautiful, hardly even looking at her while saying it. He felt it was his duty, that it was what she wanted to hear, that it would get them out of the house faster, that it would make her stop fidgeting all the way on the car journey, but tonight he found himself unable to speak. She was beautiful. It was as though all his life he had been told the sky was blue and for the first time he had actually looked up and seen it for himself. Why didn't he look at it every day? He lay on his stomach and leaned his head on his hand. Lucy imitated him. They both watched the wonder that was Ruth. Ten years of this display and he'd been pacing downstairs all this time while barking up at her.

'And remember,' she zipped up her dress at the back, while shuffling by them again, 'you got your father a cruise for his birthday.'

'I thought we were getting him golf membership.'

'Lou, he hates golf.'

'He does?'

193

'Granddad hates golf,' Lucy said.

'He's always wanted to go to St Lucia – remember the story about Douglas and Ann and how they won the trip on the back of a cereal pack, blah, blah, blah?'

'No,' Lou frowned.

'The cereal box competition.' She stopped in her flight back to the wardrobe to stare at him with surprise.

'Yeah, what about it?'

'He tells this story all the time, Lou. About how Douglas entered the competition on the back of the cereal box and they won a trip to St Lucia . . . Anything?' She looked at him for a glimmer of recognition.

Lou shook his head.

'Wow, how could you not know that?' She continued on her mission to get to the wardrobe. 'It's his favourite story. He'll be emotional.'

'Dad won't be emotional,' he smiled. 'He doesn't get emotional.'

Ruth disappeared inside and reappeared with one shoe on her foot and the other under her arm. Up, down, down and up, she made her way across the room to her dressing table.

Lucy giggled.

Ruth put her jewellery on, her earrings, her bracelet, and only then did she remove the shoe from under her arm to put it on.

Lou smiled again and watched her totter into the bathroom.

'Oh,' she raised her voice once inside. 'When you see Mary Walsh, don't mention Patrick.' She stuck her head outside the bathroom. Half of her hair was covered in rollers, the other half loose and curled. Her face was sad. 'He left her.'

'Okay,' he nodded, trying to remain as solemn as possible.

When she'd ducked her head back in again, Lou turned to Lucy. 'Patrick left Mary Walsh,' he said. 'Did you know that?'

Lucy shook her head wildly.

'Did you tell him to do that?'

She shook her head, laughing.

'Who knew that would happen?'

Lucy shrugged. 'Maybe Mary did.'

Lou laughed. 'Maybe.'

'Oh, and *please* don't ask Laura if she's lost weight. You always do that and she hates it.'

'Isn't that a nice thing to say?' He frowned.

Ruth laughed. 'Honey, she's been putting on weight consistently for the past ten years. When you say it to her, it's like you're teasing.'

'Laura's a fatty,' he whispered to Lucy, and she fell about on the bed laughing.

He took a deep breath as he noticed the time, and, strangely, dread filled his stomach. 'Okay, I really have to go. See you tomorrow,' he said to Lucy, kissing her on the head.

'I like you much better now, Daddy,' she said happily.

Lou froze, half on the bed, half off.

'What did you say?'

'I said I like you much better now,' she smiled, revealing a missing bottom tooth. 'Me, Mummy and Pud are going ice-skating tomorrow, will you come?'

Still taken aback by her comment and how it had affected him, he simply said, 'Yes. Sure.'

Ruth came back into the room again, bringing a wave of her perfume with her, her hair in loose waves down past her shoulders, her make-up flawless. He couldn't take his eyes off her.

'Mummy, Mummy!' Lucy jumped up onto the bed and started bouncing up and down. 'Daddy's coming ice-skating tomorrow.'

'Lucy, get down, you're not allowed to jump on the bed. Get down, sweetheart, thank you. Remember I told you that Daddy is a very busy man, he doesn't have time to be −'

'I'm coming,' Lou interrupted firmly.

Ruth's mouth fell open. 'Oh.'

'Is that okay?'

'Yes, sure, I just . . . Yes. Absolutely. Great.' She nodded, then headed in the other direction, clearly taken aback. The bathroom door closed softly behind her.

He gave her five minutes alone but then couldn't afford to wait any longer.

'Ruth,' Lou rapped gently on the bathroom door, 'you okay?'

'Yes, I'm fine.' She cleared her throat and sounded more perky than she intended. 'I'm just . . . blowing my nose.' There was a loud sound of her nose being blown.

'Okay, I'll see you later,' he said, wanting to go inside and hug her goodbye, but knowing that the door would open if she wanted him to.

'Okay,' she said, a little less perky again. 'See you at the party.'

The door remained closed, and so he left.

The offices of Patterson Developments were swarming with Lou Suffern's colleagues in various states of disarray. It was only seven thirty p.m. and already some were set for the night. Unlike Lou, who'd gone home after work, most people had gone straight to the pub and returned to the party to continue. There were women he barely recognised in dresses revealing bodies he had never known existed beneath their suits; and there were some whose bodies were made only for their suits. The uniformity of the day had been broken down: there was an air of adolescence, of the desire to show off and prove to one another who they really were. It was a day for rule-breaking, for saying what they felt; it was a dangerous environment to be in. Mistletoe hung from almost every doorway – in fact, Lou had already received two kisses as soon as he'd stepped out of the elevator, from opportunists hanging out there.

Suit jackets were off; novelty musical ties, Santa hats and reindeer antlers were on. Christmas-tree decorations hung from women's – and some men's – ears. They all worked hard and they were all going to play hard.

'Where's Mr Patterson?' Lou asked Alison, finding her sitting on the lap of the fifth Santa Claus he'd seen. Her eyes were glassy, the focus already gone. She was wearing a tight red dress that showed every single shape and curve of her body. He forced himself to look away.

'And what do you want for Christmas, little boy?' the voice beneath the costume bellowed.

'Oh, hi James,' Lou said politely.

'He wants a promotion,' somebody in the crowd yelled, which was followed by a few titters.

'Not just a promotion, he wants Cliff's job,' somebody with reindeer antlers shouted, and the crowd laughed again.

Smiling to hide his frustration and minor embarrassment, Lou laughed along with them, then when the conversation turned to something else, he quietly slipped away. He retreated to his office, which was quiet and still, not a glimpse of tinsel or mistletoe in sight. He sat with his head in his hands, awaiting Mr Patterson's call to his office, listening to 'Grandma Got Run Over by a Reindeer' being half-sung and half-shouted by the crowd outside. Suddenly the music got louder as the door to his office opened, then it quietened as the door closed. He guessed who it was before he looked up.

Alison walked towards him, glass of red wine in one hand, a whisky in the other, her hips swinging in the slinky red dress and looking like the dangly thing at the back of a throat. Her ankles wobbled in her platform heels and the red wine jumped up a few times to splash her thumb.

'Careful there.' Lou's eyes followed her every move, his head staying put, both sure and uncertain at the same time.

'It's okay.' She put her glass down on the table and sensually sucked her thumb, licking the spilled wine from her skin, while looking at Lou seductively. 'I brought you a whisky.' She handed it to him and sidled up beside him at the desk. 'Cheers.' She clinked his glass, and then, her eyes once again not moving from his, she drank.

Lou cleared his throat, suddenly feeling crowded, and pushed his chair back. Alison misunderstood and slid her behind along the desk so that she was directly in front of him. Her chest was in his eyeline and he tore his eyes away and instead watched the door. His position was dangerous. It looked very bad. He felt extremely good.

'We never got to finish up what we were doing before,' she smiled. 'Everybody's talking about clearing their desks before Christmas.' Her voice was low and sultry. 'Thought I'd come in and give you a hand.'

She pushed away a few files from his desk; they slid down onto the floor, scattering everywhere.

'Oops,' she smiled, sitting on the desk before him, her short red dress rising even further up her thighs, revealing long, toned, tanned legs.

Beads of sweat broke out on Lou's brow. His mind ran through every possibility. Go outside and search for Mr Patterson, or stay inside with Alison. He still had the two pills he found around the skip which were safely wrapped in a handkerchief and in his pocket. He could take a pill and do both. Remember his priorities: be with Alison, and go to his dad's party. No, be with Mr Patterson, go to his dad's party. Both at the same time.

Uncrossing her legs, Alison used her foot to pull his chair in closer to the table, red lace between her thighs greeting him as he was wheeled slowly closer to her. She inched her body to the edge of the desk, pushing her dress up even higher. So high there was nowhere else for him to look now. He could take a pill: be with Alison, and be with Ruth.

Ruth.

Alison reached out and pulled him closer, her hands on his face. He felt the acrylic nails. The tap-tap sound against the keyboard that drove him insane every day. There they were, on his face, on his chest, running down his body. Long fingers running down the fabric of his suit, the suit that was supposed to mirror his inner dignity.

'I'm married,' he spluttered as her hand reached his groin. His voice was panicked, sounding childlike. Weak and so easily convinced.

Alison threw her head back and laughed. 'I know,' she purred, and her hands continued roving.

'That wasn't a joke,' he said firmly, and she stopped suddenly to look at him. He stared back at her solemnly and they held one another's gaze, then the corner of Alison's lips lifted in a smile despite trying to prevent it. Then, when she couldn't keep it in any more, she exploded. Her long blonde hair reached down to tickle his desk top as she threw her head back to laugh.

'Oh Lou,' she sighed, finally wiping the corner of her eyes.

'It's not a joke,' he said more firmly, with dignity, with confidence. More of a man now than he was five minutes ago.

Realising he wasn't teasing now, her smile faded instantly.

'Isn't it a joke?' She cocked an eyebrow, looked him dead in the eye. 'Because you might have fooled *her*, Lou, but you haven't fooled us.'

'Us?'

She waved a hand behind her dismissively. 'Us. Everyone. Whatever.'

He pushed his chair away from the desk.

'Oh, okay, you want me to be specific? I'll be specific. Gemma in accounts, Rebecca in the canteen, Louise on training, Tracey – your secretary before me – and I never did get the nanny's name. Shall I continue?' She smiled, then took a sip of wine, watching him. Her eyes watered slightly, her corneas reddened as though the wine was travelling directly to her eyes. 'Remember all of them?'

'They were,' Lou swallowed, feeling breathless, 'they were a long time ago. I'm different now.'

'The nanny was six months ago,' she laughed. 'Christ, Lou, how much do you think a man like you can change in six months, if at all?'

Lou felt dizzy, sickened all of a sudden. He ran his sweaty hands through his hair, panic setting in. What had he done?

'Just think about it,' she perked up. 'When you become Number Two around here, you can have whoever you want, but just remember I got you first,' she laughed, putting down the wine and reaching out her foot to pull his chair towards her again. 'But if you take me with you, I can tend to all your needs.'

She took the whisky glass from his hand and placed it on the desk. Then she took his hand, pulled him to his feet, and he followed, numb and lifeless like a dummy. She rubbed her hands across his chest, grabbed his lapels and pulled him closer. Just as their lips were about to meet, he stopped, went off course and moved his lips to her ear. Ever so softly, he whispered,

'My marriage is not a joke, Alison. You are. And my wife is the kind of woman that you could only hope of being someday.'

With that, he pulled back and walked away from the desk.

Alison sat frozen on the desk. The only movement was her mouth, which had fallen open, and her hand, which fidgeted and tried to pull at the end of her skirt.

'Yeah,' he watched her fix herself, 'you should cover that

up. You can take a minute to gather your thoughts, but please replace the files on my desk before you leave,' he said calmly. Placing his hands in his pockets to hide how much his body shook, he strode out of his office and into the middle of a karaoke, where Alex from accounts was drunkenly outing himself by singing Mariah Carey's 'All I Want for Christmas'. Around Lou, streamers popped, and drunken bearded men and women smothered him with kisses as he left his office.

'I have to go,' he said, to no one in particular, trying to make his way to the elevator. He pushed right through the crowd, some people grabbing him and trying to dance with him, others blocking his path and spilling drink. 'I have to go,' he said, a little more aggressively now. His head was pounding; he was nauseous; he felt as though he had just woken up in the body of a man who had taken over his life and ballsed it right up. 'It's my dad's seventieth, I have to go,' he said, trying to make his way to the elevator. Finally, he reached the lifts, pressed the call button and didn't turn around, but kept his head down and waited.

'Lou!' He heard his name. He kept his head down, ignoring the voice. 'Lou! I need a minute with you!' He ignored it again, watching the floors rising on the elevator panel and shaking his leg anxiously, hoping he'd get inside before it was too late.

He felt a hand on his shoulder.

'Lou! I've been calling you!' a friendly voice said.

He turned around. 'Ah, Mr Patterson, hello. Sorry.' Lou was aware his voice was edgy but he needed to get out of there. He'd promised Ruth and so he pressed down on the elevator button quickly. 'I'm in a bit of a rush, it's my dad's se—'

'We won't take long, I promise. Just a word.' He felt Mr Patterson's hand on his arm.

'Okay.' Lou turned around, biting down on his lip.

'Well, I was rather hoping we could talk in my office, if

you don't mind,' Mr Patterson smiled. 'Are you okay, you look a little shaken up.'

'I'm fine, I'm just, you know, in a rush.' He allowed his boss to take him by the arm.

'Of course you are,' Mr Patterson laughed. 'You always are.' He led Lou down to his office and they sat down opposite one another on aged brown leather couches in the more informal part of Mr Patterson's office. Lou's forehead was sweating; he was aware that he could smell himself and hoped that Mr Patterson couldn't too. He reached for the glass of water in front of him; his trembling hand brought it to his lips and Mr Patterson looked on while he gulped.

'Would you like something stronger, Lou?'

'No, thank you, Mr Patterson.'

'Laurence, please.' Mr Patterson shook his head again. 'Honestly, Lou, you make me feel like a schoolteacher when you address me as such.'

'Sorry, Mr Patter—'

'Well, I'm going to have one, anyway.' Mr Patterson stood up and made his way over to the drinks cabinet. He poured himself a brandy from a crystal decanter. 'You sure you won't have one?' he offered again. 'Rémy XO,' he swirled it mid-air, tauntingly.

'Okay, I will, thank you.' Lou smiled and relaxed a little, his panic to get across the road to the party subsiding slightly.

'Good.' Mr Patterson smiled. 'So, Lou, let's talk about your future. How much time do you have?'

Lou took his first sip of the expensive brandy and he was brought back to the room, back to the present. He pulled his cuffs over his watch, taking away the distraction. He prepared for the big promotion, for his polished shoes to walk in Cliff's footsteps – though not literally to the hospital he was currently housed in, but to the top office, with panoramic views of Dublin city. He took deep breaths and ignored the clock ticking

202

away on the wall, trying to put his father's party out of his head. It would all be worth it. They would all understand. They would all be too busy partying even to notice he wasn't there.

'I've all the time you need.' Lou smiled nervously, ignoring the voice within him that shouted to be heard.

23.

Surprise!

When Lou arrived at the venue for his father's party — late — he was sweating profusely as though he'd broken out in a high fever, despite the December chill that had the power to run right through to a body's bones; squeezing into the joints and whistling around the body. He was breathless and nauseous at the same time. Relieved and exhilarated. He was exhausted, all on its own.

He'd decided to host his father's party in the famous building that Gabe had admired the very first day they'd met. Shaped like a sail, it was lit up in blue, their award-winning building, which was sure to impress his father and relatives from around the country. Directly in front of the building, the Viking longship's tall mast was decorated in Christmas lights.

When he reached the door, Marcia was outside giving out to a large doorman dressed in black. Bundled in coats, hats and scarves, a crowd of twenty or so people were standing around, stamping their feet on the pavement in order to stay warm.

'Hi Marcia,' Lou said happily, trying to break up the argument. He was bursting to tell her about the promotion but he had to bite his lip; he had to find Ruth first to tell her.

Marcia turned to face him, her eyes red and blotchy, her mascara smudged. 'Lou,' she spat, the anger not disappearing but instead intensifying and being aimed at him.

His stomach did somersaults, which was rare. He never usually cared what his sister thought of him, but tonight he was caring more than usual.

'What's wrong?'

She left the crowd behind and came firing at him. 'I've been trying to call you for an hour.'

'I was at my work party, I told you that. What's wrong?'

'*You* are what's wrong,' she said shakily, her voice somewhere between anger and deep sadness. She inhaled deeply, then slowly exhaled. 'It's Daddy's birthday, and for his sake I won't ruin it any more than it already has been, by causing an argument, so all I have to say is would you please tell this brute to let our family in. Our family –' she raised her voice to that quivering screech, 'who have travelled from all over the country to share in,' her voice went weepy again, 'in Dad's special day. But instead of being with his family, he's up there in a practically empty room, while everybody is out here being turned away. Five people have already gone home.'

'What? What?' Lou's heart leapt into his throat. He rushed to the doormen. 'Hi guys, Lou Suffern.' He held out his hand and the doormen the two men shook it with all the life of a dead kipper. 'I'm organising the party tonight.' Behind him, Marcia huffed and mumbled. 'What seems to be the problem here?' He looked around at the crowd, instantly recognising all the faces. All were close family friends whose homes he'd grown up visiting, all were over the age of sixty, some the same age as his father, some older. They stood on the freezing cold pavement in December, elderly couples hanging on to one another, trembling with the cold, some leaning on crutches, one man in a wheelchair. In their hands were sparkly bags and cards, bottles of wine and champagne, gifts that had been wrapped neatly and thoughtfully for the big night. And now there they were on the pavement, being refused entry to their lifelong friend's party.

'No invites, no entry,' one doorman explained.

One couple flagged down a taxi and slowly made their way to where it had pulled over, while Marcia chased after them, trying to convince them to stay.

Lou laughed angrily. 'Gentlemen, do you think that these people are *gatecrashing*?' He lowered his voice. 'Come on, look at them. My father is celebrating his seventieth birthday, these are his friends. There was obviously a mistake with the invitations. I arranged with my secretary Alison for there to be a guest list.'

'These people aren't on the list. This building has strict guidelines as to who comes in and who –'

'Fuck the guidelines,' he said aggressively through gritted teeth, so that those behind him couldn't hear. 'It is my father's birthday and these are his guests,' he said firmly, angry now. 'And as the person who is paying for this party, and as the man who got this building off the ground, I'm telling you to let these people in.'

Moments later the group were all shuffling inside, waiting in the grand lobby for the elevators up to the top floor, while trying to get the warmth into their old bodies.

'You can relax now, Marcia, it's all sorted out now.' Lou tried to make amends with his sister as they stood together and alone in the elevator. Marcia had refused to look at him or even speak to him for the last ten minutes while they'd managed to get everyone into the lift and up to the penthouse.

'Marcia, come on,' he laughed lightly. 'Don't be like this.'

'Lou,' the look she gave him was enough to stop his smile and make him swallow hard, 'I know you think I'm dramatic and I'm controlling and I'm annoying, and whatever else you think about me that I'm sure I don't want to know about, but I'm not being dramatic now. I'm hurt. Not for me, but for Mummy and Daddy.' Her eyes filled again and her voice, which was always so gentle and understanding, changed tone. 'Of all the selfish things you've done, this is right up there as the most selfish of them all. I have sat back and bitten my tongue while you've taken Mummy and Daddy for granted, while you've screwed around on your wife, while you've jeered and teased your brother, flirted with his wife, ignored your kids, and while you've taunted me on every possible occasion. I have been – we *all* have been – as patient as pie with you, Lou, but not any more. You don't deserve any of us. Tonight you have really done it for me. You have hurt Mummy and Daddy and you are no longer my brother.'

'Whoa, whoa, whoa, come on, Marcia.' Lou felt knocked for six. He had never been spoken to like that before and it had hit him, hurt him deeply. He swallowed hard. 'I know that all those people shouldn't have been stuck outside, but I fixed it. Where is all this coming from?'

Marcia laughed bitterly. 'What you saw outside isn't even the half of it,' she sniffed. 'Surprise,' she said dully, as the elevators opened and as the sight of the room greeted him.

Looking out, Lou's heart immediately sank, falling to his stomach where the acid began to burn it away. Around the room there were blackjack tables, roulette, scantily clad cocktail waitresses who paraded around with cocktails on trays. It was an impressive party, and one that Lou remembered being at when the building was opened, but he only realised now that it wasn't for his seventy-year-old father. It wasn't for his father, who hated celebrations for himself, who hated forcing friends and family to gather together just for him, whose idea of a good day out was alone fishing. A modest man, the very thought of a party embarrassed him, but the family had talked him into celebrating a birthday for the first time, a big occasion where his family and friends from all around the country would join in and celebrate with him. He hadn't wanted it, but somewhere along the way he had warmed to it, and there he was, standing in the middle of a casino in his best suit, where the staff wore short skirts and red bow-ties, where the DJ played dance music and where a person needed €25 minimum to play on a casino table. In the centre of one table, a near-naked man was covered in cakes and fruit.

Standing together awkwardly at the side of the room were Lou's family. His mother, with her hair freshly blow-dried, was wearing a new lilac trouser suit and a scarf tied neatly around her neck, her handbag draped over her shoulder, clasping it tight in both hands as she looked around uncertainly. His father stood with his remaining brother and sister – a nun and a priest – looking more lost in this environment than Lou had ever seen his father look. Each family member looked up at him and away again, freezing him out. The only person who smiled faintly at him was his father, who nodded and saluted him.

Lou looked around for Ruth. She stood on the far side of the room, making polite chat with the rest of the equally uncomfortable-looking partygoers. She caught his eye and her look was cold. There was an awkward tension in the room, and it was all Lou's fault. He felt embarrassed, beyond ashamed. He wanted to make it up to them; he wanted to make it up to everybody.

'Excuse me,' Lou approached the man in the suit who was standing beside him looking over the crowd, 'are you the person in charge?'

'Yes, Jacob Morrison, manager.' He held his hand out. 'You're Lou Suffern, we met at the opening night a few months ago. I recall it was a late one,' he winked at him.

'Yes, I remember,' Lou replied, at the same time not remembering him at all. 'I'm just wondering if you could help me with making some changes in here.'

'Oh.' Jacob looked taken aback. 'I'm sure we'll try to accommodate you in any way that we can. What were you thinking of?'

'Chairs.' Lou tried not to speak rudely. 'This is my father's seventieth, could we please get him and his guests some chairs?'

'Oh,' Jacob made a face, 'I'm afraid this is a standing event only. We didn't charge for –'

'I'll pay you for whatever, of course.' Lou flashed his pearly whites. 'As long as we can get those bums that aren't already on *wheelchairs* on some seats.'

'Yes, of course.' Jacob began to leave when Lou called him back.

'And the music,' Lou said, 'is there anything more traditional than this?'

'Traditional?' Jacob smiled questioningly.

'Yes, traditional Irish music. For my seventy-year-old father.' Lou spoke through gritted teeth. 'Instead of this acid jazz funky house music that my seventy-year-old father isn't so much into.'

'I'll see what we can do.'

The atmosphere between them was darkening.

'And what about food? Did Alison arrange food? Apart from the near-naked man covered in cream that my mother is currently standing beside.'

'Yes, of course. We have shepherd's pies, lasagne, that kind of thing.'

Lou quietly celebrated.

'You know, we discussed all of our concerns with Alison before,' Jacob explained.

'You did?'

'Yes, sir, we don't usually hold seventieth parties.' He smiled,

209

then it quickly faded. 'It's just that we have a standard set-up here, particularly for the Christmas period, and this is it.' He gestured to the room proudly. 'The casino theme is very successful for corporate events, that kind of thing,' he explained.

'I see. Well, it would have been nice to know that,' Lou said politely.

'You did sign off on it,' Jacob assured him. 'We have the paperwork explaining all of the details of the night. We made sure Alison had you sign the forms.'

'Right.' Lou swallowed and looked around the room. His fault. Of course. 'Of course, it just obviously slipped my mind. Thank you.'

As Lou approached his family, they stepped away and separated themselves from him as though he were a bad smell. His father, of course, didn't move with them but greeted his middle child with a smile.

'Dad, happy birthday,' Lou said quietly, reaching his hand out to his father.

'Thank you.' His father smiled, taking his son's hand. Despite all this, despite what Lou had done, his father still smiled.

'Let me get you a Guinness,' Lou said, turning around to look for the bar.

'Oh, they don't have any.'

'What?'

'Beer, champagne, and some funny-looking green cocktail,' his father said, sipping on his glass. 'I'm on the water. Your mother's happy, though, she likes champagne, though far from it she was reared,' he laughed, trying to make light of the situation.

On hearing herself being mentioned, Lou's mother turned around and threw Lou a look that withered him.

'Ah now,' his father said softly, 'I can't drink tonight anyway. I'm sailing with Quentin tomorrow in Howth,' he said proudly. 'He's racing in the Brass Monkeys and he's down a man, so yours truly is filling in.' He thumbed himself in the chest.

'You are not racing, Fred.' Lou's mother rolled her eyes. 'You can barely stand upright on a windy day, never mind on a boat. It's December, those waters are choppy.'

'I'm seventy years old, I can do what I like.'

'You're seventy years old, you have to stop doing what you like, or you won't see seventy-one,' she snapped, and the family laughed, including Lou.

'You'll have to find someone else, dear.' She looked at Quentin, whose face was crestfallen.

'I'll do it for you,' Alexandra said to her husband, wrapping her arms around him, and Lou found himself having to look away, jealousy stirring.

'You've never raced before,' Quentin smiled. 'No way.'

'What time is the race?' Lou asked.

Nobody answered.

'Of course I can do it,' Alexandra smiled. 'Isn't it just like normal? I'll bring my bikini and I'll let the rest of the crew bring the strawberries and champagne.'

The family laughed again.

'What time is the race?' Lou asked again.

'Well, if she races in her bikini, then I'll definitely let her take part,' Quentin teased.

They all laughed again.

As though suddenly hearing his brother's question, though still not looking him in the eye, Quentin responded, 'Race starts at eleven a.m. Maybe I'll give Stephen a quick call.' He took his mobile out of his pocket.

'I'll do it,' Lou said, and they all looked at him in shock.

'I'll do it,' he repeated with a smile.

'Maybe you could call Stephen first, love,' Alexandra said gently.

211

'Yes,' Quentin responded, turning back to his phone. 'Good idea. I'll just go somewhere quiet.' He brushed by Lou and left the room.

Lou felt the sting as the family turned away from him again and talked about places he'd never been, about people he'd never met. He stood by idly while they laughed at jokes he didn't understand, inside jokes that tickled all but him. It was as though they were speaking a secret language, one that Lou was entirely unable to comprehend. Eventually he stopped bothering to ask the questions that were never answered, and eventually he stopped listening, realising nobody cared about that either. He was too detached from the family to start trying in one evening to check himself into a place where there was currently no vacancy.

24.

The Soul Catches Up

Lou's father was beside him, looking around the room like a lost child, no doubt feeling nervous and embarrassed that everyone had come for him and secretly hoping that somebody else would announce it was their birthday too so the attention would be taken from him and shared with someone else.

'Where's Ruth?' his father asked.

'Em,' Lou looked around for the hundredth time, unable to find her, 'she's just chatting to guests.'

'Right. Nice view from up here.' He nodded out the window. 'City's come a long way in my time.'

'Yeah, I thought you'd like it,' Lou said, glad he'd got one thing right.

'So which one is your office?' He looked across the river Liffey at the office buildings, which remained lit up at this hour.

'That one there, directly opposite.' Lou pointed. 'Thirteen floors up, on the fourteenth floor.'

Lou's father glanced at him, obviously thinking it peculiar, and for the first time Lou felt it too, could see how it could

213

be perceived odd and confusing. This rattled him. He had always been so sure.

'It's the one with all the lights are on,' Lou explained more simply. 'Office party.'

'Ah, so that's where it is.' His father nodded. 'That's where it all happens.'

'Yes,' Lou said proudly. 'I just got a promotion tonight, Dad.' He smiled. 'I haven't told anybody yet, it's your night, of course,' he backtracked.

'A promotion?' His father's bushy eyebrows rose.

'Yes.'

'More work?'

'Bigger office, better light,' he joked. When his dad didn't laugh he became serious. 'Yes, more work. More hours.'

'I see.' His father was silent.

Anger rose within Lou. Congratulations wouldn't have gone astray.

'You're happy there?' his father asked casually, still looking out the glass, the party behind them visible in the reflection. 'No point in working hard on something if you're not, because at the end of the day that's what it's all about, isn't it?'

Lou pondered that, both disappointed by the lack of praise and intrigued by his father's thinking at the same time.

'But you always told me to work hard,' he said suddenly, feeling an anger he had never known was there. 'You always taught us not to rest on our laurels for a second, if I recall the phrase exactly.' He smiled, but it was tight and he felt tense.

'I didn't want you all to be lazy, by any means,' his dad responded, and turned to look Lou in the eye suddenly. 'In *any* aspect of your life, not just in your work. Any tightrope walker can walk in a straight line and hold a cane at the same time. It's the balancing on the rope at those dizzying heights that they have to practise,' he said simply.

A staff member, carrying a chair in her hand, broke the quiet tension. 'Excuse me, who is this for?' She looked around at the family. 'My boss told me that someone in this party asked for a chair.'

'Em, yes, I did,' Lou laughed, angrily. 'But I asked for *chairs*. Plural. For all the guests.'

'Oh, well, we don't have that amount of chairs on the premises,' she apologised. 'So who would like this chair?'

'Your mother,' Lou's father said quickly, not wanting any fuss. 'Let your mother sit down.'

'No, I'm fine, Fred,' Lou's mother objected. 'It's your birthday, you have the chair.'

Lou closed his eyes and breathed deeply. He had paid twelve thousand euro for his family to fight over the use of a chair.

'Also, the DJ said that the only traditional music he has is the Irish National Anthem. Would you like him to play it?'

'What?' Lou snapped.

'It's what he plays at the end of the night, but he has no other Irish songs with him,' she apologised. 'Shall I tell him to play it for you all now?'

'No!' Lou snapped. 'That's ludicrous. Tell him no.'

'Can you please give him this?' Marcia said politely, reaching into a cardboard box she had underneath the table. From it, party hats, streamers and banners overflowed. He even caught sight of a cake. She handed the waiter a collection of CDs. Their father's favourite songs. She looked up at Lou briefly while handing them over. 'In case you fucked up,' she said, then looked away.

It was a short comment, small and delivered quietly, but it hit him harder than anything she'd said to him that evening. He'd thought he was the organised one, the one who knew how to throw a party, the one who knew to call in all the favours and throw the biggest bash. But while he was busy thinking he was all that, his family were busy preparing Plan B, in preparation for his failures. All in a cardboard box.

Suddenly the room cheered as Quentin stepped out of the elevator along with Gabe – whom Lou hadn't known was invited – each appearing with a pile of chairs stacked up in their arms.

'There are more on the way!' Quentin announced to the crowd, and suddenly the atmosphere perked up as the familiar faces that had aged since Lou's youth looked to one another with relief, slight pain and an innocent excitement.

'Lou!' Gabe's face lit up when he saw him. 'I'm so glad you came.' He laid the chairs out for a few elderly people nearby and approached Lou, hand held out, leaving Lou confused as to whose party it was. Gabe leaned close to Lou's ear. 'Did you double up?'

'What? No.' Lou shook him off, frustrated.

'Oh,' Gabe said with surprise. 'The last I saw of you, you and Alison were having a meeting in your office. I didn't realise you left the work party.'

'Yes, of course I did. Why do you have to assume the worst, that I had to take one of those pills to show up at my own father's party?' he feigned insult.

Gabe merely smiled. 'Hey, it's funny how life works, isn't it?' He nudged Lou.

'What do you mean?'

'Well, the way one minute you can be up here, and then the next minute all the way down there?' On Lou's aggressive look, he continued, 'I just meant that when we met last week, I was down there, looking up and dreaming about being here. And now look at me. It's funny how it all switches around. I'm up in the penthouse; Mr Patterson gave me a new job –'

'He what?'

'Yeah, he gave me a job.' Gabe grinned and winked. 'A promotion.'

Before Lou had the opportunity to respond, a female staff member approached them with a tray.

'Would anybody like some food?' she smiled.

'Oh, no, thank you, I'll wait for the shepherd's pie,' Lou's mother smiled at her.

'This is the shepherd's pie.' The lady pointed to a small mini blob of potato sitting in a minuscule cupcake holder.

There was a moment's silence and Lou's heart almost ripped through his skin from its hectic beating.

'Is there more food coming later?' Marcia asked.

'Apart from the cake? No,' she shook her head, 'this is it for the evening. Trays of hors d'oeuvre.' She smiled again as though not picking up on the hostility that was currently doing the rounds.

'Oh,' Lou's father said, trying to sound upbeat. 'You can leave the tray here so.'

'The whole tray?' She looked uncertainly around and then behind her to the manager for back-up.

'Yes, we've a hungry family here,' Fred said, taking it from her hands and placing it on the tall table so that everybody had to stand up from their chairs in order to reach.

'Oh, okay.' She watched it being placed down and slowly backed away, trayless.

'You mentioned a cake?' Marcia asked, her voice high-pitched and screechy, possessed and distressed by the lack of control, by everything going wrong.

'Yes.'

'Let me see it please,' she said, casting a look of terror at Lou. 'What colour is it? What's on it? Does it have raisins? Daddy hates raisins,' they could hear her saying as she wandered off to the kitchen with the waitress, her cardboard box of damage-limitation items in her hand.

'So, who invited you, Gabe?' Lou felt tetchy, not wanting

to discuss the promotion for fear he'd throw Gabe across the other side of the room.

'Ruth did,' Gabe said, reaching for a mini shepherd's pie.

'Oh, she did, did she? I don't think so,' Lou laughed.

'Why wouldn't you think so?' Gabe shrugged. 'She invited me the night I had dinner and stayed over at your house.'

'Why do you say it like that? Don't say it like that,' Lou said childishly, squaring up to him. 'You weren't invited to dinner in my house. You dropped me home and ate leftovers.'

Gabe looked at him curiously. 'Okay.'

'Where is Ruth anyway? I haven't seen her all night.'

'Oh, we've been talking all evening on the balcony. I really like her,' Gabe responded, mashed potato dribbling down his chin and landing on his borrowed tie. Lou's tie.

At that, Lou's jaw clenched. 'You really like her? You really like *my wife*? Well, that's funny, Gabe, because I really like my wife too. You and I have so fucking much in common, don't we?'

'Lou,' Gabe smiled nervously, 'you might want to keep your voice down just a little.'

Lou looked around and smiled at the attention they'd attracted and playfully wrapped his arm around Gabe's shoulder to show all was good. When eyes looked away, he turned to face Gabe and dropped the smile.

'You really want my life, don't you, Gabe?'

Gabe seemed taken aback, but hadn't the opportunity to respond as the elevator doors opened and out fell Alfred, Alison and a crowd from the office party, who – despite the noise of Lou's father's favourite songs blaring out through the speakers – managed to announce themselves to the room, loud and clear, while dressed in their Santa suits and their party hats, blowing their party blowers at anyone who so much as looked their way.

Lou darted from his family and ran up the steps to the elevator, blocking Alfred's path. 'What are you all doing here?'

'We're here to partaaay, my friend,' Alfred announced, swaying and blowing a party horn in his face.

'Alfred, you weren't invited,' Lou said loudly.

'Alison invited me,' Alfred laughed. 'And I think you know better than anyone how hard it is to turn down an invitation from Alison,' he smiled. 'But I don't mind being sloppy seconds,' he laughed, wavering drunkenly on the spot. Suddenly his eyeline moved to above Lou's shoulder and his face changed. 'Ruth! How are you?'

Lou's heart almost failed as he turned around and saw Ruth behind them.

'Alfred.' Ruth folded her arms and stared at her husband.

There was a tense silence.

'Well, this is awkward,' Alfred said uncertainly. 'I think I'm going to go and join the party. I'll leave you two to bludgeon each other in private.'

Alfred disappeared, leaving Lou alone with Ruth, and the hurt on her face was like a dagger through his heart. He'd gladly have anger anytime.

'Ruth,' he said, 'I've been looking for you all evening.'

'I see the party planner, Alison, joined us too,' she said, her voice shaking as she tried to remain strong.

Lou looked over his shoulder and saw Alison, little dress and long legs, dancing in the middle of the floor seductively with Santa.

Ruth looked at him questioningly.

'I didn't,' he said, the fight going out of him, not wanting to be that man any more. 'Hand on heart, I didn't. She tried tonight, and I didn't.'

Ruth laughed bitterly. 'Oh, I bet she did.'

'I swear I didn't.'

'Anything? Ever?' She studied his face intently, clearly hating herself; embarrassed, angry at having to ask.

He swallowed. He didn't want to lose her, but he didn't

want to lie. 'A kiss. Once, is all. Nothing else,' he spoke faster now, panicking. 'But I'm different now, Ruth, I'm –'

She didn't listen to the rest of it, she turned away from him, trying to hide her face and her tears from him. She opened the door to the balcony and cold air rushed in at Lou. The balcony was empty, the smokers inside eating as many mini shepherd's pies as it took to fill a hole.

'Ruth –' He tried to grab her arm and pull her back inside.

'Lou, let go of me, I swear to God, I'm not in the mood to talk to you now,' she said angrily.

He followed her out to the balcony and they moved away from the window so that they couldn't be seen by anyone inside. Ruth leaned on the edge and looked out at the city. Lou moved close behind her, wrapped his arms tightly around her body and refused to let go, despite her body going rigid as soon as he touched her.

'Help me fix this,' he whispered, close to tears. 'Please, Ruth, help me fix this.'

She sighed, but her anger was still raw. 'Lou, what the hell were you thinking? How many times did we all tell you how important this night was?'

'I know, I know,' he stuttered, thinking fast. 'I was trying to prove to you all that I could –'

'Don't you dare lie to me again.' She stopped him short. 'Don't you dare lie when you've just asked for my help. You weren't trying to prove *anything*. You were fed up with Marcia ringing you, fed up with her trying to get it right for your father, you were too busy –'

'Please, I don't need to hear this right now,' he winced, as though every word brought on a migraine.

'This is *exactly* what you need to hear. You were too busy at work to care about your father, or about Marcia's plans. You got a stranger who knew nothing of your father's seventy years on this earth to plan the whole thing for you. Her?' She pointed inside at Alison, who was doing the limbo underneath the chocolate fondue stand, revealing the red lace underwear to all that were looking. 'A little tramp that you probably screwed while dictating the party guest list,' she spat.

Lou thought better of informing Ruth that Alison was actually a well-qualified business graduate and, apart from party planning, a competent employee. It didn't seem appropriate to defend her honour; Alison's behaviour at the office and then at his father's party was doing little to defend her own honour.

'That didn't happen, I swear. I know I messed everything up. I'm sorry.' He was so used to saying that word now.

'And what was it all for? For a promotion? A pay rise that you don't even need? More work hours in a day that just aren't humanly possible to achieve? When will you stop? When will it all be enough for you? How high do you want to climb, Lou? You know what, last week you said that only a job can fire you, but a family can't. But I think you're about to realise that the latter is possible after all.'

'Ruth,' he closed his eyes, ready to jump off the balcony then and there if she was going to leave him, 'please don't leave me.'

'Not me, Lou,' she said. 'I'm talking about them.'

He turned around and watched his family join a convoy, as the room danced around in a train, kicking their legs every few steps. 'I'm racing with Quentin tomorrow. On the boat.' He looked at her for praise.

'I thought Gabe was doing that?' Ruth asked in confusion. 'Gabe offered his time to Quentin right here in front of me. Quentin said yes.'

Anger rose as Lou's blood boiled. 'No, I'm definitely going to do it.' He would see to it.

'Oh, really? Is that before or after you're coming ice-skating with me and the kids?' she asked, before walking off and leaving him alone on the balcony, cursing himself for forgetting his promise to Lucy.

As Ruth opened the door to the balcony, music rushed out and cold air rushed in. Then the door closed again, but he felt a presence behind him. She hadn't gone inside. She hadn't left him.

'I'm sorry about everything I've ever done. I want to fix it all,' he said with exhaustion. 'I'm tired now. I want to fix it. I want everyone to know that I'm sorry. I'd do anything for them to know that and to believe me. Please help me fix it,' he repeated.

Had Lou turned around then he would have seen that his wife had indeed left him; that she'd rushed off to a quiet place to once again cry her tears of frustration for a man who had convinced her only hours previously in their bedroom that he had changed. No, it was Gabe that had stepped in when Ruth had rushed off, and it was Gabe who heard Lou's confessions on the balcony.

Gabe knew that Lou Suffern was exhausted. Lou had spent so many years moving so quickly through the minutes, hours and days, through the moments, that he'd stopped noticing life. The looks, gestures and emotions of other people had long since stopped being important or visible to him. Passion had driven him at first, and then, while on his way to the some-where he wanted to be, he'd left it behind. He'd moved so fast, he'd taken no pause for breath; his rhythm was too quick, his heart could barely keep up.

As Lou breathed in the cold December air and lifted his face up to the sky, to feel – and appreciate – the icy droplets of rain that fell onto his skin, he knew that his soul was coming to get him.

He could feel it.

25.

The Best Day

At nine a.m. on Saturday morning, the day after his father's seventieth birthday party, Lou Suffern sat out in his back garden and lifted his face and closed his eyes to the morning sun. He'd clambered over the fence that separated their two-acre landscaped garden – where pathways and pebbles, garden beds and giant pots signposted the way to walk – from the rugged and wild terrain that lay beyond human meddling. Splashes of yellow gorse were everywhere, as though somebody in Dalkey had taken a paintball gun and fired carelessly in the direction of the northside headland. Lou and Ruth's house sat at the very top of the summit, their back garden looking out to the north with vast views of Howth village below, the harbour, and out further again to Ireland's Eye. Often, Snowdon in Snowdonia National Park in Wales, 138 kilometres away, could be seen from the headland; though on this clear day it was forever that Lou Suffern had his eye on.

Lou sat on a rock and breathed in the fresh air. His numb nose dribbled, his cheeks were frozen stiff, and his ears ached from the nip in the wind. His fingers had turned a purplish blue, as though they were being strangled at the knuckles; not good weather for vital parts, but ideal weather for sailing. Unlike the carefully maintained gardens of his and his neighbours' houses, the wild and rugged gorse had been even more lovingly left to grow as it wanted, like a second child who was given more space and less rules. It had roamed the mountainside and stamped its authority firmly around the headland. The land was hilly and uneven, it rose and fell without warning, apologised for nothing and offered no assistance to trekkers. It was the student in the back row in class, quiet but suggestive, sitting back to view the traps it had laid. Despite Howth's wild streak in the mountains and the hustle and bustle of a fishing village, the town itself always had a sense of calm. It had a patient, grandparental feel about it: lighthouses that guided inhabitants of the waters safely to shore; cliffs that stood like a line of impenetrable Spartans with heaving chests and muscles that rippled through abdomens, fierce against the elements. There was the pier that acted as a mediator between land and sea and dutifully ferried people out as far as humanly possible; the Martello tower that stood like a lone ageing soldier who refused to leave his zone long after the trouble had ended. Despite the constant gusts that attacked the headland, the town was steady and stubborn.

Lou wasn't alone as he pondered his life. Beside him sat himself. They were dressed differently: one ready for sailing with his brother, the other for ice-skating with the family. They stared out to sea, both watching the shimmer of the sun on the horizon, looking like a giant silver dime had been dropped in for luck and now glimmered under the waves. They'd been sitting there for a while, not saying anything, merely comfortable with their own company.

Lou on the mossy grass looked at Lou on the rock and smiled. 'You know how happy I am right now? I'm beside myself,' he chuckled.

Lou, sitting on the rock, fought his smile. 'The more I hear myself joke, the more I realise I'm not funny.'

'Yeah, me too.' Lou pulled a long strand of wild grass from the ground and rolled it around his purple fingers. 'But I also notice what a handsome bastard I am.'

They both laughed.

'You talk over people a lot, though,' Lou on the rock said, recalling witnessing his other self commanding conversations unnecessarily.

'I noticed that. I really should –'

'And you don't really listen,' he added, deep in thought. 'And your stories are always too long. People don't seem to be as interested as you think,' he admitted. 'You don't ask people about what they're doing. You should start doing that.'

'Speak for yourself,' Lou on the grass said, unimpressed.

'I am.'

They sat in silence again because Lou Suffern had recently learned that much ascended from silence and from being still. A gull swooped, squawked, eyed them suspiciously and then flew off.

'He's off to tell his mates about us,' Lou on the rock said.

'Let's not take whatever they say to heart; they all look the same to me,' the other Lou said.

They both laughed again.

'I can't believe I'm laughing at my own jokes.' Lou on the grass rubbed his eyes. 'Embarrassing.'

'What's going on here, do you think?' Lou asked seriously, perched on his rock.

'If you don't know, I don't know.'

'Yes, but if I have theories, well then, so do you.'

They looked at one another, knowing exactly what the other was thinking.

Lou chose his words wisely, letting them roll around his mouth before saying, 'I'm not superstitious, but I think we should keep those theories to ourselves, don't you? It is what it is. Let's keep it at that.'

'I don't want anybody to get hurt,' Lou on the grass spoke up.

'Did you just hear what I said?' he said angrily. 'I said don't talk about it.'

'Lou!' Ruth was calling them from the garden and it broke the spell between them.

'Coming!' he yelled, peeping his head above the fence. He saw Pud, new to his feet, escaping to freedom through the kitchen door, racing around the grass unevenly like an egg that had prematurely hatched where legs alone had broken free. He shuffled along after the ball, trying to catch it but mistakenly kicking it with his running feet each time he got near. Finally learning, he stopped running before reaching the ball, and instead slowly sneaked up behind it as though it was going to take off again by itself. He lifted a foot. Not used to having to balance on one leg, he fell backwards onto the grass, landing safely on his padded behind. Lucy ran outside in her hat and scarf and helped to pull him up.

'She's so like Ruth.' He heard a voice near his ear and realised Lou had joined him.

'I know. See the way she makes that face.' They watched Lucy giving out to Pud for being careless. They both laughed at exactly the same time she made the face.

Pud screeched at Lucy's attempt to take him by the hand and lead him back into the house. He pulled away and threw his hand up in the air in a mini tantrum, then chose to waddle to the house by himself.

'Who does he remind you of?' Lou said.

'Okay, we'd better get moving. You walk down to the harbour, I'll drive Ruth and the kids into town. Make sure you're there on time, won't you? I practically had to bribe Quentin into saying yes about helping him today.'

'Of course I'll be there. Don't you break a leg.'

'Don't you drown.'

'We'll enjoy the day.' Lou reached out and shook hands with himself. Their handshake turned into an embrace, and Lou stood on the mountainside giving himself the biggest and warmest hug he'd received in a very long time.

Lou arrived down at the harbour two hours in advance of the race. He hadn't raced for so many years, he wanted to get accustomed to the talk, get a feel for being on the boat again. He also needed to build up a relationship with the rest of the team: communication was key and he didn't want to let anybody down. Not true – he didn't want to let Quentin down. He found the beautiful *Alexandra*, the forty-foot sailboat Quentin had bought five years ago and that he had since spent every spare penny and every waking moment on. Already on board, Quentin and five others were in a tight group, going over the course and their tactics.

Lou did the math. There were only supposed to be six on the boat; Lou joining them made seven.

'Hi there,' he said, approaching them.

'Lou!' Quentin looked up in surprise and Lou realised then why there were already six people. Quentin hadn't trusted him to show up.

'Not late, am I? You did say nine thirty.' He tried to hide his disappointment.

'Yeah, sure, of course.' Quentin tried to hide his surprise. 'Absolutely, I just, eh . . .' He turned around to the other men waiting and watching. 'Let me introduce you to the rest of the team. Guys, this is my brother, Lou.'

Surprise flitted across a few faces.

'We didn't know you had a brother,' one smiled, stepping forward to offer his hand. 'I'm Geoff, welcome. I hope you know what you're doing.'

'It's been a while,' Lou looked uncertainly at Quentin, 'but Quentin and I were sent on enough sailing courses over the years, it'd be hard for us ever to forget. It's like riding a bike, isn't it?'

They laughed and welcomed him aboard.

'So where do you want me?' He looked at his brother.

'Are you really okay to do this?' Quentin asked him quietly, away from the others.

'Of course.' Lou tried not to be offended. 'Same positions as we used to?'

'Foredeck man?' Quentin asked.

'Aye, aye, Captain,' Lou smiled, saluting him.

Quentin laughed and turned back to the rest of the crew. 'Okay, boys, I want us all working in harmony. Remember, let's talk to each other, I want information flowing up and down the boat at all times. If you haven't done what you should have done, then shout, we all need to know exactly what's going on. If we win, I'll buy the first round.'

They all cheered.

'Right, Lou,' he looked at his brother and winked, 'I know you've been looking forward to this for a long time.'

Though untrue, Lou didn't feel it was a good idea to object.

'Finally you get your opportunity to see what *Alexandra*'s made of.'

Lou punched his brother playfully in the side.

Ruth pushed Pud's buggy through Fusiliers Arch and they entered St Stephen's Green, a park right in the centre of Dublin city. An ice rink had been set up in the grounds, attracting shoppers and people from all around the country to join in the unique experience. Passing the duck-filled lake and walking over O'Connell Bridge, they soon entered a wonderland. Instead of the usual manicured gardens, a Christmas market had been set up, lavishly decorated and looking like it had come straight out of a Christmas movie.

Stalls selling hot chocolate with marshmallows, mince pies and fruit cakes lined the paths and the smell of cinnamon, cloves and marzipan oozed into the air. Each stall owner was dressed as an elf, while Christmas tunes blared out of the speakers, icicles dripped from the roof of every stall and machines blew fake snow through the air.

Santa's Igloo was the centre of attention, a long queue forming outside, while elves dressed in green rags and pointy shoes did their best to entertain the waiting masses. Giant red and white striped candy canes formed an archway into the igloo, while bubbles blew from the chimneytop and floated up into the sky. On one patch of grass a group of children – umpired by an elf – played tug of war with an oversized Christmas cracker. A Christmas tree twenty feet tall had been erected and decorated in oversized baubles and tinsel. Hanging from the branches were giant water balloons, which a queue of children – but more daddies – threw holly-covered balls at in an attempt to burst the balloons and release the gifts inside. A red-faced elf, wet from the exploding balloons, ran around collecting gifts from the floor, while his accomplice filled more balloons and passed them to another team-mate to hang on the branches. There was no whistling while they worked.

Pud's chubby little forefinger pointed in every direction as something new caught his eye. Lucy, who was usually all chat, had suddenly gone very quiet. Her chocolate-brown hair was cut bluntly at her chin, her fringe stopped above eyebrows that shaped big brown eyes. She was dressed in a bright red coat that went to her knees, double-breasted with oversized black buttons and a black fur collar, cream tights and shiny black shoes. She held on to Pud's buggy with one hand and floated along beside them all, drifting away in a heaven of her own. Every now and then she'd see something and look up to Lou and Ruth with the biggest smile on her face. Nobody said anything. They didn't need to. They all knew.

Further away from the Christmas market they found the ice rink, which was swarmed by hundreds of people young and old, the queue snaking alongside the rink so that those who crashed and fell could be viewed by spectators who chuckled at every comedy fall.

'Why don't you all go and watch the show?' Lou said, referring to the mini-pantomime that was being performed in the bandstand. Dozens of children sat on deckchairs, entranced by the magical world before them. 'I'll queue for us.'

It was a generous gesture and a selfish one both at the same time, for Lou Suffern couldn't possibly change overnight. He had made the attempt to spend the day with his family, but already his BlackBerry was burning a hole in his pocket and he needed time to check it before he quite simply exploded.

'Okay, thanks,' Ruth said, pushing Pud over to join Lou in the queue. 'We shouldn't be too long.'

'What are you doing?' Lou asked, panicked.

'Going to watch the show.'

'Aren't you taking him?'

'No. *He* is asleep. He'll be fine with you.'

She headed off hand-in-hand with a skipping Lucy, while Lou looked at Pud with mild panic and full of prayer for him not to wake. He had one eye on his BlackBerry, the other on Pud, and a third eye that he had never known he had on the group of teenagers in front of him, who had suddenly started shouting and jumping around as their hormones got the better of them, each screech from their mouths and jerk of their gawky hand movements a threat to his sleeping child. He suddenly became aware of the level of 'Jingle Bells' being filtered through the speakers, of the feedback that sounded like a five-car pile-up when a voice cut in to announce a separated family member that was waiting by The Elf Centre. He was aware of every single solitary sound, every squeal of a child on the ice, every shout as their fathers fell on their arses, every crack of bones. On high alert, as though waiting for somebody to attack at any moment, the BlackBerry and its flashing red light went back in his pocket. The queue moved on and he ever so slowly pushed the buggy up the line.

In front of him, a greasy-haired adolescent telling a story to his friends through the use of serious explosion sounds and occasional epileptic-fit movements caught Lou's eye. The boy, getting to the climax of the story, leapt back and landed against the buggy.

'Sorry,' the boy said, turning around and rubbing his arm, which he'd bumped. 'Sorry, mister, is he okay?'

Lou nodded. Swallowed. He wanted to reach out and throttle the child, wanted to find the boy's parents so that he could tell them about teaching their son the art of storytelling without grand gestures and spittle-flying explosions. He peeped in at Pud. The monster had been woken. Pud's eyes, glassy, sleepy and tired, and not yet ready to come out of hibernation, opened slowly. They looked left, they looked right, and all around, while Lou held his breath. He and Pud looked at one another for a while in a tense silence, and then, deciding he didn't like the horrified expression on his father's face, Pud spat out his soother and began screaming. Scream. Ing.

'Eh, shhhh,' Lou said awkwardly, looking down at his son.

Pud screamed louder, thick tears forming in his tired eyes.

'Em, come on, Pud.' Lou smiled at him, giving him his best porcelain-toothed smile that usually worked on everyone in business.

Pud cried louder.

Lou looked around in embarrassment, apologising to anybody whose eye he caught, particularly the smug father who had a young baby in a pouch on his front and two other children holding each of his hands. He grumbled at the smug man and turned his back on him, trying to end the screech of terror by pushing the buggy back and forth quickly, deliberately clipping the heels of the greasy teen who'd put him in this predicament. He tried pushing the soother in Pud's mouth, ten times over. He tried covering Pud's eyes with his hand, hoping that the sight of darkness would make him want to sleep. That didn't work. Pud's body was contorting, bending backwards as he tried to break out of his straps like the Incredible Hulk from his clothes. He continued to wail, sounding like a cat who was being hung by the tail and then dunked head first in water, followed by a strangling. He fumbled with the baby bag and offered him toys, which were flung rather violently out of the buggy and around the ground.

Smug Family Man with the front pouch bent over to assist Lou in his gathering of dispersed toys. Lou grabbed them while failing to make eye contact, grunting his thanks. After most things from the baby bag lay scattered on the ground, Lou decided to release the dough monster. He struggled with the trickiness of the catch for quite some time while Pud's screams intensified and they gathered more stares, and, just as someone was close to calling social services, he finally broke his son free. Pud didn't stop crying and continued to yell with snot bubbling from his nostrils, his face as purple as a Ribena berry.

Ten minutes of pointing at trees, dogs, children, planes, birds, Christmas trees, presents, elves, things that moved, things that didn't move, anything that Lou could lay his eye on, and Pud was still crying.

Ruth came running over with Lucy.

'What's wrong?'

'Woke up as soon as you left, he won't stop crying.' Lou was sweating.

Pud took one look at Ruth and reached his arms out towards her, almost jumping out of Lou's arms. His cries stopped instantly, he clapped his hands, his face returned to a normal colour, he babbled. He looked at his mother, played with her necklace and acted as though nothing had happened to him at all. Lou was sure that when nobody else was looking, Pud smiled cheekily at him.

Feeling in his element, Lou's stomach churned with anticipation as he watched the coastline move further away, as they made their way to the starting area, north of Ireland's Eye. Bundled-up family members and friends waved their support from the lighthouse on the end of the pier, with binoculars in hands.

There was a magic about the sea. People were drawn to it. People wanted to live by it, swim in it, play in it, look at it. It was a living thing that was as unpredictable as a great stage actor: it could be calm and welcoming, opening its arms to embrace its audience one moment, but then could explode with its stormy tempers, flinging people around, wanting them out, attacking coastlines, breaking down islands. It had its playful side too, as it enjoyed the crowd, tossed children about, knocked lilos over, tipped over windsurfers, occasionally gave sailors helping hands; all done with a secret chuckle. For Lou there was nothing like the feel of the wind in his hair, gliding through the water with the rain in his face or the sun beating down. It had been a long time since he'd sailed – he and Ruth, of course, had had many holidays on friends' yachts over the years, but it was a long time since Lou had been a team player in any aspect of his life. He was looking forward to the challenge; he was looking forward to not only being in competition with thirty other boats, but trying to beat the sea, the wind and all the elements.

In the starting area they sailed near the committee boat *Free Enterprise* for identification purposes. The starting line was between a red and white pole on the committee boat and a cylindrical orange buoy which was left to port. Lou got into position at the bow of the boat as they circled the starting area, trying to get into the right position to time it perfectly so that they'd cross the starting line at just the right time. The wind was north-east force four and the tide flooding, which added to the sea's bad humour. This would have to be watched to keep the boat moving fast through the choppy, lumpy sea. Just like old times, Lou and Quentin had talked this out so both knew what was required. Any premature passing of the starting line would mean an elimination, and it was up to Lou to count them down, position them correctly, and communicate with the helmsman, who was Quentin. They used to have it down to a fine art when they were in their teens, back then they'd won numerous races and could have competed with their eyes closed, merely feeling the direction of the wind; but it had been so long ago and the communication between them had broken down rather dramatically over the past few years.

Lou blessed himself as the warning signal appeared at 11.25. They moved the boat around, trying to get into position so that they'd be one of the first to cross the starting line. At 11.26 the preparatory flag went up. At 11.29 the one-minute signal flag went down. Lou waved his arms around wildly, trying to signal to Quentin where to place the boat.

'Right starboard, starboard right, Quentin!' he yelled, waving his right arm. 'Thirty seconds!' he yelled.

They came dangerously close to another yacht. Lou's fault. 'Eh, left port! LEFT!' Lou yelled. 'Twenty seconds!'

Each boat fought hard to find a good position, but with thirty boats in the race there could only be a small number that would make it across the starting line in the favoured position close to the committee boat. The rest would have to do their best with stolen wind on the way up the beat.

Eleven thirty heralded the start signal, and at least ten boats crossed the start line before them. Not the best start, but Lou wasn't going to let it get to him. He was rusty, he needed some practice, but he didn't have time for that, this was the real thing.

They raced along, with Ireland's Eye on their right, the headland to their left, but there was no time to take in the view now. Lou didn't move, thinking fast, looking around him at all the yachts racing by, with the wind blowing in his hair, his blood pumping through his veins, feeling more alive than he'd ever felt. It was all coming back to him, what it felt like to be on the boat. Perhaps his speed was down, but he hadn't lost his instincts. They raced along, the boat crashing over the waves as they headed towards the weather mark, one mile up in the wind from the starting line.

'Tacking!' Quentin shouted, watching and steering as they all prepared. The runners trimmer, Alan, checked that the slack on the old runners had been pulled in. The genoa trimmer, Luke, made sure that the new sheet had the slack pulled in and gave a couple of turns on the winch. Lou didn't move an inch, thinking ahead about what he needed to do and watching the other boats around them to make sure nothing was too close. He instinctively knew they were tacking onto port and would have no right of way over boats on starboard. His old racing tactics came flooding back and he was quietly pleased with how he had positioned the boat right on the layline to the weather mark. He could sense Quentin's confidence in him gaining at their now favourable position when the tack was completed, powering towards the mark with a clear passage in. It was Quentin's belief in him that Lou was fighting to win, just as much as first place.

Quentin made sure that there was room to tack and started the turn. Geoff, the cockpit man, moved quickly to the old genoa, and as the genoa backwinded, he released it. The boat went through the wind, the mainsheet was eased a couple of feet and the boom came across. Luke pulled as fast as possible, and when he couldn't pull any more he put a couple more turns on the winch and the grinding began. Quentin steered the new course.

'HIGH SIDE!' Lou yelled, and they all raced to hang their legs over the windward side.

Quentin whooped and Lou laughed into the wind.

After rounding the first mark and heading towards the second with the wind on their side, Lou jumped into action in time to hoist the spinnaker, then gave Quentin the thumbs up. The rest of the team instantly got busy, tending to their individual duties. Lou was a little too much fingers and thumbs but he could tell it was coming together.

Watching it raise to the top, Lou happily called, 'UP!'

Alan trimmed the spinnaker while Robert grinded. They sailed fast and Lou punched the air and roared. Behind the wheel, Quentin laughed as the spinny filled with wind like a windsock, and with the wind with them they raced to the next mark. Quentin allowed himself a quick look astern and it was some sight: there must have been twenty-five boats with spinnakers filling, chasing them down. Not bad. He and Lou caught one another's eyes and smiled. They didn't say anything. They didn't need to. They both knew.

After thirty minutes of queuing for the ice rink, Lou and his family finally reached the top.

'You guys all have fun,' Lou said, clapping his hands together and stamping his feet to keep warm. 'I'll just go to the coffee place over there and watch you.'

Ruth started laughing. 'Lou, I thought you were coming skating.'

'No.' He scrunched up his face. 'I've just spent the last half an hour watching men older than me on the ice and they look like right eejits. What if someone sees me? I'd rather stay here, thank you. Plus, these are new and dry-clean only,' he added, referring to his trousers.

'Right,' Ruth said firmly, 'you won't mind taking care of Pud then, while Lucy and I skate.'

'Come on, Lucy,' he instantly grabbed his daughter's hand, 'let's get us some skates.' He winked at a laughing Ruth and made off for the ice-skates. He got to the counter ahead of Smug Family Man, who, like the Pied Piper, was leading even more children now. Ha. He had a sense of silent victory at arriving at the counter first. The ice was nearby and child in Lou had come out to play.

'What size?' The man behind the desk looked at him.

'Ten please,' Lou responded, and looked down at Lucy to speak up. Her big brown eyes stared back up at him.

'Tell the man your size, sweetheart,' he said, feeling Smug Family Man breathing down his neck as he waited.

'I don't know, Daddy,' she said, almost in a whisper.

'Well, you're four, aren't you?'

'Five,' she frowned.

'She's five,' he told the man. 'So whatever size a five-year-old would take.'

'It really depends on the child.'

Lou sighed and took out his BlackBerry, refusing to have to queue again. Behind him, Smug Family Man with the baby in the pouch called over his head, 'Two size fours, a size three, and an eleven, please.'

Lou rolled his eyes and mimicked him as he waited for his call to be answered. Lucy laughed and copied his face.

'Hello?'

'What size is Lucy?'

Ruth laughed. 'She's a twenty-six.'

'Okay, thanks.' He hung up.

Once on the ice, he held on to the side of the rink carefully. He took Lucy's hand and guided her along. Ruth stood by with Pud, who kicked his legs excitedly while bouncing up and down and pointing at nothing in particular.

'Now, sweetheart,' Lou's voice and ankles wobbled as he stepped on the ice, 'it's very dangerous, okay, so you have to be very careful. Hold on to the sides now, okay?'

Lucy held on to the side with one hand and slowly got used to moving along the ice while Lou's ankles wobbled on the thin blades.

Lucy started to skate faster. 'Honey,' Lou said, his voice shaky as he looked down at the cold, hard ice, dreading what it would feel like to fall. He couldn't remember the last time he'd fallen, as a child most probably, and childhood was where falling belonged.

The distance between Lucy and Lou widened.

'Keep up with her, Lou,' Ruth called from the other side of the barrier, walking alongside him as he moved, and he could hear the smile in her voice.

'I bet you're enjoying this.' He could barely look up at her, he was concentrating so much.

'Absolutely.'

He pushed with his left foot, which skidded further than he planned, and he almost broke into the splits. Feeling like Bambi getting to his feet for the first time, he wobbled and spun, arms waving around in circles like a fly trapped in a jam jar, while not too far away he heard Ruth's distinctive laugh. But he was making progress. He looked up now and then to keep his eye on Lucy, who was clearly visible in her fire-engine-red coat, halfway around the rink.

Smug Family Man went flying by him, arms swinging as though he was about to take part in a bobsleigh race, the speed of him almost toppling Lou. Behind him, Smug Family Man's kids raced along, holding hands, and were they singing? That was it. Slowly letting go of the barrier at the side, his wobbly legs tried to balance. Then, bit by bit, he slid a foot forward, almost toppling backwards, his back arching as though about to fall into a crab position, but he rescued himself.

'Hi Daddy,' Lucy said, speeding by him as she completed the first round of the rink.

Lou moved out from the side of the rink, away from the beginners who were shuffling around inch by inch, determined to beat Smug Family Man, who was racing around like the roadrunner.

Halfway between the centre and the barrier, Lou was out on his own now. Feeling a little more confident, he pushed himself further, trying to swing his arms for balance like the others were doing. He picked up speed. Dodging children and old people, he quite unsophisticatedly darted around the rink, hunched over and swinging his arms, more like an ice-hockey player than a graceful skater. He bumped against children, knocking some over, causing others to topple. He heard a child cry. He broke through a couple holding hands. He was concentrating on not falling over so much that he could barely find the time to apologise. He passed Lucy but, unable to stop, had to keep moving, his speed picking up as he went round and round. The lights that decorated the park trees blurred as he raced around. The sounds and colours of the skaters around him whirled around. Feeling like he was on a merry-go-round, he smiled and relaxed a little bit more, as he raced round, and round, and round. He passed Smug Family Guy; he passed by Lucy for a third time; he passed by Ruth, who he heard call his name and take a photograph. He couldn't stop and he wouldn't stop; he didn't know how. He was enjoying the feel of the wind in his hair, the lights of the city around him, the crispness of the air, the sky so filled with stars as the evening began to close in at the early hour. He felt free and alive, happier than he remembered being for a long time. Round and round he went.

Alexandra and the crew had taken on the course for the third and final time. Their speed and coordination had come together better over the last hour, and Lou had fixed any previous hiccups that he'd had. They were coming up to rounding the bottom mark and they needed to once again execute the spinnaker drop.

Lou made sure that the ropes were free to run. Geoff hoisted the genoa, Lou guided it into the luff groove and Luke made sure that the genoa sheet was cleated off. Robert positioned himself to grab the loose sheet under the mainsail so that it could be used to pull in the spinnaker. As soon as he was in position, everyone prepared for everything to happen at once. Geoff released the halyard and helped to stuff the spinnaker down below. Joey released the guy and made sure it ran out fast so that the spinnaker could fly flaglike outside the boat. When the spinnaker was in the boat, Luke trimmed the genoa for the new course, Joey trimmed the main, Geoff lowered the pole and Lou stowed the pole.

Spinnaker down for the last time and approaching the finishing line, they radioed the race officer on Channel 37 and waited for recognition. Not first in, but they were all happy. Lou looked at Quentin as they sailed in and they smiled. Neither of them said anything. They didn't need to. They both knew.

Lying on his back in the middle of the rink with people flying by him, Lou held on to his sore rib-cage and tried to stop laughing, but he just couldn't. He had done what he had been dreading all his life and achieved the most dramatic and comical fall of the day. He lay in the centre of the rink, with Lucy laughing too, trying to lift his arm and pull him up. They had been holding hands and skating around slowly together when, too cocky, Lou had tripped over his own feet, gone flying and landed on his back. Nothing was broken, thankfully, other than his pride, but even that he surprisingly didn't care about. He allowed Lucy to believe she was helping him up from the ice as she pulled on his arm. He looked over to Ruth and saw a flash as she took yet another photo. They caught one another's eyes and he smiled.

They didn't say anything about the day that evening. They didn't need to. They all knew.

It had been the best day of all of their lives.

26.

It All Started with a Mouse

On the Monday following his weekend of sailing and skating, Lou Suffern found himself floating down the corridor to the room with the bigger desk and better light. It was Christmas Eve and the office block was near empty, but the few souls that haunted the halls – dressed in their casuals – offered pats on the back and firm handshakes of congratulations. He had made it. Behind him, Gabe helped carry a box of his files. Being Christmas Eve, it was the last day he would have the opportunity to prepare himself before the Christmas break. Ruth had wanted him to accompany her and the kids into the city and wander around absorbing the atmosphere, but he knew the best thing to do was to get a headstart in his new job, so that he could come back in the New Year and not have to waste time settling in. Christmas Eve or no Christmas Eve, he was intent on familiarising himself with the job now.

Down he and Gabe went to his bigger office with better light. When they opened the door and entered, it was almost as though angels were singing, as the morning sun lit a pathway from the door to the desk, shining directly on his new oversized leather chair as though it were an apparition. He'd made it. And although he could breathe a sigh of relief, he was about to take another deep breath for the new task ahead of him. No matter what he achieved, the feelings of having to reach again were endless. Life for him felt like an endless ladder that disappeared somewhere in the clouds, wobbling, threatening to topple and bring him down with it. He couldn't look down now or he would freeze. He had to keep his eyes upward. Onward and upward.

Gabe placed the boxes down where Lou directed and he whistled as he looked around.

'Some office, Lou.'

'Yeah, it is,' Lou grinned, looking around.

'It's warm,' Gabe added, hands in pockets and strolling around.

Lou frowned. 'Warm is . . . a word I wouldn't use to describe this', he spread his hands out in the vast space, 'enormous fucking office.' He started laughing, feeling slightly delirious. Tired and emotional, proud and a little fearful, he tried to take it all in.

'So what exactly is it that you do now?' Gabe asked.

'I'm the Business Development Director, which means I now have the authority to tell certain little shits exactly what to do.'

'Little shits like you?'

Lou's head snapped around to face Gabe, like a radar that had found a signal.

'I mean, just a few days ago you would have been one of those little shits being told what to . . . never mind,' Gabe trailed off. 'So how did Cliff take it?'

'Take what?'

'That his job was gone?'

'Oh.' Lou looked up. He shrugged. 'I don't know. I didn't tell him.'

Gabe left a silence.

243

'I don't think he's well enough yet to talk to anyone,' Lou added, feeling the need to explain.

'He's seeing visitors now,' Gabe told him.

'How do you know?'

'I know. You should go and see him. He might have some good advice for you. You could learn from him.'

Lou laughed at that.

Gabe didn't blink, and stood staring at him in the silence.

Lou cleared his throat awkwardly.

'It's Christmas Eve, Lou. What are you doing?' Gabe's voice was gentle.

'What do you mean, what am I doing?' Lou held his hands up questioningly. 'What does it look like? I'm working.'

'Bar security, you're the only person left in the building. Haven't you noticed? Everybody's out there.' Gabe pointed out at the busy city.

'Yeah, well, everybody out there isn't as busy as I am,' Lou said childishly. 'Besides, you're here too, aren't you?'

'I don't count.'

'Well, that's a great answer. I don't count then, either.'

'You keep on going like this and you won't. You know, one of the most successful businessmen of all time, a certain Walt Disney, I'm sure you've heard of him, he has a company or two here and there,' Gabe smiled, 'said that "A man should never neglect his family for business."'

There was a long, awkward silence where Lou clenched and unclenched his jaw, trying to decide whether to ask Gabe to leave or physically throw him out.

'But then,' Gabe laughed, 'he also said, "It all started with a mouse."' Gabe smiled.

'Okay, well, I'd better get to work now, Gabe. I hope you have a happy Christmas.' Lou tried to control his tone so that if he didn't exactly sound happy, he at least didn't sound like he wanted to strangle Gabe.

'Thank you, Lou. A very happy Christmas to you too. And congratulations on your warm, enormous fucking office.'

Lou couldn't help but laugh at that, and as the door closed he was alone for the first time in his new office. He made his way to the desk, ran his finger along the walnut border to the pigskin surface. All that was on the desk was a large white computer, a keypad and a mouse.

He sat down on the leather chair and swung around to face towards the window, watching the city below him preparing for the celebrations. A part of him felt pulled outside, yet he felt trapped behind the window that showed him the world yet wouldn't let him touch it. He often felt as though he were trapped inside an oversized snow globe, responsibilities and failures sprinkling down around him. He sat in that chair, at that desk, for over an hour, just thinking. Thinking about Cliff; thinking about the events of the past few weeks, and the best day of all, only two days ago. He thought about everything. When a mild panic began inside him, he turned in his chair and faced the office, facing up to it all.

He stared at that keypad. Stared at it hard. Then he followed the thin white wire that was connected to the mouse. He thought about Cliff, about finding him underneath this very desk, clutching this very keyboard, swinging that very mouse at him with wide, terrified, haunted eyes.

In honour of Cliff – something that Lou realised he hadn't managed to do in the entire time that the man had been out of work – he kicked off his shoes, unhooked the keyboard from the computer monitor, and he pushed back the leather chair. He got onto his hands and knees and crawled underneath the desk, clutching the keyboard close to him. He looked at the windows that were floor to ceiling and watched the city racing by. He sat there for another hour, just pondering.

The clock on the wall ticked loudly in the silence. Gone was the usual hustle and bustle of the office block. No phones ringing, no photocopiers going, no hum of the computers, no voices, no footsteps passing by. Before looking at the clock, he hadn't heard the seconds at all, but now the ticking seemed to get louder and louder as soon as he'd registered it. Lou looked at the keypad, and then he looked at the mouse. He had a jolt, felt it smack him in the head for the second time that year, but for the first time, Cliff's message finally reached him. Whatever Cliff had been so afraid of coming to get him, Lou sure as hell didn't want it chasing him either.

He clambered out from under the desk, shoved his feet into his polished black leather shoes and walked out of the office.

27.

Christmas Eve

Grafton Street, the busy pedestrian street in Dublin city, was awash with people doing their last-minute shopping. Hands were fighting to grab the last remaining items on shelves, budgets and all thought had gone out of the window as rash decisions were made according to availability and time, and not necessarily with the recipient in mind. Presents first; for who, later.

For once not keeping up the pace of the panicked around him, Lou and Ruth held hands and slowly wandered the streets of Dublin, allowing others to rush and push by them. Lou had all the time in the world. Ruth had been more than taken aback when he'd arranged to meet her after his earlier brusque no, but, as usual, hadn't asked any questions. She'd welcomed his new change with a silent delight but with equal amounts of cynicism that she'd refuse to ever speak aloud. Lou Suffern had much to prove to her.

They walked down Henry Street, which was filled with market stalls as hawkers cleared the last of their stock: toys and wrapping paper, leftover tinsel and baubles, remote-control cars that ran up and down the street, everything on show for the last few hours of manic Christmas shopping. On the ever-changing Moore Street, alongside traditional market stalls, displays included a lively ethnic mix of Asian and African stores. Lou bought Brussels sprouts from the sharp-tongued stall-sellers whose stream-of-consciousness outpourings were enough entertainment for anyone. They attended early Christmas Eve Mass and ate lunch together in the Westin Hotel in College Green, the historic nineteenth-century building, formerly a bank, that had been transformed to a five-star hotel. They ate in the Banking Hall, where Pud spent the entire time lopsided with his head tilted to the ceiling, watching in awe the intricately hand-carved ornate ceiling and the four chandeliers that glistened with the eight thousand pieces of Egyptian crystal, shouting over and over again just to hear the echo of his voice in the high ceiling.

Lou Suffern saw the world differently that day. Instead of viewing it from thirteen floors up, behind tinted, reinforced glass in an oversized leather chair, he had chosen to join in. Gabe had been right about the mouse; he'd been right about Cliff teaching him something – in fact it had happened six months ago as soon as the plastic mouse had hit him across the face, causing Lou's fears and his conscience to resurface after long being buried. In fact, when Lou thought about it, Gabe had been right about a lot of things. The voice that had grated so much on his ear had in fact been speaking the words he hadn't wanted to hear. He owed Gabe a lot. As the evening was closing in, and the children had to return home before Santa took to the skies, Lou kissed Ruth and the kids goodbye, saw them safely into her car and then headed back to the office. He had one more thing to do.

In the office lobby, while waiting at the elevators, the doors opened, and as Lou was about to step in Mr Patterson stepped out.

'Lou,' he said in surprise, 'I can't believe you're working today, you really are a piece of work.' He eyed the box in Lou's hand.

'Oh no, I'm not working. Not on a holiday,' Lou smiled, trying to make a point, subtly attempting to set the ground rules for his new position. 'I just have to, em,' he didn't want to get Gabe into trouble by revealing his whereabouts, 'I just left something behind in the office.'

'Good, good. Well, Lou,' Mr Patterson rubbed his eyes tiredly, 'I'm afraid I have to tell you something. I deliberated over whether to or not, but I think it's best that I do. I didn't come in this evening to work either,' he admitted, 'Alfred called me in. Said it was urgent. After what happened to Cliff we're all on tenterhooks, I'm afraid, and so I made my way in quickly.'

'I'm all ears,' Lou said, the panic building inside him. The elevator doors closed again. Escape route gone.

'He wanted to have a few words about . . . well, about you.'

'Yes,' Lou said slowly.

'He brought me these.' Mr Patterson reached into his pocket and retrieved the container of pills that Gabe had given Lou. There was only one pill inside. Alfred, the rat, had obviously scuttered to the skip to collect the evidence to destroy him.

Lou looked at the container in shock and tried to decide whether to deny them or not. Sweat broke out on his upper lip as he thought quickly for a story. They were his father's. No. His mother's. For her hip. No. He had back pain. He realised Mr Patterson was talking and so tuned in.

'He said something about finding them under the skip. I don't know,' Mr Patterson frowned, 'but that he knew them to be yours . . .' He studied Lou again, searching for recognition.

Lou's heart beat loudly in his ears.

'I know that you and Alfred are friends,' Mr Patterson said, a little confused, his face showing his sixty-five years. 'But his concern for you seemed a little misguided. It seemed to me that the purpose of this was to get you into trouble.'

'Em,' Lou swallowed, eyeing up the brown container, 'that's not, em, they're not, em . . .' he stuttered while trying to formulate a sentence.

'I'm not one to pry into people's personal lives, Lou – what my colleagues do in their own time is their own business, so long as it's not going to affect the company in any way. So I didn't take too kindly to Alfred giving me these,' he frowned. When Lou didn't answer but continued to sweat profusely, Mr Patterson added, 'But maybe that's what you wanted him to do?' he asked, trying to make sense of it all.

'What?' Lou wiped his brow. 'Why would I want Alfred to bring these to you?'

Mr Patterson stared at him, his lips twitching slightly. 'I don't know, Lou, you're a clever man.'

'What?' Lou responded, totally confused. 'I don't understand.'

'Correct me if I'm wrong, but *I* assumed,' his twitching lips eventually grew to a smile, 'that you deliberately tried to mislead Alfred with these pills. That you somehow made him believe they were more than they were. Am I right?'

Lou's mouth fell open and he looked at his boss in surprise.

'I knew it.' Mr Patterson chuckled and shook his head. 'You are good. But not that good. I could tell from the blue mark on them,' he explained.

'What do you mean? What blue mark?'

'You didn't manage to scratch the entire symbol off them,' he explained, opening the container and holding it out so that he could empty it into his palm. 'See the blue mark? And if you look close enough you can also see the trace of the *D* where it used to be. I should know, believe me, working in here, I swear by these fellas.'

Lou swallowed. 'That was the only one with the blue mark?' Lazy till the end, Alfred couldn't even reach into a skip to save his own skin, he'd had to scrape an initial off a simple headache tablet.

'No, there were two pills. Both with blue marks. I took one, I hope you don't mind. Found under a skip or no skip, my head was pounding so much I had to have one. This bloody Christmas season is enough to drive me to an early grave.'

'You took one?' Lou gasped.

'I'll replace it.' He waved his hand dismissively. 'You can get them at every pharmacy. Newsagents even, they're just over-the-counter pills.'

'What happened when you took one?'

'Well, it got rid of my headache, didn't it?' he frowned. 'Though to tell you the truth, if I don't get home in the next hour I'll be given another one, before I know it.' He looked at his watch.

Lou was gobsmacked into silence.

'Anyway, I just wanted to let you know that I didn't like what Alfred was trying to do, and that I don't think you're a . . . well, whatever Alfred was trying to make me believe. There's no place in the company for people like him. I had to let him go. Christmas Eve, Christ, this job makes a monster of us sometimes,' he said, tiredly now, appearing older than his sixty-five years.

Lou was silent, his mind screaming questions at him. Either Alfred had replaced them, or Lou too had taken headache pills on the two occasions he had doubled up. Lou took out the handkerchief from his pocket, unwrapped it and examined the one remaining pill. His heart froze in his chest. The faint initial of the headache tablet could be seen. Why hadn't he noticed it before?

'Ah, I see you have another one there,' Mr Patterson

chuckled. 'Caught red-handed, Lou. Well, here you go, you can have the last one. Add it to your collection.' He handed him the container.

Lou looked at him and opened and closed his mouth like a goldfish, no words coming out, as he took the remaining pill from Mr Patterson.

'I'd better go now.' Mr Patterson slowly backed away. 'I have a train set to put together and batteries to insert into a Little Miss something-or-other with a mouth as dirty as a toilet bowl, which I'll no doubt be forced to listen to all week. Have a lovely Christmas, Lou.' He held his hand out.

Lou gulped, his mind still in a whirl about the headache tablets. Was he allergic to them? Had the doubling-up been some sort of side-effect? Had he dreamed it? No. No, it had happened, his family had witnessed his presence on both occasions. So if it wasn't the pills, then it was . . .

'Lou,' Mr Patterson said, his hand still in mid-air.

'Bye,' Lou said croakily, and then cleared his throat. 'I mean, Happy Christmas.' He reached out and shook his boss's hand.

As soon as Mr Patterson had turned his back, Lou ran to the fire escape and charged down the stairs to the basement. It was colder than usual and the light at the end of the hall had finally been fixed, no longer flashing like eighties strobe lighting. Christmas music drifted out from under the door, 'Driving Home for Christmas' by Chris Rea echoing down the long, cold, sterile hallway.

Lou didn't knock before entering. He pushed the door with his foot, still carrying the box in his arms. The room was significantly emptier than it had been. Gabe was down the second aisle, rolling up the sleeping bag and blanket.

'Hi Lou,' he said, without turning around.

'Who are you?' Lou asked, his voice shaking as he laid the box down on a shelf.

Gabe stood up and stepped out of the aisle. 'Okay,' he said slowly, looking Lou up and down. 'That's an interesting way to start a conversation.' His eyes went to the box on the shelf and he smiled. 'A gift for me?' he said softly. 'You really shouldn't have.' He stepped forward to receive it and Lou took a step backward while eyeing him quite fearfully.

'Hmm,' Gabe said, frowning at him, then turned to the gift-wrapped box on the shelf. 'Can I open it now?'

Lou didn't answer. Sweat glistened on his face and his eyes moved sharply to follow Gabe's every movement.

Taking his time, Gabe carefully opened the perfectly wrapped gift. Approaching it from the ends, he slowly removed the tape, taking care not to rip the paper.

'I love giving people gifts,' he explained, still keeping the same easy tone. 'But it's not often that people give them to me. But you're different, Lou. I've always thought that.' He smiled at him. He unwrapped the box and finally revealed the gift inside, an electric heater for his store room. 'Well, this is certainly very thoughtful. Thank you. It will certainly warm up my next space, but not here, unfortunately, as I'm moving on.'

Lou had moved up against the wall now, as far away from Gabe as he could before he spoke with a tremble. 'The pills you gave me were headache tablets.'

Gabe kept studying the heater. 'Mr Patterson told you that, I suspect.'

Lou was taken aback, having expected Gabe to deny it. 'Yes,' he responded. 'Alfred took them from the skip and gave them to him.'

'The little rat.' Gabe shook his head, smiling. 'Predictable old Alfred. I thought he might do that. Well, we can give him points for persistence, he *really* didn't want you to have that job, did he?'

When Lou didn't answer, Gabe continued, 'I bet running to Patterson didn't do him any favours, did it?'

'Mr Patterson fired him,' Lou said quietly, still trying to figure the situation out.

Gabe smiled, not seeming at all surprised. Just satisfied – and very much satisfied with himself.

'Tell me about the pills,' Lou found his voice shaking.

'Yeah, they were a packet of headache pills I bought at a newsagent. Took me ages to scrape the little letters off; you know there aren't many pills without branding on them these days.'

'WHO ARE YOU?' Lou shouted, his voice drenched in fear.

Gabe jumped, then looked a little bothered. 'You're frightened of me now? Because you found out it wasn't a bunch of pills that cloned you? What is it with science these days? Everyone is so quick to believe in it, in all these new scientific discoveries, new pills for this, new pills for that. Get thinner, grow hair, yada, yada, yada, but when it requires a little faith in something, you all go crazy.' He shook his head. 'If miracles had chemical equations then everybody would believe. It's disappointing. I had to pretend it was the pills, Lou, because you wouldn't have trusted me otherwise. And I was right, wasn't I?'

'What do you mean *trust you*, who the hell are you, what is this all about?'

'Now,' he said, looking at Lou sadly, 'I thought that was pretty clear by now.'

'Clear? As far as I'm concerned, things couldn't be more messed up.'

'The pills. They were just a science con. A con of science. A conscience.' He smiled.

Lou rubbed his face tiredly, confused, afraid.

'It was all to give you your opportunity, Lou. Everybody deserves an opportunity. Even you, despite what you think.'

'Opportunity FOR WHAT?' he yelled.

The following words that Gabe spoke sent shivers running up and down Lou's spine, and had him wanting to run immediately to his family.

'Come on, Lou, you know this one.'

They were Ruth's words. They belonged to Ruth.

Lou's body was trembling now and Gabe continued.

'An opportunity to spend some time with your family, to really get to know them, before . . . well, just to spend time with them.'

'To get to know them before what?' Lou asked, quiet now.

Gabe didn't respond, looking away, knowing he'd said too much.

'BEFORE WHAT?' Lou yelled again, coming close to Gabe's face.

Gabe was silent but his crystal-blue eyes bored into Lou's.

'Is something going to happen to them?' His voice shook as he began to panic. 'I knew it. I was afraid of this. What's going to happen to them?' He ground his teeth together. 'If you did something to them, then I will –'

'Nothing has happened to your family, Lou,' Gabe responded.

'I don't believe you,' he panicked, reaching into his pocket and retrieving his BlackBerry. He looked at the screen: no missed calls. Dialling the number of his home quickly, he backed out of the basement stock room, giving Gabe one last vicious look, and ran, ran, ran.

'Remember to buckle up, Lou!' Gabe shouted after him, his voice ringing in Lou's ears as Lou ran to the underground car park.

With the BlackBerry on autodial to Lou's home, and still ringing out, Lou drove out of the underground car park at a fierce speed. Thick, heavy rain plummeted against his windscreen. Putting the wipers on the fastest speed, he drove out of the empty car park and put his foot down on the by-then-empty quays. The beeping of the seat-belt warning got louder

255

and louder but he couldn't hear it for all the worrying he was doing. The wheels of the Porsche slipped a little on the wet roads as he raced down the backroads of the quays, then up the Clontarf coast road to Howth. Across the sea, the two red and white striped chimneys of the electricity generating station stood 680 feet tall, like two fingers raised at him. Rain bucketed down, leaving visibility low, but he knew these streets well, had driven up and down them all his life, and all he cared about was driving over the small thread of land that separated him from his family and getting to them as quickly as possible. It was six thirty and pitch black as the day had closed in. Most people were at Mass or in the pubs, getting ready to put presents together and leave a glass of milk and Christmas cake out for Santa, a few carrots for his chauffeur. Lou's family were at home, having an evening meal – that he'd promised them he'd join – but Lou's family weren't answering the phone. He looked down at his BlackBerry to make sure it was still dialling, taking his eye off the road. He swerved a little as he moved over the middle line. A car coming at him beeped loudly and he quickly moved back into his lane again. He flew up past the Marine Hotel at Sutton Cross, which was busy with Christmas parties. Seeing a clear road ahead of him, he put his foot down. He raced by Sutton Church, raced by the school along the coast, passed through safe, friendly neighbourhoods where candles sat in the front windows, Christmas trees sparkled and Santas dangled from roofs. Across the bay, the dozens of cranes of Dublin's skyline were laced in Christmas lights. He said goodbye to the bay and entered the steep road which began to ascend to his home on the summit. Rain bucketed down, falling in sheets, blurring his vision. Condensation was appearing on the windscreen, and he leaned forward to wipe it with his cashmere coat sleeve. He pressed the buttons on the dashboard to hopefully clear the screen. The ping, ping, ping of the seat-belt warning rang in his ears, and the condensation rapidly filled the windscreen as the car got hotter. Still he sped on, his phone ringing out, his desire to be with his family overtaking any other emotion he should have felt then. It had taken him twelve minutes to get to his street on the empty roads.

Finally, his phone beeped to signal a call coming through. He looked down and saw Ruth's face – her caller ID picture. Her big smile; her eyes brown, soft and welcoming. Glad she was at least safe enough to call him, he looked down with relief and reached for the BlackBerry.

The Porsche 911 Carrera 4S has a unique four-wheel-drive system which grips the road far better than any rear-wheel-drive sports car. It allots five to forty per cent of the power to the front wheels, depending on how much resistance the rear wheels have. So if you accelerate out of a corner hard enough to spin the rear wheels, power is channelled to the front, pulling the car in the right direction. All-wheel-drive basically means that the Carrera 4S could negotiate the icy road with far more control than most other sports cars.

Unfortunately, Lou did not have that Porsche model. He had it on order. It would be arriving in January, only a week away.

And so when Lou looked down at his BlackBerry, so overwhelmed with relief and emotion to see his wife's face, he had taken his eye off the road and had dived into the next corner much too fast. He reflexively lifted his foot from the accelerator, which threw the car's weight forward and lightened the rear wheels; then he got back on the accelerator and turned hard to make the corner. The rear end broke traction and he spun across to the other side of the road, which was the deep decline down the cliff's edge.

The moments that followed for him were ones of sheer horror and confusion. The shock numbed the pain. The car turned over, once, twice and then a third time. Each time, Lou let out a yell as his head, his body, his legs and arms thrashed about wildly like a doll inside a washing machine. The emergency airbag thumped him in the face, bloodying his nose, knocking him out momentarily so that the next few moments passed in a still but bloody mess.

Some amount of time later, Lou opened his eyes and tried to survey the situation. He couldn't. He was surrounded by blackness and found himself unable to move. A thick, oily substance covered one of his eyes, preventing him from seeing, and with the one hand he could move, he found that every part of his body he touched was covered in the same substance. He moved his tongue around his mouth, tasted rusty iron and realised it was blood. He tried to move his legs, but couldn't. He tried to move his arms, and could just about move one. He was silent while he tried to keep calm, to figure out what to do. Then, when for the first time in his life he couldn't formulate one single thought, when the shock wore off and the realisation set in, the pain hit him at full force. He couldn't get the images of Ruth out of his mind. Of Lucy, of Pud, of his parents. They weren't far above him, somewhere on the summit; he had almost made it. In the darkness, in a crushed car, in the middle of the gorse and the hebe, somewhere on a mountainside in Howth, Lou Suffern began to whimper.

Raphie and Jessica were doing their usual rounds and bickering over Raphie's country-music tape, which he liked to torment Jessica with, as they passed the scene where Lou's car had gone off the road.

'Hold on, Raphie,' she interrupted his howling about his achy breaky heart.

He sang even louder.

'RAPHIE!' she shouted, punching the music off.

He looked at her in surprise.

'Okay, okay, put your Freezing Monkeys on, or whatever you call them.'

'Raphie, stop the car,' Jessica said, in a tone that made him immediately pull over. She leapt out of the car and jogged the few paces back to the scene that had caught her eye, where the trees were broken and twisted. She took her torch out and shone it down the mountainside.

'Oh God, Raphie, we need to call emergency services,' she shouted to him. 'Ambulance and fire brigade!'

He stopped his brief jog towards her and made his way back to the car, where he radioed it in.

'I'm going down!' she yelled, immediately making her way through the broken trees and down the steep incline.

'You will not, Jessica!' she heard Raphie yell back, but she didn't listen. 'Get back here, it's too dangerous!'

She could hear, but quickly zoned out from his shouts and could soon only hear her own breath, fast and furious, her heart beating in her ears.

Jessica, new to the squad, should never have seen a sight like this mangled car, upside down and totally unrecognisable, in her life. But she had. For Jessica, it was all too familiar; it was a sight that haunted her dreams and most of her waking moments. Coming face to face with her nightmare, and the replaying of a memory, dizziness overcame her and she had to hunker down and put her head between her knees. Jessica had secrets, and one of them had come back to haunt her. She hoped to God nobody was in that car; the car was crushed, unrecognisable, with no licence plate, and in the darkness she couldn't tell whether it was blue or black.

She climbed around the car, the icy wet rain pelting down on her, soaking her in an instant. The surface was wet and mucky beneath her, causing her to lose her footing numerous times, but as her heart beat wildly in her chest and as she found herself back in a distant memory, reliving it, she couldn't feel the pain in her ankle as she went over on it; she couldn't

259

feel the scrapes of branches and twigs on her face, the hidden rocks among the gorse that bruised her legs.

Around the far side of the car, she saw a person. Or a body at least, and her heart sank. She shone the light near him. He was bloodied. Covered in it. The door had been smashed shut, she couldn't pull it open, but the window pane of the driver's side had shattered, so at least she had access to his upper half. She tried to keep calm as she shone the flashlight.

'Tony,' she breathed as she saw the figure. 'Tony.' Tears welled in her eyes. 'Tony.' She clawed at the man, ran her hands across his face, urged him to wake. 'Tony, it's me,' she said. 'I'm here.'

The man groaned but his eyes remained closed.

'I'm going to get you out of here,' she whispered in his ear, kissing him on the forehead. 'I'm going to get you home.'

His eyes slowly opened and she felt a jolt. Blue eyes. Not brown. Tony had brown eyes.

He looked at her. She looked at him. She was taken out of her nightmare.

'Sir,' she said, her voice shakier than she wanted. She took a deep breath and started again. 'Sir, can you hear me? My name is Jessica, can you hear me? Help is on the way, okay? We're going to help you.'

He groaned and closed his eyes.

'They're on their way now,' Raphie panted from above her, starting to make his way down.

'Raphie, it's dangerous down here, it's too slippy, stay up there so they can see you.'

'Is anyone alive?' he asked, ignoring her request and continuing to slowly move down one foot at a time.

'Yes,' she called back. 'Sir, give me your hand.' She shone the torch to look at his hand and her stomach flipped at the sight. She took a moment to adjust her breathing and she brought the flashlight up again. 'Sir, take my hand. Here I am, can you feel it?' She gripped him tight.

He groaned.

'Stay with me now, we're going to get you out of here.'

He groaned some more.

'What? I can't . . . em . . . don't worry, sir, an ambulance is on its way.'

'Who is it?' Raphie called. 'Do you know?'

'No,' she called back simply, not wanting to take her attention away from this man, not wanting to lose him.

'My wife,' she heard him whisper, so quietly it could have been mistaken for an exhale. She moved her ear to his lips, so close she could feel them on her ear lobe, the stickiness of the blood.

'You have a wife?' she asked gently. 'You'll see her. I promise, you'll see her. What's your name?'

'Lou,' he said, then he started to cry softly, and even that was such an effort that he had to stop.

'Please hang in there, Lou.' She fought back the tears and then put her ear to his lips again as he breathed some more words.

'A pill? Lou, I don't have any –'

He let go of her hand suddenly and started pulling at his coat, thumping his chest with a lifeless hand as though that movement was the equivalent to lifting a car. He grunted with the effort; he whimpered from the pain. Reaching into his breast pocket, which was soaked with blood, Jessica took out the container. There was one white pill left inside.

'Is this your medication, Lou?' she asked unsurely. 'Do I –?' She looked up to Raphie, who was trying to figure out how to make it down through the tricky terrain. 'I don't know if I'm supposed to give you –'

Lou took her hand and squeezed it with such strength that she immediately opened the container, with a shaking hand, and shook the single pill onto her palm. With trembling fingers she lifted his mouth open, placed the pill on his tongue and

261

closed his mouth. She quickly looked around to see if Raphie had seen her. He was still only halfway down the slope.

When she looked back at Lou, he was looking at her, wide-eyed. He gave her such a look of love, of absolute gratitude for that one simple thing, that it filled her heart with hope. Then he gasped for air and his body shuddered, before he closed his eyes and left the world.

28.

For Old Time's Sake

At exactly the same time as Lou Suffern left one world and entered another, he stood in the front garden of his Howth home, drenched to the very core. He was trembling from the experience he'd just had. He didn't have much time, but there was nowhere in the world he'd rather have been right at that moment.

He stepped through the front door, his shoes squelching on the tiles. The fire in the sitting room was crackling, the floor below the tree was filled with presents, wrapped with pretty ribbons. Lucy and Pud were so far the only children in the family, and so family tradition decided that his parents, Quentin and Alexandra, and this year the newly separated Marcia, would be staying overnight in his house. Their joy at seeing Lucy's reaction on Christmas morning was too immense to deny them of. Tonight he couldn't imagine not being with them; he couldn't think of anything that would fill his heart with any more joy. He entered the dining room, hoping they would see him, hoping that Gabe's last miraculous gift wouldn't fail him now.

'Lou.' Ruth looked up from the dinner table and saw him

first. She leapt out of her chair and ran to him. 'Lou, honey, are you okay? Did something happen?'

His mother rushed to get a towel for him.

'I'm fine,' he sniffed, cupping her face with his hands and not taking his eyes off her. 'I'm fine now. I was calling,' he whispered. 'You didn't answer.'

'Pud hid the phone again,' she said, studying him with concern. 'Are you drunk?' she asked in a whisper.

'No,' he laughed. 'I'm in love,' he whispered back, then raised his voice so that the whole room could hear. 'I'm in love with my beautiful wife,' he repeated. He kissed her fully on the lips, then breathed in her hair, kissed her neck, kissed her everywhere on her face, not caring who was there to see. 'I'm sorry,' he whispered to her, barely able to get words out of his mouth, his tears were so heavy.

'Sorry about what? What happened?'

'I'm sorry for the things that I've done to you. For being the way I was. I love you. I never meant to hurt you.'

Ruth's eyes filled. 'Oh, I know that, sweetheart, you already told me, I know.'

'I just realised that when I'm not with you, I'm ruthless,' he smiled, and his tearful mother — who'd returned with a towel — laughed and clapped her hands, before grabbing her husband's hand at the table.

'To all of you,' he pulled away from Ruth, but wouldn't let go of her hand, 'I'm so sorry to all of you.'

'We know that, Lou,' Quentin smiled, emotion thick in his voice. 'It's all water under the bridge now. Okay? Stop worrying and sit down for dinner, it's all okay.'

Lou looked to his parents, who smiled and nodded. His father had tears in his eyes and nodded emphatically that it was all okay. His sister Marcia was blinking fiercely to stop her tears, moving the silverware around on the table.

They dried him, they loved him, they kissed him, they fed

him, though he wouldn't eat much. He told them in turn that he loved them, over and over again, until they were laughing and telling him to stop. He went upstairs to get a change of clothes before, according to his mother, he caught pneumonia. While upstairs, he heard Pud crying and immediately left his bedroom and hurried to his son's room.

The room was dark, with just a night light. He could see Pud wide awake and standing up against the railings of his cot, like a woken prisoner held captive by the sleep army. Lou switched the light on and went inside. Pud viewed him angrily at first.

'Hey there, little man,' Lou said gently. 'What are you doing awake?'

Pud just gave a quiet little moan.

'Oh, come here.' Lou leaned over the railings and lifted him up, holding him close in his arms and shushing him. For the first time ever, Pud didn't scream the house down when his father came near him. Instead, he smiled, pointed a finger in Lou's eye, in his nose, then in his mouth, where he tried to grab his teeth.

Lou started laughing. 'Hey, you can't have them. You'll have your own soon, though.' He kissed Pud on the cheek. 'When you're a big boy, all sorts of things will happen.' He looked at his son, feeling sad that he would miss all of those things. 'Mind Mummy for me, won't you,' he whispered, his voice shaking.

Pud laughed, suddenly hyper, and blew bubbles with his lips.

Lou's tears quickly disappeared at the sound of Pud's laughter. He lifted him up, put Pud's belly on his head and started jiggling him about. Pud laughed so hard, Lou couldn't help but join in.

From the corner of his eye, Lou saw Lucy at the door watching them.

'Now, Pud,' he spoke loudly, 'how about you and I go into Lucy's room and jump on her bed to wake her up – what do you think?'

'No, Daddy!' Lucy laughed, exploding into the room. 'I'm awake!'

'Oh, you're awake too! Are you both the little elves that help Santa?'

'No,' Lucy laughed. Pud laughed too.

'Well then, you'd better hurry to bed, or else Santa won't come to the house if he sees you awake.'

'What if he sees you?' she asked.

'Then he'll leave extra presents,' he smiled.

She ruffled up her nose. 'Pud smells of poo. I'm getting Mummy.'

'No, I can do it.' He looked at Pud, who looked back at him and smiled.

Lucy stared at him as though he were insane.

'Don't look at me like that,' he laughed. 'How hard can this be? Now come on, buddy, help me out here.' He smiled at Pud nervously. Pud's open palm smacked his father across the face playfully. Lucy howled with laughter.

Lou laid Pud down on the ground, so that he wouldn't wriggle off the changing mat on top of the unit that Ruth used.

'Mummy puts him up there.'

'Well, Daddy doesn't,' he said, while trying to figure out how to undo the babygro.

'The buttons are at the bottom.' Lucy sat down beside him.

'Oh. Thanks.' He opened the buttons and rolled it up Pud's body, evacuating all clothes from the area. He untaped the new nappy and slowly opened it. Turned it around in his hands, trying to figure out which way it went.

'Oh pooh!' Lucy dove backwards, her fingers pinching her nose. 'Piglet goes on the front,' she said through her blocked nose.

Lou moved quickly to try to get the situation in hand, while Lucy rolled around fanning the air with exaggerated drama. Impatient with his father's progress, Pud began kicking his legs, forcing Lou away from him. With Pud on his knees, his rear end in Lou's face, Lou crawled around behind him, approaching his bottom with a baby wipe, as though attacking him with a feather duster. His light swipes were not helping the situation. He needed to get in there. Holding his breath, he went for it. With Pud momentarily under control and playing with a ball that had caught his eye, Lucy handed the various apparatus to Lou.

'You're supposed to put that cream on next.'

'Thanks. You'll always take care of Pud, won't you, Lucy?' She nodded solemnly.

'And you'll take care of Mummy?'

'Yessss.' She punched the air.

'And Pud and Mummy will take care of you,' he said, finally grabbing Pud's podgy legs and pulling him from under the cot and along the carpet while Pud screeched like a pig.

'And we'll all take care of Daddy!' she hurrahed, dancing around.

'Don't worry about Daddy,' he said quietly, trying to figure out which way to put the nappy on. Finally he got the gist, and quickly closed the buttons on Pud's suit. 'Tonight we're going to let him sleep without his pyjamas.' He tried to sound sure of himself.

'Mummy puts the lights out so that he gets sleepy,' Lucy whispered.

'Oh, okay, let's do that,' Lou whispered, turning off the lights so that the Winnie the Pooh night light was all that circulated on the ceiling.

Pud made a few gurgles and spurts, non-words as he watched the lights.

Lou hunkered down in the darkness, pulling Lucy close to him, and he sat on the carpet hugging his little girl and watched the pooh bear of very little brain chasing a honeypot on the ceiling. It was his moment to tell her now.

'You know that no matter where Daddy is, no matter what's happening in your life, no matter if you're sad or happy or lonely or lost, remember that I'm always there for you. Even if you don't see me, know that I'm in here,' he touched her head, 'and I'm in here,' he touched her heart. 'And I'm always looking at you, and I'm always proud of you and of *everything* you do, and when you sometimes question how I ever felt about you, remember right now, remember me saying that I love you, my sweetheart. Daddy loves you, okay?'

'Okay, Daddy,' she said sadly. 'What about when I'm naughty? Will you love me when I'm naughty?'

'When you're naughty,' he thought about it, 'remember that Daddy is somewhere always hoping that you'll be the best that you can be.'

'But where will you be?'

'If I'm not here, I'll be elsewhere.'

'Where is that?'

'It's a secret,' he whispered, trying to hold back his tears.

'A secret elsewhere,' she whispered back, her warm sweet breath on his face.

'Yeah.' He hugged her tight, and tried not to let a sound pass his lips as his tears fell, hot and thick.

Downstairs in the dining room, there wasn't a dry eye in the house as they listened to the conversation in Pud's nursery over the baby intercom. For the Sufferns they were tears of joy because a son, a brother and a husband had finally come back to them.

That night, Lou Suffern made love to his wife, and afterwards held her close to him, rubbing his hands down her silky hair until he drifted away, and even then his fingertips continued to trace the contours of her face: the little turn-up of her nose, her high cheekbones, the tip of her chin, along her jawline then all the way along her hairline, as though he were a blindman seeing her for the first time.

'I'll love you forever,' he whispered to her, and she smiled, halfway to her dream world.

It was in the middle of the night that the dream world was shattered when Ruth was awakened by the gate buzzer. Half-asleep, she stood in her dressing gown and welcomed both Raphie and Jessica into her home. Quentin and Lou's father accompanied her, keen to protect the house against such late-night dangers. But they couldn't protect her from this.

'Morning,' Raphie said sombrely as they all gathered in the living room. 'I'm sorry to disturb you at such a late hour.'

Ruth looked the young garda beside him up and down, at her dark black eyes that seemed cold and sad, at the grass and dried muck splattered on her boots, which clung to the bottom of her navy-blue trousers. At the small scrapes across the face and the cut that she was trying to hide behind her hair.

'What is it?' Ruth whispered, her voice catching in her throat. 'Tell me, please.'

'Mrs Suffern, I think you should sit down,' Raphie said gently.

'We should get Lou,' she whispered, looking to Quentin. 'He wasn't in bed when I woke up, he must be in his study.'

'Ruth,' the young garda said, so softly that Ruth's heart sank even further, and as her body went limp she allowed Quentin to reach for her and pull her down to the couch beside him and Lou's father. They grabbed one another's hands, squeezed one another so tightly that they were linked like a chain, and they listened as Raphie and Jessica told them how life for them had changed beyond all comprehension, as they learned that a son, a brother and a husband had left them as suddenly as he'd arrived.

While Santa laid gifts in homes all across the country; while lights in windows began to go out for the night; while wreaths upon doors became fingers upon lips and blinds went down as the eyelids of a sleeping home drooped, hours before a turkey went through a window at another home in another district, Ruth Suffern had yet to learn that despite losing her husband she had gained his child, and together the family realised – on the most magical night of the year – the true gift that Lou had given them in the early hours of Christmas morning.

29.

The Turkey Boy 5

Raphie watched the Turkey Boy's reaction as he heard the last of the story. He was silent for a moment.

'How do you know all of this?'

'We've been piecing it all together today. Talking to the family and to his colleagues.'

'Did you talk to Gabe?'

'Briefly, earlier. We're waiting for him to come to the station.'

'And you called to Lou's house this morning?'

'We did.'

'And he wasn't there.'

'Nowhere to be seen. Sheets still warm from where he'd lain.'

'Are you making this up?'

'Not a word of it.'

'Do you expect me to believe this?'

'No, I don't.'

'Then what was the point?'

'People tell stories, and it's up to those who listen whether to believe them or not. It's not the job of the storyteller.'

'Shouldn't the storyteller believe it?'

'The storyteller should tell it,' he winked.

'Do you believe it?'

Raphie looked around the room to make sure nobody had sneaked in without him noticing. He shrugged awkwardly, moving his head at the same time. 'One man's lesson is another man's tale, but often, a man's tale can be another's lesson.'

'What's that supposed to mean?'

Raphie avoided the question by taking a slug of coffee.

'You said there was a lesson – what was the lesson?'

'If I have to tell you that, boy . . .' Raphie rolled his eyes.

'Ah, come on.'

'Appreciating your loved ones,' Raphie said, a little embarrassed at first. 'Acknowledging all the special people in your life. Concentrating on what's important.' He cleared his throat and looked away, not comfortable with preaching.

The Turkey Boy rolled his eyes and faked a yawn.

Raphie tossed his embarrassment to the side, giving himself one more opportunity to get through to the teen before he gave up altogether. He should have been at home on his second helping of Christmas dinner instead of being here with this frustrating boy.

He leaned forward. 'Gabe gave Lou a gift, son, a very special gift. I'm not going to bother asking you what that was, I'm going to tell you, and you'd better listen up, because right after this I'm leaving you and you'll be alone to think about what you did and if you don't pay attention then you'll go back out to the world an angry young man who'll feel angry for the rest of his life.'

'Okay,' the Turkey Boy said defensively, sitting up in his seat as though being told off by the headmaster.

'Gabe gave Lou the gift of *time*, son.'

The Turkey Boy ruffled up his nose.

'Oh, you're fourteen years old, and you think you've all

the time in the world, but you haven't. None of us have. We're spending it with all the might and indifference of January sales shoppers. A week from now they'll be crowding the streets, swarming the shops, with open wallets, just throwing all their cash away.' Raphie seemed to crawl into the shell on his back for a moment, his eyes tucked under his grey bushy eyebrows.

The Turkey Boy leaned forward and glared at him, amused by Raphie's sudden emotion. 'But you can earn more money, so who cares?'

Raphie snapped out of his trance and looked up as though seeing the Turkey Boy in the room for the first time. 'So that makes time more precious, doesn't it? More precious than money, more precious than anything. You can never earn more time. Once an hour goes by, a week, a month, a year, you'll never get them back. Lou Suffern was running out of time, and Gabe gave him more, to help tie things up, to finish things properly. That's the gift.' Raphie's heart beat wildly in his chest. He looked down at his coffee and pushed it away, feeling his heart cramp again. 'So we should fix things before . . .'

He ran out of breath and waited for the cramping to fade.

'Do you think it's too late to, you know,' the Turkey Boy twisted the string of his hoody around his finger, speaking self-consciously, 'fix things with my, you know . . .'

'With your dad?'

The boy shrugged and looked away, not wanting to admit it.

'It's never too late —' Raphie stopped abruptly, nodded to himself as though registering a thought, nodded again with an air of agreement and finality, then pushed back his chair, the legs screeching against the floor, and stood.

'Hold on, where are you going?'

'To fix things, boy. To fix some things. And I suggest you do the same when your mother comes.'

The young teenager's blue eyes blinked back at him, innocence still there, though lost somewhere in the mist of his
confusion and anger.

Raphie made his way down the hall, loosening his tie. He
heard his voice being called but continued walking anyway.
He pushed his way out of the staff quarters, into the public
entrance room that was empty on Christmas Day.

'Raphie,' Jessica called, chasing after him.

'Yes,' he said, turning around finally, slightly out of breath.

'Are you okay? You look like you've seen a ghost. Is it your
heart? Are you okay?'

'I'm fine,' he nodded. 'Everything's fine. What's up?'

Jessica narrowed her eyes and studied him, knowing he was
lying. 'Is that boy giving you trouble?'

'No, he's fine, purring like a pussy cat now. Everything's
fine.'

'Then where are you going?'

'Eh?' He looked towards the door, trying to think of another
lie, another untruth to tell somebody for the tenth year running.
But he sighed – a long sigh that had been held in for many
years – and he gave up, the truth finally sounding odd yet
comfortable as it fell from his tongue.

'I want to go home,' he said, suddenly appearing very old.
'I want today to be over so that I can go home to my wife.
And my daughter.'

'You have a daughter?' she asked with surprise.

'Yes,' he said, simple words filled with emotion. 'I do. She
lives up there on Howth summit. That's why I'm there in the
car every evening. I just like to keep an eye on her. Even if
she doesn't know it.'

They stared at one another for a while, knowing that something strange had overcome them that morning, something
strange that had changed them forever.

'I had a husband,' she said finally. 'Car crash. I was there.

274

Holding his hand. Just like this morning.' She swallowed and lowered her voice. 'I always said I'd have done anything to give him at least a few more hours.' There, she'd said it. 'I gave Lou a pill, Raphie,' she said firmly, looking him straight in the eye now. 'I know I shouldn't have, but I gave him a pill. I don't know if all that stuff about the pills is true or not – we can't locate Gabe now – but if I helped Lou have a few more hours with his family, I'm glad, and I'd do it again if anyone asks.'

Raphie simply nodded, acknowledging her two confessions. He'd put it in their statement but he didn't need to tell her that; she knew.

They just looked at one another, staring at but not seeing each other. Their minds were elsewhere; on the times gone by, the lost time that could never return.

'Where's my son?' A woman's urgent voice broke their silence. As she had opened the door, light filled the dark station. The cold of the day crept in, snowflakes were trapped in the woman's hair and clothes and fell from her boots as she stamped them on the ground. 'He's only a boy,' she swallowed. 'A fourteen-year-old boy.' Her voice shook. 'I sent him out to get gravy granules. And the turkey's missing now.' She spoke as though delirious.

'I'll take care of this.' Jessica nodded at Raphie. 'You go home now.'

And so he did.

One thing of great importance can affect a small number of people. Equally so, a thing of little importance can affect a multitude. Either way, a happening – big or small – can affect an entire string of people. Occurrences can join us all together. You see, we're all made up of the same stuff. When something happens, it triggers something inside us that connects us to a situation, connects us to other people, lighting us up and linking us like little lights on a Christmas tree, twisted and turned but still connected on a wire. Some go out, others flicker, others burn strong and bright, yet we're all on the same line.

I said at the beginning of this story that this was about a person who finds out who they are. About a person who is unravelled and their core is revealed to all that count. And that all that count are revealed to them. You thought I was talking about Lou Suffern, didn't you? Wrong. I was talking about us all.

A lesson finds the common denominator and links us all together, like a chain. At the end of that chain dangles a clock, and on the face of the clock the passing of time is registered. We hear it, the hushed tick-tock sound that breaks any silence, and we see it, but often we don't feel it. Each second makes its mark on every single person's life; comes and then goes, quietly disappearing without fanfare, evaporating into air like steam from a piping hot Christmas pudding. Enough time leaves us warm; when our time is gone, it too leaves us cold. Time is more precious than gold, more precious than diamonds, more precious than oil or any valuable treasures. It is time that we do not have enough of; it is time that causes the war within our hearts, and so we must spend it wisely. Time cannot be packaged and ribboned and left under trees for Christmas morning.

Time can't be given. But it can be shared.